THE BOY WHO HATCHED MONSTERS

Books by T.C. Shelley

The Monster Who Wasn't
The Werewolves Who Weren't
The Boy Who Hatched Monsters

T.C. SHELLEY

THE BOY WHO HATCHED MONSTERS

BLOOMSBURY
CHILDREN'S BOOKS

LONDON OXFORD NEW YORK NEW DELHI SYDNEY

BLOOMSBURY CHILDREN'S BOOKS
Bloomsbury Publishing Plc
50 Bedford Square, London WC1B 3DP, UK
29 Earlsfort Terrace, Dublin 2, Ireland

BLOOMSBURY, BLOOMSBURY CHILDREN'S BOOKS and the Diana logo
are trademarks of Bloomsbury Publishing Plc

First published in Great Britain in 2022 by Bloomsbury Publishing Plc

A catalogue record for this book is available from the British Library

ISBN: PB: 978-1-5266-0079-0; eBook: 978-1-5266-0078-3

2 4 6 8 10 9 7 5 3 1

Typeset by RefineCatch Limited, Bungay, Suffolk

Printed and bound in Great Britain by CPI Group (UK) Ltd, Croydon CR0 4YY

To find out more about our authors and books visit www.bloomsbury.com
and sign up for our newsletters

To Holly and Tess for your advice. You are both very clever and know how to make fictitious characters very miserable. You have the opposite effect on your aunt and mother

The Sirens

Where the sirens live, you sail their oceans;
Their singing makes fools love their destruction.
Wretched is the soul, whom the music calls
To siren shores and under their spell falls.
That poor chump will not see the joys of life,
His growing kids, or his beautiful wife!
On rocky outcrops, they wait; human bones
Nestle and settle in the cracks of stones.
Away now, escape this horrible coast.
Avoid listening to them or you'll be toast!

The Odyssey, Book XII, attrib. Homer, translated by
Solomon Jedidiah (1865)

CHAPTER 1

Kylie whimpered as she watched the red-haired woman wandering along the kerb on the opposite side of the street. Russell was busying himself in the alcove, unrolling his sleeping mat and bag, readying himself for sleep. He stopped and threw a few chips in Kylie's direction. When she ignored them and growled, he put a comforting hand on her head. But Kylie didn't want to be comforted.

Russell peered up and down. He couldn't see anything for Kylie to growl at; they were alone on the street, but he didn't have her corgi's nose or eyes, so he returned to patting down his bedding and pulling out a couple of treats for her from a paper bag. She didn't even sniff them.

'S'all right, girl. What are you whining at?' he asked.

This wasn't the first visit the red-haired woman had made. Kylie had smelt her before. She'd been over at the square the week before throwing sparkly air at Maxie. Then

Maxie'd wandered over to Russell blathering about how they had to keep a lookout for a fairy-boy and someone called Sam. 'Gotta watch for him,' Maxie had said to Russell.

'What you talking about, Max?' Russell had asked, then looked googly-eyed as Maxie had taken off his shoes, laid himself down on Russell's bedding and had a nap for an hour. Kylie had breathed in his scent until the madness-making sparkle wore off. Maxie had woken up jittery and confused. It was a nasty business, Kylie knew that much. And now the woman was back.

Underneath the red-haired woman's smell of awful, Kylie detected desperation. Humans were scary enough when they got desperate, let alone this ... this monster. Yes, Kylie's nose agreed with her, You got that right. She wasn't human, no more than Kylie. Even less so: at least Kylie had a soul. You could smell a soul in a body; a good one gave off a scent warmer and more sugar-spiced than Christmas. Russell's soul smelt like that. This woman left sour soulless-ness everywhere, like that horrible stuff people put over sores and wounds. It stung Kylie's nose just like that stuff, but unlike that stuff, it meant no good.

Kylie snarled as the strange woman turned her atten-tion to Russell. He bustled under the alcove as she pushed back her red hair and strode in their direction.

Kylie barked. 'Back off! Don't want your kind here.'

'What are you making noise about, Ky?' Russell asked, and patted her, studying the street as he did so.

'It's time to go,' Kylie said, pulling at Russell's trouser leg.

'Whatsa matter, girl? Timmy got stuck in a well?' He chuckled at his own joke.

'Get goin', you drongo!' Kylie barked at him. 'I'll bite you if I have to.'

'Don't you like our nice little nest, then? You coulda told me before I started unpacking.' Russell, God bless him, started packing. He was a good soul and Kylie was his best mate. He'd leave a spot if she didn't like it. Not many humans would do that.

Kylie jittered about as Russell moved too slowly, rolling up the bag, looking around for its cover, chatting to himself, giving the horrible woman time to get halfway across the road.

A car came drifting out of the night, bearing down on the woman as if it didn't see her. It looked like it might crash into her and run her down, but it swerved a couple of metres beforehand, clipped the kerb and forced the car's front wheel on to the pavement. The driver, a young man, stopped and stared at nothing. As Kylie watched his perplexed face, she realised he couldn't see the woman. He had no idea why he'd veered.

Shaken, the driver peered around, saw Kylie and her human and decided not to get out. They wouldn't hurt the poor love, but Kylie supposed he didn't know that. The awful sound of grating metal dragged over the concrete as the car took off again, leaving Russell gawping after it.

'Wonder why ... ?' he started.

The incident was over in a couple of seconds, but the red-haired woman hadn't flinched, hadn't slowed at all.

Soon she stood a metre or two away from them on the footpath.

'Go away', Kylie barked at her. 'Begone, whatever you are.'

Russell turned back to his packing. 'I'm hurrying, I'm hurrying.'

Kylie couldn't wait. She bit his trouser leg.

'Hey, what you doing?'

Kylie nipped at him again, and Russell backed off, at last putting distance between himself and the monster woman. Kylie would have sunk her teeth into him, made him bleed, if only he'd run. He had no idea how close to a monster he stood.

Russell tapped Kylie on the nose. 'Stop it! Stop it! What you doing?'

'Have you seen Sam?' the monster woman asked.

'Wha'?' Russell turned and saw her for the first time, startled by her sudden appearance.

'Sam! I'm looking for my Sam! If you see him, tell him I need him, he's in danger. Tell him, he has to be careful. There's danger coming.'

Kylie crouched at Russell's feet and turned to the monster, growling so low and constant no one would take it as anything but threat. 'I don't know if you bleed, but I'm willing to take a bite out of you to find out,' the corgi said.

The monster woman blew a kiss at Kylie. Tiny sparkling lights flew from her fingers and they fluttered towards the dog's nose. Kylie held her breath. She couldn't let any get inside her. Maxie had gone nutty when he'd breathed it in.

She blew air out of her nose and the twinkly dust floated up and settled in her eyes instead. Her sight blurred. She felt sleepy, but at least her mind was still her own.

'Sam's worth a thousand humans and ten thousand dogs. You've got to help me help him', the monster woman said.

'What?' Russell asked.

Despite her sleepiness, Kylie smelt fear on Russell, almost as sour as the desperation the woman gave out. The corgi dropped to the concrete, too tired to stand.

'I want to know where my Sam is. He's in this town and one of you creatures must know.'

'Lady, I don't know a Sam', Russell replied. 'What you do to my dog?'

'Yes, you do, you must know Sam. Where is he?' the woman said. 'It's a simple enough question. If he doesn't show up, they will talk like waves.'

'Sam? Is he the old bloke who lives near the racing course?' Russell asked.

'He's as young as dawn, is my boy. He needs me.'

The sleepiness took a stronger hold on Kylie, but Russell picked her up, and she smelt his fear again, and the scent cleared her head a little. She cracked open an eye to see the monster woman's chin a few centimetres from her furry snout.

Kylie growled deep in her throat.

'Kylie, settle', Russell said.

'Yes, settle the beast before I break its neck. What is wrong with this place? A thousand years ago I could go into any town and ask any human to locate someone and they would know how.'

'A thousand years ago?' Russell laughed shakily. 'You aren't that old, love. Still, if you'd been looking thousands of years ago, towns were a lot smaller.' He turned to go. 'Look, lady, I don't know your problem, but I gotta get my dog some help.'

The woman grabbed Russell by the throat and lifted him. Kylie rose with him, clutched in his clenched arms. Kylie yelped as she saw his widening eyes, then found herself squashed between Russell and the woman. Above her the woman's face changed, her humanity seeping away, the colour leaching from her hair, so Kylie and Russell both saw a grey-haired, grey-faced witch. At last Russell could see she was a monster, but it was too late to do anything. He wriggled in her grasp, his breath trapped in his throat as she clamped his windpipe.

As Russell's hands grew cold, Kylie fought off the sleepiness. She didn't know how long she could hold on; the sparkly stuff weighed down her eyes so heavily.

Russell gagged. With the last of her energy, Kylie lunged up and dug her teeth into the bony wrist of the hagged monster. The creature screamed and released Russell's throat. Kylie's head fell back, limp.

Russell's instincts and the size of his terror did the rest. He ran. Kylie bobbed in his arms and let the sleep take her. She didn't have to fight it any more.

'Saaaaaaaaaaammmmmmmmm!' the monster wailed.

* * *

Sam loved sitting high up on the roof of his house, peering at Brighton Beach. He looked out to sea. Daniel, Sam's guardian angel, had promised to visit, and Sam missed him. The angel hadn't been around for over a week, which was longer than Sam liked. Sometimes Sam saw him in town, or at school, but Daniel had said he'd definitely show at the house today. Here they could actually talk, not just nod at each other as Sam pretended he couldn't see his friend.

With his sensitive gargoyle hearing, Sam could just make out his family downstairs. Michelle, Richard and Nick were being particularly quiet, their movements heavy and sluggish. Nobody had given Sam so much as a smile since he'd woken up, so it was good to get outside to spend some time with the gargoyles.

Wheedle lay semi-snoozing on his back behind Sam. The stone bull hardly left the roof these days, due to his parenting responsibilities. Spigot the marble eagle watched the street, giving short, informative shrieks every now and then, and Bladder leaned against Sam's leg while Nugget cuddled into Sam's lap. Wheedle put up his head every time the baby gargoyle peeped.

'She's a little grotesque,' Bladder said, pointing at the newest addition to their pack.

Sam stared at Nugget, whose cute monkeyish face grinned up at his. He patted her head. 'I don't think you should say that. She's gorgeous.'

'He don't mean she's ugly, Sam,' Wheedle said, dark granite shadows deepening under his grey eyes. 'He means she's a mixed gargoyle. They're very common. Gargoyles

7

like us, made of a single animal – a bull, an eagle, a lion –
are rare.'

'Mixed gargoyle?' Sam asked.

'Yeah, she's a mixture of monkey and dog an', an' ...'
Wheedle trailed off. 'I got no idea ...'

Spigot squawked.

'Yeah, she's got bat wings for sure,' Wheedle agreed.

'Whatever she is, I think she's beautiful,' Sam said.

'Stunted though,' Bladder replied. 'She's nearly three
months old and hardly grown. An' in the last month, she's
taken to ...' Bladder's voice dropped. 'Sleepin'.'

'Dada,' Nugget said, rubbing her face in Bladder's
mane.

Sam loved that she could call Bladder that with such
confidence. To be honest, he was jealous.

'An' her words ...' Bladder started.

'What's wrong with her words?'

'Mama.' Nugget looked at Wheedle with fond grey
eyes.

Bladder winced.

'What's the matter? That's a nice word,' Sam replied.

'But what *real* words does she know?'

Nugget sat up. 'Tham, chocklit, sleep, nap, hungee,
play, Mama, Dada.' Nugget's nose nuzzled into Sam's hand.
'Nuggee sleep, Tham.' She shuffled around on his lap, and
her eyes fluttered closed.

'What's wrong with what she says? They're lovely
words.' Sam peered at Bladder.

'Exactly. Lots of warm, cosy, cutesy words, like a

human baby. Not like a monster at all. Where'd she get 'em? What about "maim", "thump", "tease"? "Belch"? Where are her full sentences? I've been trying to teach her, "Wipe that look off your face, ya twit." All she does is hug me.'

Wheedle sighed. 'Well, she's Sam's first attempt. He likes nice words. Maybe she'll get more knowledge as she grows. We did.'

'But *we* started with enough to keep ourselves alive, all breathed in right from the get-go. It means she's not safe, Sam. We gotta get more fairy dust, breathe the important stuff into her head. She's all hugs and kisses and can't look after herself. Look, she's napping. It's morning.' Bladder's volume dropped. 'An' Wheedle's started on it too.'

'She sleeps better on Sam than on me,' Wheedle said. 'I'd like a nice rest as well.'

'Which ain't right. Wheedle won't petrify, so he's doing this instead ...' Bladder pointed as the stone bull yawned. 'It's not natural for gargoyles. The worst thing is, Sam ...' Bladder stared at Nugget. 'You did this.'

Wheedle groaned. 'We know Sam did this. You've been going on non-stop about it since it happened. An' I can barely think about my next minute. What's your point, Bladder?'

'My point? My point is no one but an ogre king has ever hatched any kind of monster before. Every month for decades me, you, Spigot and the whole of monsterkind went down to see Thunderguts sigh those beads into being, and never once has anyone else done it. Only an ogre has ever been able to do it before.'

9

'It's not me', said Sam, 'it's the fairy dust. It made me sneeze and then ...'

'Pop, pop, pop ... a beautiful little gargoyle came into the world.' Wheedle stared at Nugget and sighed.

'I think I'm gonna throw up my breakfast', Bladder said, then his voice dropped. 'The point is, what if Maggie finds out all she has to do is blow a bit of fairy dust into Sam's face and monster eggs'll be hatching left, right an' centre ... ?'

'Ah, I see', Wheedle said. 'Dada is worried little Sammy may be an ogre.'

Bladder harrumphed. 'Of course I'm not. An' he's not an ogre, he's a gargoyle, but I worry about all of you. You're my pack. If Maggie finds out about this, she'll want him making monsters *for her*.'

'You're such a fusspot. Sam is safe here at the Kavanagh house, Maggie hasn't shown up for ages, so she's probably lost all trace of him, an' it don't matter if she's got a tonne of fairy dust. If she can't find him, she can't spray him, an' he can't hatch any other beads. Her plans to force him to make more monsters ain't going to help an' ...' Wheedle faltered. 'Something, something. Too tired.'

Sam didn't want to think of it either. What good would it do? He wished he could forget everything: the monsters roaming the earth because he'd set them free by breaking the soul sword, the fact Maggie might be looking for him because she thought he could make more ogres to build her a monstrous army. He also suspected there was an outraged fairy queen stomping about somewhere, angry with him because he'd stopped her trapping his friends' souls in a weapon to force Maggie and her minions back in The Hole. He wondered if there was anyone outside of his house who wasn't annoyed with him.

It was November, and getting colder. He hadn't seen monsters (other than gargoyles) since he'd accidentally hatched Nugget three months before. Nothing from The Hole had bothered him, no were-people were sniffing around, no fairies tried to pull him into a war, and Maggie had been unheard of for ages. The blessings and wardings over the Kavanagh house held strong. When the sun hit them, which was happening less and less as the temperature fell, Sam saw them glowing on the paintwork where Daniel had traced them. Those sigils kept the wrong kinds of monsters and non-humans away.

'You do need to think about it though, Sam,' Bladder said, cutting through his thoughts. 'You hatching Nugget is reason to worry.'

There was so much to think of that little Nugget wasn't getting any of his worry time.

Actually, Sam thought as he stroked her grey chin, *she's one of the good things*. Sam pulled his coat over Nugget so she could snuggle closer to his belly.

'It's not her herself,' Bladder continued, as if he knew what Sam had been thinking. Sam saw the soft glow in the lion's eye. 'We're all happy to have another gargoyle in the world, aren't we, Wheedle?'

Wheedle replied with a snore.

'It's that *you* made her. *You* did that. *You* got fairy dust up your nose and sneezed on her and she came about.

Maggie won't stop looking for you if she finds that out. You can't ever let your guard down. There's no new ogre king, so you and a handful of fairy dust are the closest thing to an heir she's got. Even your angel Turkey Breath is worried, an' if he thinks ...'

Wheedle's hoofs stopped mid-trot. He opened one eye. 'What you saying about the angel? What I miss?'

'What if Maggie shows up and tries to get Sam to make more ... ?' Bladder waved his paw over Nugget.

Wheedle yawned. 'Maybe his next one will be better.'

'We don't want there to be a next one! And we especially don't want it to be better!' Bladder said. 'That *would* make Sam the ogre king.'

'Not an ogre,' Wheedle muttered. 'All gargoyle, aren't you Sam?' Another yawn.

Sam sighed. 'I think she's lovely the way she is.' He stroked Nugget's ears again. His hand felt gritty and he rubbed it on his trousers. 'She will grow up though, won't she? She's a bit bigger than when she hatched.'

'We don't know.' Bladder stared at Nugget. 'I wish she could talk better. She gets these looks on her face and can't tell us nothing.' He shook his head before letting out an enormous burp. 'Pardon.'

'How's your tummy?' Sam asked. Nothing seemed to agree with Bladder any more, even chocolate. Especially chocolate.

'What do you mean?' Bladder replied. 'There's nothing wrong with my tum. Don't get me off-topic. We was discussing Nugget.'

'Who is a baby. Babies don't do what you want.' Wheedle dragged himself over and put his heavy head on Sam's leg.

'Not supposed to be a baby,' Bladder replied.

Nugget woke. Wheedle picked her up in one limp hoof and cuddled her. The little gargoyle shivered, nuzzled Sam's hand one more time and bounced on to Wheedle's back. 'All your whingeing, Bladder, now that's what's ruining everyone's sleep,' Wheedle said.

'No one. Is supposed. To sleep.' Bladder's voice came out in a roar and Nugget started to cry.

'Bladder, not today, hey?' Wheedle said.

'Bladder went to reply, then stopped with his jaw ajar. He frowned, blinked as if he'd remembered something and glanced at Sam, his mouth still open. The stone lion gave an artificial laugh. 'Yes, that's right. I forgot.'

'Why don't you go down and get yourself a warm drink, Sam? It's cold up here.' Wheedle winked at Bladder.

'What? Oh, yeah, good idea, Wheedle. You should definitely do that, Sam,' Bladder said.

Sam did feel cold, but he wondered about the wink and what Bladder had forgotten.

Sam jumped through his bedroom window, landing on the floor with a soft bump.

'Tham?' a voice called. Nugget peered in from the window sill.

'Go back up,' he whispered, pointing at the roof.

Nugget watched him with a sad face, her eyes growing larger as she pouted.

'Oh, all right, come in.'

Nugget bounced to the bedroom floor and in three quick jumps landed on Sam's bed. 'Nuggee hungee, Tham.'

'You want some chocolate?' Sam opened his desk drawer and pulled out a bar. He spent most of his pocket money on chocolate, to keep the gargoyles happy.

Nugget shook her head. 'Nuggee hungee.' She rubbed her gurgling tummy.

'You want something else?'

Nugget nodded.

'I don't have any sugar mice. Would you like some milk?'

Nugget frowned. She didn't know what milk was. Until recently, she'd been fine with chocolate and sugar mice, but last night she'd pushed away third and fourth helpings and looked for something else. Just like Bladder.

'Are you getting tummy aches like Bladder?'

Nugget rubbed her tummy again. 'Yucky.'

'All right, we'll try some milk. But you stay here.'

Sam tucked the quilt around Nugget and she put her small head on the pillow. Sam kissed her forehead like Michelle kissed his and pulled the door to as he left.

Michelle and Richard sat in the kitchen. They stopped talking as Sam entered the room. He hadn't been listening – Daniel had had a few words about Sam snooping too much, so he'd trained himself to stop eavesdropping.

Nick stood peering into the fridge. 'Sorry, Mum, I'm not feeling hungry,' he said. 'Do you mind if I go back to bed?'

'You do that, son', Richard replied. He comforted a cup of coffee in one hand and held a pencil in the other, but there were no words written in his crossword puzzle.

'Thanks, Dad.'

Mum, Dad. They were every second word Nick said.

'What about you, Sam – you still have your appetite?'

'Mu ... Mu ... Michelle', Sam started.

Michelle peered at him expectantly.

'I just wanted a warm drink. Maybe some milk too, if that's OK.'

'Warm milk? You can get that yourself.'

'Hey, Sammy.' Nick mussed his hair, then plodded off to the stairs.

Whatever was making them all down, Sam guessed it wasn't anything he'd done. Hair mussing was a sign of affection, Daniel had told him. Sam went to the fridge. Today's date on the calendar had been marked with a hand-drawn heart. Sam wondered why. Everything else was written out: *Nick's app: Dentist; Aunt Colleen's hip surgery; board meeting.*

Sam poured out a large glass of milk and, as he microwaved it, he studied the heart.

He heard a bump upstairs. So did Michelle and Richard. Something solid, possibly stone, hitting the floor.

'What's that?' Michelle asked.

Not 'What?' Sam thought. *'Who?'*

'Nick's dropped something', Richard said. 'I hear it all the time. Actually, that's more your thing, isn't it, Sam? You bang that chair around a lot. It's surviving very well, considering.'

Sam didn't respond. The banging from his room was never his chair; it was generally the heavy footfall of a careless gargoyle. Sam listened. The solid bumping was not coming from his part of the house.

He heard baby Beatrice giggling from her room. *Oh boy.* If she yelled, Michelle would be up the stairs in a shot.

He grabbed the milk and moved with quick intent to the stairs.

He wasn't really out of earshot, so Daniel couldn't call it snooping, but as he left he heard Richard sigh, then say, 'I'm glad he's here with us, especially today.'

'Yeah,' Michelle replied. 'I know he's not ... but he ... anyway, it's good.'

The heart on the calendar. What's today?

He followed the bumping to Beatrice's room to find Nugget in the cot with the baby. They were each sucking an arm of a tortured teddy, its resigned face staring at Sam.

'Tham!' Nugget said.

'Ah, you've finally met,' Sam said.

'Tham!' Beatrice said.

'And introduced yourselves, I see.'

The teddy forgotten, both babies jumped up and leaned on the cot railing. 'Tham! Tham! Tham!' They slapped hands and paws on the wood.

'Is Beatrice awake?' Michelle called out.

'Yes, she is,' Sam called back. He put the milk on the changing table, rushed to the cot and grabbed Nugget. The baby gargoyle clutched the wooden edge, her stone claws holding tight. 'No, Tham. Nooooo. Play.'

16

'What's the matter, Beatrice?' Michelle called out from the top of the stairs.

'Let go, Nugget!' Sam said.

'No, Tham,' Nugget repeated.

'I have milk.'

Sam pointed his chin at the milk on the table. Nugget stared at it as Michelle's tired feet clumped nearer.

Nugget's tummy grumbled and she let go of the rail and reached towards the cup.

Baby gargoyle in arms, Sam rushed to the changing table, put the cup in Nugget's paws and pushed the straw into her mouth. She knew exactly what to do and sucked up the warm liquid. Sam shoved Nugget into the box of nappies on the lower shelf of the table as Michelle came in the door.

'Mama!' Beatrice called.

Sam sighed. Even Beatrice called Michelle 'Mum'.

'Oh, you're such a good boy, Sam,' Michelle said. 'You don't have to change her.' Michelle reached the cot. She studied Beatrice's face. 'There's dust everywhere.' She patted Beatrice and the cot mattress. Nugget quietly drank up her milk. Sam watched her eyes widen in pleasure.

Michelle brought the human baby to the table. 'Out the way,' she said to Sam, and popped Beatrice down on the pad. With two quick motions she had Beatrice un-nappied and clean.

Nugget sat a paw's reach from Michelle's knees, and Sam wagged a warning finger at the gargoyle. Michelle leaned over. Her hand moved towards Nugget's nose, and

Sam realised what she wanted. He ducked and pulled out a fresh nappy. As Nugget stretched to touch Michelle's fingers, he pushed down the gargoyle's paw and handed the nappy to Michelle. 'Here you go,' he said.

'What's this?' Michelle asked.

'A nappy?'

'More dust.' Michelle replied and shook out the nappy before turning it over, making sure the clean side was under Beatrice.

Sam stepped back so he could watch Nugget. The gargoyle let the empty cup fall to the floor. Bump!

'Huh?' Michelle said.

'It's my cup, it's all right.' Sam grabbed it and glared at Nugget, shaking his head. The gargoyle reached for Sam. 'In a second,' he whispered.

'What?' Michelle asked.

'I'll take it downstairs in a second,' Sam replied.

'Good boy. You put that milk away quickly – maybe you need something more filling.' She scooped Beatrice into her arms and walked to the door. Sam put himself in front of the table, blocking the view of the gargoyle as Michelle turned to look at him. 'I'm so glad you're here, Sam,' she said.

'Me too.' Sam smiled, which was hard as Nugget butted her stone head on the backs of his knees.

Sam listened until he heard Beatrice burbling at Michelle downstairs. He knelt down. 'Bad girl,' he said.

Nugget burped in his face. 'Mik,' she said and patted her protruding tum. 'Yum.'

CHAPTER 2

Bladder was still grumbling as Sam climbed back on the roof, Nugget in his arms. She played with the collar of his jumper.

'Gargoyles sleeping, Sam! Sleeping, for goodness sake! Wheedle looks exhausted. Can't just petrify the way we're supposed to, he says. Can't turn to stone cos it might wake the baby, might hurt the baby, might scare the baby. Up all day and awake all night. It's just "Nugget, Nugget, Nugget". As soon as she followed you, Wheedle actually petrified, solid. Finally. You really breathed her wrong.'

Sam sighed.

Bladder sighed too. 'Oh, Sam, I'm sorry, you know what a grump I can be.'

Sam did, but he was surprised. He couldn't remember Bladder apologising before.

* * *

Sam remembered the sneeze that had hatched Nugget's bead. She'd arrived far too small and almost completely wordless. Her first word had been 'Mama' as she peered into Wheedle's adoring face, and 'Dada' as Bladder's bottom jaw hit the ground with a clunk and a piece of his lower mane fell off. She also knew 'Tham', which was odd. Poor Spigot was just 'Birdie', but he didn't seem to mind as he gifted her with affectionate pecks and let her hide under his wing. She hadn't felt the need to say much more until recently. For the first month she'd been happy to lie on top of Wheedle as they turned to stone together, but later she started to sleep, not petrifying like a gargoyle should, just closing her eyes and curling into Wheedle's belly. Lately, Wheedle said Nugget whimpered and cried all night, and now she only slept when Sam showed up, crawling into his lap and passing out.

Sam didn't want to tell Bladder about this incident with the 'milk'. Sure, the older gargoyle's appetite had changed in the last few months too, but he was embarrassed by it, and no one was allowed to mention it. Maybe it had something to do with Nugget's arrival.

The day after Nugget hatched, Bladder had said he noticed something off. The lion had gathered the remaining motes of dust from his mane and encouraged Sam to sneeze her bigger, better, smarter, but it made no difference. She developed slowly. She grew faster than Beatrice, but not as fast as a normal gargoyle. By a month old she should have been adult-sized and speaking fluently. A week after this failed stage of development, Bladder had suggested they get a good dose of fresh dust to fix her, and Wheedle got angry, hating the word 'fix', then burst into tears.

Sam had thought it was a good thing. Maybe his hatchlings wouldn't impress Maggie much, even if she did find out; then she'd lose interest in using him. That would be excellent.

'I don't think Maggie'll be that easily put off. Nugget's like Spigot,' Bladder had replied. 'Did we ever tell you Spigot was one of Thunderguts's early tries, before he got good at making monsters? That's all Maggie will see Nugget as: a first attempt.'

'Anyway, she'll be big and beautiful too, one day,' Wheedle had said. 'Just like you, Sam. You're so lovely, luvvly-wubbly.' Wheedle had rubbed noses with Nugget. The baby gargoyle giggled.

And Bladder had rolled his eyes.

A wing tickle woke Sam from the memory, as Yonah flew over his shoulder and landed with a soft drop next to him. A second after the dove, Daniel appeared, a bright, shining grin on his face. 'Hello, all.'

Nugget cheered and threw herself at the angel, hiding in his wings and peering out between downy plumes.

Wheedle shook off his stoniness and grunted himself awake. 'What you want?'

'My reason for visiting you is something we talked about earlier. Remember?'

Wheedle looked confused, then sat up. 'Oh? Oooooh! Of course. How could I ... ? It's the lack of sleep.' The gargoyle stared at Sam. 'I am so sorry. An' we were supposed to ...'

'Hey up there!' Voices rose from the street. Sam peered down. His school friends Wilfred, Amira and Hazel waited on the pavement.

'Looks like we've lost a bit of time. So, let's hurry it along, hey?' Wheedle said. 'Spigot, chuck down the rope.'

'Yonah?' Daniel said.

Yonah nodded and fluttered away.

'What's going on, Daniel? Wheedle?' Sam asked.

'No time,' Wheedle said. 'Gotta haul these shifters up.'

Wilfred raced around on the footpath. Sam suspected that if the other boy had been in his dog-shape he'd have been chasing his tail.

As Wheedle and Spigot pulled them up one at a time, Sam helped the three shifter kids clamber over the edge of the roof. They hugged and greeted him as if they hadn't spent the previous day together at school.

'Congratulations,' Hazel said to Sam.

'Er, thanks.' Sam wondered what that was about.

'Wow!' Wilfred said. 'Great view. Oooh.' The shifter boy gazed at Daniel with glowing eyes.

'Hello, Wilfred.' The angel shot a beautiful smile at him.

Wilfred grinned at the angel and elbowed Amira, pointing in Daniel's direction.

'Yes, yes, why don't you get his autograph, fanboy?' Amira asked.

'It's nice to see you all here for Sam's special day,' Wheedle said.

'My special day? What's so special about today?' Sam looked at the faces crowding around him. Bladder, Spigot and Wheedle bunched up with Daniel on the edge of the roof. Nugget peered out from under his wing and Wilfred shuffled as close as he could to the angel. Hazel and Amira settled in near Wilfred.

'We'll just wait for Yonah, shall we?' Daniel asked.

As Sam scanned the sky, a bevy of pretty pigeons arrived and established themselves behind the gargoyles. They all peered up to wait for Yonah.

Sam's stare followed theirs. *What is so special about today?* It *was* a lovely day. Despite it being late November and brisk on the rooftop, the sun above them picked out pretty colours from the sea and town.

They were high enough to see all around, from the green expanse near the marina all the way to the i360 Tower.

Maybe that was the 'special day' thing.

Sam had discussed climbing to the top of the i360 Tower with Wheedle. Richard had already taken him up the lift, and the gargoyles had done the ascent one evening, but they hadn't done it together. Maybe that's what Wheedle meant by 'special'. Maybe they'd figured out a way to get up the tower during the day.

But that didn't explain the shifters' presence. Or the shifters' presents. Wilfred, Amira and Hazel had nicely wrapped gifts in their laps. Maybe it was a Christmas thing? Sam still didn't get Christmas, but Michelle was going mad shopping for it. Sam was trying to figure out what to get everyone. Chocolate for gargoyles, that was easy, but what do you get humans?

Maybe it was an anniversary thingy. Michelle and Richard had had their wedding anniversary in October. Nick had dragged him out to buy Michelle a platinum bracelet. They'd had a bit of money each and Richard gave them the rest. It couldn't be an anniversary though; Sam hadn't been around a year. Maybe half a year?

'What special day?' he asked again.

Daniel peered at a low-hanging cloud and clicked his fingers. A white shape appeared. At first, Sam didn't recognise Yonah. Her tiny talons clutched a pale box twice her size. As she got closer, Sam saw it was plastic, something like the containers Michelle put food in so they could eat it another day. The dove flapped over Daniel's head and the angel stretched up to take the container. Then Yonah fluttered to Spigot and sat on his neck. The two birds rubbed their heads together in greeting.

Wheedle peeked at the two birds and chuckled. When he saw Sam looking too, he winked as if they shared some bizarre secret. Sam had no idea what it could be. Yonah preened her wings so they fluffed up as she settled on the eagle. Spigot's head did a happy waggle.

Wheedle winked at Sam again.

With the arrival of the plastic container, the pigeons pushed closer.

Daniel lifted a brown object from the tub. It looked like a chocolate cake. It smelt like a chocolate cake. The

24

gargoyles huddled around it like it was chocolate cake, as did the press of birds.

Daniel shoved some thin cylindrical objects into the top of the cake. Each one was as long as Sam's forefinger and there were thirteen of them. What did they mean? Thirteen was an unlucky number, Sam had heard. The angel lit them with the end of his finger, which set the pigeons squawking. Wheedle and Bladder oohed and aahed. The flames flickered.

Candles. The Kavanaghs had used candles in a blackout, but they'd been thick and short.

'Happy birthday, Sam', Daniel said. 'You've changed all of us, and we wanted to celebrate your special day.'

Birthday? It wasn't his birthday. 'No, I was hatched at the end of May sometime.'

'You were, but Samuel Ethan Kavanagh, the child of Michelle and Richard Kavanagh, was born thirteen years ago to this day. November thirtieth, to be exact. As you are Samuel Kavanagh, both born and hatched, you have two birthdays.'

'Go with it', Bladder said. 'More opportunities for cake. You'll get one in May too.'

'Now blow out your candles and wish for something', Wheedle said.

Sam knew exactly what he wanted. He'd like to be able to celebrate this day with Richard and Michelle. If not today, then maybe the following year. It was all very well and good being *their* Samuel Kavanagh, the child they'd lost and found again, but rather pointless if they didn't know the truth about it. He couldn't even call them 'Mum' and 'Dad'. He blew out the candles.

'He looks in pain,' Bladder said. 'Is the cake all right?'

'Made in Heaven,' Daniel said.

It tasted like it too. It was rich, deeply chocolatey, with a hint of joy running through it. Sam felt happy eating it.

Bladder and Wheedle shoved their indelicate snouts into the soft spongy goodness and wolfed it down before eyeing the piece of cake Sam had just started.

Wilfred, Amira and Hazel barely said anything. Their eyes closed as they *mmmm*ed.

Spigot and Yonah fed each other crumbs from their slices of cake. Wheedle seemed to find this entertaining and poked Bladder to watch, who smirked. Neither the stone eagle nor the dove paid attention to Wheedle and Bladder.

Nugget got cake in her eyes. Daniel flung broken bits at the pigeons.

Bladder burped. ''Scuse me. You got any Tummy Times?' he asked the shifters. They shook their heads.

Wheedle took out a blue packet from under his front leg and tossed it to Bladder. The gargoyle scoffed the lot and burped again.

'What exactly are you eating that's causing this trouble?' Daniel asked. 'How does a gargoyle's digestive system even work? Where does it all go?'

'Bit personal, don't you think?' Wheedle replied.

Bladder belched. The smell that rode out was reminiscent

of sugary sewerage or rubbish bins out the back of a sweet shop.

'I'm getting tummy aches all the time.' Bladder's stone paled down to white marble.

'And weird cravings. Do you think he's pregnant?' Wheedle asked. Sam guessed he was a little serious too. The arrival of Nugget had unnerved them, and all three grown-up gargoyles jumped whenever Sam sneezed.

'What kind of weird cravings?' Daniel asked.

'Salad, boiled eggs, sandwiches, pie, fruit. Don't worry, I haven't given in to any of them. Oh, bother ...' Bladder ran to the edge of the building, and a heavy 'yurk' erupted from him. Everyone, birds included, turned their backs, pretending not to hear. Bladder would be deeply ashamed to be caught vomiting.

'Is that normal for a gargoyle?' Sam asked.

'Not even slightly,' Wheedle answered.

CHAPTER 3

'Sam, Nick. I'm off to the centre,' Michelle yelled up the stairs, and with Sam's window open, her voice carried to the roof. 'Do you want to come?'

'Not today, Mum,' Nick replied.

'That means she's going in to town, doesn't it?' Amira asked. 'Would she give us all a lift?'

'I think so,' Sam replied. 'Just ask.'

'You should come too, Sam. Spend the voucher I got you,' Wilfred said.

Sam held the voucher. It had 'Happy Birthday, Sam' written over it in Wilfred's scrawl. Then he looked at the new notebook and jigsaw Amira and Hazel gave him. Both had dogs on them: specifically a Saluki and a Kokoni.

'We better get you back on the pavement, then,' Bladder said to the shifters.

Sam popped into the house through his window, making sure to close it behind him. Nugget was getting far too curious, and if one of the older gargoyles didn't watch her, she was likely to go off on her own.

'Sam?' Michelle called again.

'Coming!' He headed downstairs and saw Michelle giving Richard a fond farewell pat on the head. She turned and looked at the fridge again, sighing at that striking red heart.

She strained a smile at Sam.

It clicked. The hand-drawn heart on the calendar. It was a birthday. His birthday. Their original Sam's. They would be quietly remembering when they lost him as an infant, not realising they'd got him back. Not realising their Sam's soul was in the boy standing right next to them.

'Are you all right, Michelle?' Sam asked.

'I didn't sleep well last night', Michelle replied. 'I think there's another baby on the street. It woke me with its crying.'

'I swear it sounded like it came from the roof,' Richard said. 'I thought I was dreaming.'

'It's just the way sound carries in these streets,' Michelle said.

Richard grunted. Beatrice looked sleepy, and Sam thought Richard looked ready to curl up next to her.

The shifters were waiting on the pavement when they stepped outside. Wilfred was chatting to Hoy Poy, the neighbour's pug, about the best lamb bones.

Michelle smiled brighter this time. 'Hello, you three. What are you doing here?'

'Hello, Mrs Kavanagh', Hazel replied. 'We just came to see Sam. Are you off?'

'Yeh, sorry, everyone, I'm going to town to help Michelle', Sam replied.

Hazel winked a bit too obviously.

'I'm volunteering at the soup kitchen. Sam and Nick sometimes help me carry the boxes in. But that's OK, Sam, you can go with your friends', Michelle said. 'I can do it myself.'

'Why don't we come too?' Hazel asked. 'We can all help.'

'That would be lovely', Michelle said.

'Many hands make light work, Mrs Kavanagh', Amira said as she took a box from Michelle's hands.

Wilfred, Amira and Hazel jostled to see who would have a window seat. When Sam realised they all wanted one, he volunteered to sit in the middle-back. Even with the cold Channel wind flying up the streets, the three shifters put the windows down, and Michelle had to tell them three times to pull in their heads. Wilfred's tongue hung out as they rounded the corner up to North Street.

'Here we are', Michelle said. She opened the back of the car and the three shifters grabbed a box each, letting Sam lead the way to the kitchen.

The group plunged down an alley marked by a cardboard sign that read 'Lunch' in big blue letters. A man sat on a blanket on the footpath with a plump beige dog next to him. The dog lifted her head slightly, politely sniffing the air as Sam and the shifters approached.

* * *

Kylie shot up as soon as she got a whiff of the first person coming down the alleyway. He looked like a boy, but he wasn't one. He smelt like the red-haired woman, but he was chatting happily to the other three children behind him, and they had the distinct pong of people who lived with warm-hearted, lovely dogs ... In fact, they didn't just smell like they had dogs in the family but as if they *were* dogs. And the boy with the odd scent, well – now she whiffed deeper – there was a magical undercurrent there, like being a pup and rolling in high grass, or sleeping by a warm fire. There was cinnamon and nutmeg in it too, like the best of souls in one body. She swallowed her growl and cocked her head. It was very confusing.

Russell startled at Sam's footsteps. 'Some guard dog you are.' He shuffled inside his coat.

Kylie saw the four children sniff at Russell. They wrinkled their noses. Russell stank, she knew it. They'd both slept in the alley outside the soup kitchen the previous night, and small spaces always held in a body's sourness. Russell needed a shower.

'They smell like dog lovers. I'm not barking at a friendly,' Kylie told Russell. 'They don't much like your particular aroma though.'

The odd-smelling boy's cheeks reddened.

'Coming through, coming through.' A woman pushed past the kids and rummaged in her bag.

'The kitchen's not open for an hour,' Russell said.

'I know,' the woman replied. 'I'm here to get things started. The others will be along shortly.'

'Are you in charge, missus?'

The woman shook her head. 'No, I just volunteer some Saturdays and make sure the supplies get here. Sometimes cut up some things for the crew. I've got four helpers today.'

Kylie liked this woman. She didn't talk to Russell the way un-homeless people normally did, all huffy and uncomfortable.

'I'm all right waiting here, aren't I?' Russell asked.

'Course you are. I'm Michelle. You new here?'

'Nah, come here lots. Just not normally for Saturday lunch. My name's Russell.'

'Well, when the others get here, you get inside and grab a warm seat. Your dog too.' Michelle leaned down and gave Kylie a scratch behind her ears.

Kylie sniffed the kids again. Whatever she'd found odd about that boy, it was gone now.

It must have been her nerves from the night before. It had taken Russell two hours to go back and retrieve his things, and that was only because he was so cold he couldn't get to sleep. When they finally went back to get their stuff, he packed up and ran away so fast Kylie wondered if his arthritis had disappeared. Afterwards, he was jittery again. As he drifted off to sleep, somewhere around 2 a.m., he pulled her close and kept murmuring, 'Was a weird dream, that's all, just a dream.' It had chilled Kylie's tail to the tip, freezing her wag right out.

32

The woman, Michelle, opened the door and ushered in the three doggy kids holding the boxes. Only the strange-smelling boy was left, and the scent got nicer every second. Kylie edged towards him.

'Block his path like the mammoth you are, why don't you?' Russell said.

Kylie rolled her eyes at this. *Yep, Russell's back in form.*

'She's got a bit of Australian corgi in her', Russell said to the boy. 'When I first got her she was blonde and slim, so I called her Kylie. Not so slim now, are you, darlin'?'

Kylie snapped at his leg. 'You wanna see how big a corgi can get when she's eaten a lug called Russell?' she barked. 'Just keep fat-shaming the dog.'

'She's spirited too. I never know what will set her off,' Russell said. 'Been really grumpy lately.'

'Because I'm stuck with an idiot who doesn't know when he's in danger and sometimes he can be a little insensitive. I'm just the right size for my breed, you know.'

'You look lovely.' The boy stared at her for a second then peered at Russell. 'Maybe you shouldn't say things about her weight. Corgis are supposed to be nice and chunky.'

You read my mind, Kylie thought.

Russell laughed. 'Think the dog is sensitive, do you?'

A delightful aroma wafted from the kitchen.

'She's got bacon.' Kylie sighed. She never managed to get any of the scraps from the kitchen.

'I'll see if there's anything left', the boy said.

Kylie gazed at the boy. He was watching her. 'That almost sounded like you were talking to me', she said.

'I was.'

Kylie woofed.

'What are you barking about now?' Russell asked.

'I think he understood me, ya drongo. Settle yourself, Kylie', the corgi told herself. 'It's probably just a coincidence.' Still, she danced over to the kid's legs. 'If you answer this with a "yes", I will love you for life. Could you could get me some bacon?'

'Yes', the boy replied. 'I will try to get you some bacon.'

Kylie yapped like a pup and chased her tail; she'd never been so excited. He understood her! He really did.

'Calm down, you idiot', Russell said to her. 'They won't let us in to lunch if you make too much noise.'

The door opened again and the woman, Michelle, was there. 'Sam', she said, 'help me cut up some carrots.'

The boy smiled at Kylie and walked past Michelle into the kitchen.

She'd been so ecstatic he understood her, the woman's words only registered to Kylie after the door shut.

'What? She called him Sam? His name's Sam!' Kylie yapped at Russell, then she scratched at the door and yelped, 'Let me in. Sam? Sam. I've gotta talk to you.'

On the other side of the door, Sam listened to the dog calling him. *She must really want bacon*, he thought, so he grabbed a handful of fat and rind from Wilfred's board.

'Hey! She didn't even say "please". Don't let her have it all,' Wilfred whined.

'She was grateful someone understood her. Hand it over. You can have some at your own house. Cooked,' Hazel said.

Amira grunted.

They could hear Kylie still scratching at the door, barking, 'Sam! Sam!' Then she howled.

'All right! All right!' Wilfred dropped a few meatier bits into Sam's hand.

Sam went back out to the alley, cupping the cured fat and pork in his fingers. As soon as he appeared, Kylie settled.

'Whatsat for?' Russell asked.

'She asked for it,' Sam replied.

'My dog talked to you?'

Sam nodded. He knew real humans couldn't understand dogs, but he couldn't lie.

'So, they let fruit cakes work here,' Russell said to Kylie.

'All this time,' Kylie muttered to herself. 'All this time.' She grinned doggedly at Sam.

'So, how long you been able to talk to animals?' Russell asked, and chuckled.

'Shut up and let the grown-ups talk.' Kylie nipped Russell's calf then sat down at Sam's feet. 'Sam, I need you to tell Russell he was out last night across from Churchill Square. A red-haired woman almost throttled him.'

'A red-haired woman?' Sam asked.

Russell startled. 'What about a red-haired woman?'

'Your dog said one almost throttled you last night.'

'She did?' Russell gulped. He stared at Sam. Then at Kylie.

Sam listened as the dog told a hurried and horrid story about the previous night. Kylie managed to yap out the whole thing while taking quick mouthfuls of bacon.

After the dog finished, Sam zipped up his jacket against the sudden chill.

'You're the Sam she's looking for, aren't you?' Kylie asked.

The door opened and the shifters returned to the alley. 'I finished cutting your carrots for you,' Amira said. She peered at him. 'You don't look well, Sam.'

'What? Who's Maggie?' Russell asked.

'The red-haired woman. You need to stay away from her,' Sam said to Russell. 'She's dangerous.'

'Tell him about his friend,' Kylie said.

'She sprinkled Markie a few nights ago ...' Sam started.

'Maxie,' Kylie yapped.

'Maxie,' Amira corrected.

Russell looked between Kylie and Amira. 'Nope, Kylie did not say that. It's some sort of trick. A trick.' Russell's face paled so much his lips went white, but Sam could see understanding unfold on his face. It looked painful. 'Did my dog really tell you all that?' Russell gave a resigned sigh. 'She was pretty. Young and pretty, but scary, then ... she changed ...' Russell said.

'Into an old crone', Hazel finished. 'Yeah, Sam's told us about her.'

'And you know she's dangerous.' Sam met Russell's gaze, willing the man to believe him. 'You ran away from your swag and didn't go back for ages.'

'Kylie really told you all that?' Russell asked. His voice had dropped to a whisper.

'She did. And she also doesn't like your rude comments about her weight.'

Kylie nipped Russell at that point to prove it.

Russell's eyes were ringed in blue circles.

'What are you going to do, Sam?' Hazel asked.

'She said she had a message for Sam. A warning,' Russell said. 'Something about him being in danger, about someone "talkin' like waves". Didn't make any sense.'

'Stay off the streets, if you can,' Sam said.

'How are we supposed to stay off the streets?' Russell asked. 'It's where I live. Don't have a nice home to lob up to.'

Sam dropped a little more of the bacon, but Kylie ignored it. 'I don't want Russell hurt again, Sam, and she's been coming at us homeless lot for a while. We can't just avoid her.'

Sam felt deflated. 'Well, it's me she wants. If you see her this evening, tell her I'll be in town tomorrow night. I can't avoid her forever either.'

CHAPTER 4

That night, Sam couldn't sleep. He sat on the Kavanagh roof with his eyes closed. It was 2 a.m.

Daniel had visited, hung around for two minutes, then flown off, saying he'd find out what could be done. He hadn't returned, and Sam had given up on seeing the angel again that night and was waiting for his thoughts to settle so he could go back to bed. Time seemed to slow when he was tired.

He wasn't getting much conversation out of anyone else. Wheedle lay belly up on the tiles and rock solid like a toppled statue. Bladder had slid off to the furthest corner of the roof and was rocking Nugget in gentle paw. The tiny gargoyle whined at him. When Bladder thought someone was watching, he grimaced as if it were all too difficult, but as soon as Wheedle fell to stony sleep, the lion's face softened and he purred at the baby gargoyle. Spigot looked content with Yonah snoozing on his back, peering over his shoulder repeatedly as if he was worried the dove might disappear.

Time whispered on. Eventually even Nugget fell asleep between Bladder's paws and the lion gargoyle turned to stone to stand over and protect the baby. Sam put his back to them and tried hard to fall into a nap.

The air whooshed and in a blurring glow of white Daniel sat next to him, his legs dangling by Sam's over the edge of the roof. They sat together in silence for a bit and watched owls wing from tree to tree through the park opposite.

'She's getting desperate to find you,' Daniel said finally.

'Yes. Did you find out what the stuff about talking waves meant? And about the coming danger? Who's in danger? Does she mean the gargoyles? The rest of the pack? The Kavanaghs?'

Daniel shrugged. 'We don't know, but it wasn't very wise of you to say you'd meet her, and to let her know you were coming. That's if she shows up. Perhaps she won't find Kylie and her human ... Here's hoping.'

'Russell and Kylie were going to tell all their friends at the centre, and others in the street. It's likely she'll find one of them.'

'You haven't had any sleep tonight, have you?'

Sam shook his head. 'Only a little. And it wasn't good. I want this over and done with. I've got to let her know I can't help her, that I'm not who she thinks I am. You have to help me. The Kavanaghs aren't going to let me go out tomorrow night by myself, unless you give them a strong suggestion. You can come with me. She can't do anything while you're around, right?'

'Theoretically,' Daniel agreed. 'But in a lot of situations, especially ones humans get themselves into, an angel's wings are tied. We aren't allowed to do anything that is a challenge to free will, you know that. If you choose to go, you have to deal with the consequences. What if she sends monsters to grab you?'

'I don't want to fight monsters either, so the best way to do that is not to make them in the first place. She has to know I won't help her.'

'She's a banshee, Sam, remember that. She's been manipulating your family for millennia. She'll think she can get you to do anything she wants if she puts it the right way.'

'I don't want her hurting strangers because she's looking for me, and what if she finds my friends or my family? Or my pack? They're not up to fighting an army of monsters.'

Sam peered at Wheedle. He was snoring. Bladder's eyes were open, but stone. Nugget lay awake, curled into a ball between Bladder's paws with her thumb stuck in her mouth. She stared at Sam with bright, interested eyes. 'Tham? Snuggy Nuggee?'

'Sure, Nugget.'

The little gargoyle lunged over to him, buried herself beneath his jacket and cuddled up to his face. Her little stone cheek chilled him, but he couldn't turn her away. In seconds, her eyes fluttered closed.

'I had a nightmare about what Kylie told us,' he said.

'That's not good.'

'No,' Sam replied. He shuffled over and leaned on Daniel, stealing his warmth. 'Can you check on Kylie and Russell? Then I can ...' He couldn't remember what the other thing was.

'Let me do something to help for tonight at least,' Daniel said.

Daniel put up two more blessings. It took about ten minutes.

'They're pretty,' Sam said. He yawned.

'Appearance doesn't matter. What matters is that nothing will come looking for you.' Daniel dusted his hands. They glowed pink. 'Even if Maggie sends troops to search for you, they won't notice the house. They won't even see a street here; they'll wander right by and go somewhere else. The whole Kavanagh family is as invisible as you can get. You could just stay in hiding ...'

'No, I can't, Daniel. Some problems need to be faced.'

'All right, but not now. You look worse than Wheedle.' Daniel put his hand on Sam's head. 'There. That's a touch of sleep.'

'A touch of sleep?'

'You have about ten minutes before it hits you. Nothing will wake you for the next few hours, and your sleep will go back to normal.'

Sam gave a weak smile. He did want to sleep.

Daniel waved and left. Sam needed to get back to bed. He tried to put Nugget down, but she clung to him. Finally, he gave in, scaling back to his room with the gargoyle at his chest. He tucked her into his bed and she scooched over, her thumb back in her mouth. He climbed in beside her and fell asleep.

Sam's bedroom door clicked as Richard opened it. 'You are still there!' he said. 'I've been calling and calling you. We went to church without you. Thought you'd be up when we got back. It's three p.m. Your ... Michelle has been worried.' Richard shook his head. 'But you obviously needed the sleep, you're looking much better than you did last night at dinner. Thought you were coming down with something.'

Sam looked at his clock – it did read 3 p.m. That wasn't right. He'd gone to bed more than twelve hours before.

Sam pushed back the bedclothes. Nugget had gone, but his sheets were dust grey.

Sam liked Sundays. They were lazy even without the extra sleep, and he ended up by himself watching TV. Nick had gone out with his friends.

He listened to Michelle and Richard pottering around the house, until they started one of their low-voice conversations. He filtered it out. Their talks about him always left him confused and bothered. At one point in the day, he did feel quite solitary, but he didn't mind. It was nice being alone sometimes. He needed to be alone to think about what he would say to Maggie tonight. He also knew, if Daniel wouldn't prompt the Kavanaghs to let him out when he asked, he'd have to sneak out. He hated even thinking about doing that to them. It seemed so dishonest.

When Nick came home, Sam heard the front door give a shrill whine on hinges that needed oiling, and dark settled over the street outside. Maggie would be out soon and he could catch the bus to town. He put on his puffer jacket and shoved pocket money into his jeans. He took a deep breath. He hadn't seen Daniel all day and he guessed even an angel's suggestions could only go so far. People could ignore them if they chose, and the Kavanaghs had never let him out at night before. He wondered how to bring it up.

He walked into the kitchen.

'There you are, Sam,' Michelle said. 'Don't you look handsome? And ready to go out. You must have read my mind.' Michelle and Richard exchanged a look. 'We're thinking of a family outing. Fancy going out to dinner?'

That blasted angel, Sam thought. Then he realised that the only way for Daniel to get Richard and Michelle to let him into town in the evening would have been for them to take him. Oh well, Sam did fancy a dinner out. He felt hungry. He'd been stressed, and at least he'd be with family. He'd have to work out how to keep them far away from where he met Maggie. He hoped he wasn't walking them into a trap.

When Sam didn't answer, Richard felt his forehead. 'You look pale again, like yesterday. You sure you're not coming down with something? We don't have to go out.'

Sam faked a smile. 'Nope, I feel fine. Let's do this.'

Sam and Nick sat in the back of the car. Beatrice burbled between them. 'Tham, Tham, Tham', she said at Sam, and then turned her attention to Nick. 'Ni, Ni, Ni.'

'I think she's saying your names', Michelle said. 'Mama? Can you say Mama?'

'Mama', Beatrice replied, and flew a handful of pink stars at Michelle.

'Dada.' Michelle pointed at Richard.

Beatrice mimicked her. 'Dada.'

Sam envied her. Michelle was never going to point at herself and Richard and expect Sam to say those words. Sigh.

'Nick', Michelle carried on.

'Ni.'

'Sam?'

'Tham, Tham, Tham.' Beatrice smacked Sam with a stuffed giraffe and laughed.

'Clever girl', Michelle said.

Sam stroked Beatrice's hand and she threw coloured sparkles through his hair.

Despite Sam's misgivings, the night started out great. There were people everywhere, and no sign of Maggie. They went to the pier and played in the arcade. Richard held Beatrice so that Michelle could challenge the boys, and then Michelle proceeded to complain about how many coppers she'd lost. Nick and Sam went on a few of the driving games by themselves. When the last of the shops closed on the high street, they wandered towards a quiet restaurant down The Lanes.

Sam had a piece of pie. He drank lemonade and ate ice cream. It had been dark before they left the pier, and it was even darker by the time they left the restaurant. The angelic sleep lifted him and he felt good, despite himself.

'Come on, time to go home,' Michelle said.

'Do we have to?' Nick asked.

Sam remembered why he was in town in the first place. He couldn't leave.

'Can I stay out too?' he asked.

Beatrice hung limply in Michelle's arms. 'She really needs to go to bed.'

Richard sighed.

'You don't want to go home either?' Michelle asked him.

Richard half-smiled. 'It's fine. Beatrice needs her beauty sleep.'

'Beatrice is tired and so am I, but there's no reason you can't spend some time with the boys by yourself. How about you drop me home?'

Nick cheered.

Sam didn't want to cheer, but he needed to end this with Maggie, so he did.

'You're old enough to be out together while I drop your mum home, aren't you?' Richard winked at the boys.

Nick wanted to play pool and led Sam to an all-ages games place. Sam stopped outside the door, scanning the street for Maggie. It was late enough for her to be out. Where was she? He was almost alone, this would be the best time to go looking for her.

'I might just go up and grab a kebab,' Sam said, pointing to a place three shops up.

'Dad would kill me if I let you go by yourself,' Nick said. 'Why d'you want a kebab? You had a huge dinner. You were eating like it was your last meal.'

'Was I?' Sam peered along the road. People wandered up and down, great crowds of them. Sam had never been out on a Sunday night before. It made him nervous, reminded him of tunnels full of imps running from the Great Cavern. There were people everywhere. He tried to tell himself that they were hurrying to get out of the cold, chatting and laughing on the way, not desperate and full of fear like the creatures down in The Hole.

'You know, I could eat a nice piece of baklava though,' Nick said.

Sam's skin prickled. He smelt the beginning of fairy dust in the air.

'Sam?' The Irish lilt had not changed. Her voice was as familiar as Michelle's. The crowd seemed to hear it too, their expressions growing foggy and distant, as if she were sending magic through her words.

'What was I saying?' Nick asked. He looked faint.

Sam pulled money out of his pocket. 'You were going to get me a kebab and get yourself a balaclava.'

'Baklava,' Nick said. 'Yeah, OK.' He wandered off to the shop.

Sam did not know what to feel. He'd come looking for her, after all, but he didn't feel relieved. He had been haunted by the idea of her for months, but the real her, the real Maggie, still meant something to him. When she stepped on to the footpath, her red hair streaming in the wind of a passing bus, he even smiled.

She turned and looked straight at him.

'Sam?' Maggie said. 'They said you'd come. I didn't believe them.' People passed her, their eyes looking rabbit-wild as they skittered around her, unseeing, pulling in jackets and skirts to avoid touching her. The atmosphere changed, got colder, and conversations that had been jolly and excited became dreamy. 'I've been looking for you for so long. You've finally heard my call. Why have you not come back?'

'Maggie, I can't come back to you. I have a new life now.'

'We need you, my darlin'. Do you not understand? All monsters need you. We know what you can do. An' I can protect you.'

Sam stared at her. 'Protect me from who?'

'You *can* sneeze them, can't you? You can make more of us.'

'It doesn't work the same. I sneezed a hatchling. It's stunted and it can't look after itself.'

'Oh, on the first few tries Thunderguts brought nothing into being. He thought he'd missed getting the magic.'

'But Nu ...' Sam stopped; he didn't want to tell Maggie Nugget's name. 'It's stunted. Wrong. It doesn't understand anything.' He hated talking about Nugget that way, but it was true. She wasn't a real monster, not even a real gargoyle if you thought about it. Even though Spigot couldn't talk, at least he understood things and could look after himself.

And the more useless Maggie believed Nugget to be, the greater chance she would leave Sam alone. 'It has to sleep. For all I know, all my sneezes won't hatch anything else.'

'What does that mean to me? I've collected enough fairy dust to protect me and mine. It's you we need.'

'What for? I thought ...' Sam paused. 'How do you even know about the sneezing?'

'That day you left The Hole, all surrounded by light, a pixie followed you and your gargoyle mates. He saw your little gargoyle hatch after you brought the dark bead to life. Did it not happen that way? But he told too many your secret. It's not just me and mine who have this knowledge. Now the wrong ones know.' Maggie looked weary. 'There's so few of us left. We need to stick together.'

'What wrong ones?'

'Sam, it's not only humans who are vulnerable now.' Her face twisted and she looked ready to cry. 'Besides, you can't be happy being human. There's more to you than being ordinary.'

'Actually, I'm really happy being human. I want to stay here.'

'Without me?' She looked so sad, so lonely. Sam wanted to comfort her. 'If you must, Sam. You must do what you want. I can't make you. But you will visit me sometime?'

'Really?' Sam had been ready to tell Maggie 'no, never'. He hadn't expected her to ask so little of him. Something, despite it all, he found he actually wanted to do. She had held his soul inside her for twelve years and it was hard not to feel that connection.

'Of course, my darlin'. Of all the other creatures walking this world, you're the only one who's found his way into my heart. You're my boy.'

Sam let her pull him into her arms. She kissed his head. The relief was huge. He felt for the first time he could have everything. He could be with the Kavanaghs, his pack, his friends and maybe even with Maggie sometimes.

'But I'm not the only one who wants this. I cannot say how the others will be should you refuse to come.'

Sam peered at Maggie's face. 'Who?'

'The old, old ones. The wet witches. They're the ones you've got to watch for.'

'What have I done to them?'

'They've just become tired of waiting, my darlin'. All monsters know of you and your magical sneezes, and certain ones think this means you belong with us. And my wet-sisters, well, they're getting angry, which could put everyone around you in danger. All your fragile human toys. I've heard them in the darkness. They've been singing a ditty to the ocean.' She sang:

'The sea, the sea, the hungry sea,
Send out your damp reply to me,
Eat the children, swallow them down,
Silence their breath. We'll watch them drown.'

Her voice sounded empty of emotion, deathly and cold. People stopped, their faces etched in pain, grief twisting their features. One man covered his face and broke into tears.

'Maggie, stop', Sam said.

She peered about, and looked surprised. 'I forget, Sam, when I'm singing. You know the power of a banshee's voice?'

Sam nodded. He was born with the knowledge. Maggie was the Kavanaghs' own banshee. She forewarned them of death in the family, she came wailing at their funerals – he'd first met her at Old Samuel Kavanagh's wake. He knew a banshee could fill her voice with death, but he'd never heard her do it before.

'It's the nature of the song. Let me try again.'

She sang it again, her voice loud, eerie and inhuman, but this time it was lovely. He could hear the chant over the noise of the cars and the people on the street.

She sang it a third time. Sam frowned. What did it mean? Did someone mean to drown all the children?

Nick appeared, a wrapped kebab in one hand and a brown paper bag in the other. 'Go away', he said to Maggie.

Maggie smiled at Nick. 'Oh, a Kavanagh. I always recognise them in the street. They see me as well as I see them. It's the touch of the "other" they've got. I'm here as your friend, Nick.'

'Go away', Nick said again.

'It's Kavanaghs keepin' you from me, isn't it?' Maggie asked. 'Why don't you bring them with you? We could all be together. A family.'

Nick trembled.

Maggie kissed Sam again, soft lips on his forehead, strangely motherly and possessive all at once. She wagged a finger at him, still smiling as she moved off with the crowd. 'Bye, my darlin'.' A man looking at his phone stepped sideways to get around her.

Sam wondered what the song meant. He had to get home, to see Daniel. The angel would know what to do. He watched as Maggie walked away. She looked alone and little on the street. He noticed her feet were bare. It was so cold and she had bare feet.

Richard came up the street. 'So, what do you want to do now? A movie?'

Nick shook his head. His face was white.

Richard put his hand on Nick's forehead. 'You don't look good.'

'Yeah, I feel all queasy. That girl ...' Nick pointed, but Maggie had blended in with the people on the footpath. They couldn't see her any more.

'Let's get you home.'

'Yes, as quickly as possible,' Sam said.

Richard frowned.

They moved in the direction of the car park. As they walked further from Maggie, Nick's colour returned and the furrow between Richard's eyes softened.

Sam followed. He'd lost interest in his kebab.

'Sam.' Maggie's voice followed him along the street. 'You'll always be my boy.'

Eleven p.m. Sam's sleep the night before had made him far too alert. He and Daniel had had a long chat, and the angel had gone off to ward the shifters' houses against water damage. It took an age for Daniel to reappear. The gargoyles danced with agitation and no one could stop Nugget crying until the angel returned.

'Your house has been flood-warded too. Yonah's got a real talent for it', Daniel said. 'But you can't drown anyway, Sam, even if the sea rises to here. The angel patted the roof.

'But Michelle, Richard ...'

'Up on a hill. We've got tonnes of time to get them out.'

'I'll keep watch. If the sea starts looking funny ...' Bladder said.

'Call me', Daniel finished.

Sam exhaled and when he inhaled, sleepiness came with it. He yawned. Relief was tiring.

'Take Nugget with you.' Wheedle pushed the little gargoyle at Sam. 'Then the rest of us can take turns on guard duty.'

Sam woke with a shrill burn filling his ears and head. He screamed with sudden, hot pain. The noise came from everywhere, as if it were in the room, on the street, and in his head too.

The clamour went on and on.

His practice of not eavesdropping had given him a lot of ear control, and normally he'd be able to drive loud sounds down and away a bit, but this cacophony was different. It was insistent and invasive.

He jumped out of bed and Nugget slid into the soft space left by his body, sleeping soundly through it. Sam shoved his fingers into his ears as hard as he could. It muffled the drilling a little, but that was all. For some reason, he thought it was a song. He'd heard music many times: he loved singing himself, even though there were songs he didn't like. When singers and musicians hit painful high notes it left him very unimpressed – the shifters too – but he'd come to realise those with human ears couldn't hear the shrieking tones. This pained pitching made him think of those songs – sneaky notes, secret chords, a furtive melody that only an imp or a dog could hear.

He forced his head into his mattress to smother the hideous noise.

'Block it! Block it! Block!' he yelled at himself, and it worked a little, enough for him to regain his own head.

The piercing trill lessened. It didn't disappear, but it softened and he could hear Beatrice's cries through the walls.

Soon his ears blocked the strange song altogether, although pain still brewed behind his eyes. The noise pricked at his skin, even as his ears refused it.

He gave himself a few seconds to shake off the awful choir and right himself before he followed the cry to Beatrice's room.

Neither Michelle nor Richard was with her. How could they sleep through the noise?

Beatrice had clambered to the side of her cot. She barely knew how to crawl and yet she was standing, holding the bars between clenched hands, doing her best to get one stumpy, lumpy leg over the top. It wasn't working.

What struck Sam most was the colour of her sparkles. She was shooting out strange, awful colours, frazzled reds and harsh oranges, like a fire alarm going off. Their sharpness made him duck as she flung them at him, but the sparkles hit no harder than normal, bouncing off and shooting back at Beatrice.

For a moment Sam thought someone was calling his name, but then Beatrice spotted him and squawked, reaching for him with angry fists, losing her balance and tottering over the edge of the railing. Sam swept over and plucked her from the cot, meaning to comfort her, but she writhed and wriggled in his arms, a tough bundle of starter muscles and fat. She was winning the fight.

When she wouldn't stop twisting, he dropped rather than put her back in her cot. It made her more desperate to escape than he'd ever seen her. Her sparkles flew at him and her face grew redder and redder, her bellows doubling in fury. Sam patted her but stopped when she went to bite his arm with her new white teeth.

Then the song grew more powerful. His ears still blocked it out, but his skin bristled with it; his bones vibrated as if he too were being played like a wooden instrument.

Beatrice stared at him, her mouth and eyes wide and leaking. She wailed and then a gust of wind rushed past him towards his bedroom, and a door slammed.

The wind stopped.

As if there wasn't enough noise, at that moment Bladder yelled for him from the ground floor.

CHAPTER 5

Sam lunged down the stairs, fell the last five steps, and managed to land on all fours like a cat-shaped gargoyle. The front door was open and the black shape of Bladder was framed in the doorway.

'Sam!' Bladder called out so loudly, Sam was sure it would wake Richard and Michelle. The gargoyle's eyes were clenched shut. Sam saw him take a pipeful of breath and get ready to yell again.

'What?' Sam yelled back.

'I've been screaming for ages.'

'I've been distracted. I think Beatrice is trying to get out of the cot.' Upstairs, Beatrice let out a frustrated wail.

'She is,' Bladder replied. 'Come on!' The stone cat raced into the street.

Sam dashed after him.

He stopped on the footpath and glanced about. There were young people everywhere: little children all the way up to high-schoolers not much older than Nick. Some carried babies in their arms and others were hardly more than babies themselves pattering barefoot down the road, thumbs in mouths, like a carnival or parade. They all marched in the same direction.

Their eyes stared blankly, unblinking. Sam still didn't know everything there was to know about humans, but he was pretty sure this was not normal behaviour.

'What in the world ... ?' Sam stared about him. He felt very glad that he had shut the door to Beatrice's bedroom before he'd run to answer Bladder's call.

'Oh, it gets better.'

Bladder pushed through the crowd. Sam followed as the mob washed around him on their continued hike, and the song needled into Sam's skull again.

In the midst of the hypnotised mob, Nick, Spigot and Wheedle tussled on the road.

A lump grew on Nick's forehead, and he was punching his fists raw into Wheedle's stone flanks, his face vacant and emotionless.

'Stop fighting!' Sam yelled at the mess of gargoyles and human boy.

'Tell that to HIM!' Wheedle said between *oophs*. 'We're trying to stop this idiot running off with the crowd. Look at them.'

Bladder jumped in, pinning Nick's wrists under his huge forepaws.

They were high enough on the hill that Sam could see the multitude as they moved further down, heading south. Those nearer him tramped on after them. He jumped in front of a boy carrying a silent baby. The boy stepped around him. He clapped his hands right up close in someone's face; the person did not blink. He grabbed the arm of one of the walkers, a girl of about ten. 'Where are you going?' he asked.

The girl did not look at him, but she growled and twisted Sam's wrist so hard he cried out.

Nursing his hand, he faced the gargoyles still fighting Nick. 'Do any of you know what's happening?'

Bladder replied with an *ugh* as Nick kicked him in the belly.

Nick was bleeding and Sam was sure he heard something crack when the older boy kicked Bladder's solid underside.

As the crowd about them thinned away, the awful song softened too. Then other noises returned; ones Sam hadn't realised he'd missed. Birds sang again, a bin clanged and a dog barked.

Hoy Poy. He let out a relieved breath as he listened for Beatrice. She sounded content as she resettled herself. Michelle and Richard remained sleeping inside his home. The other noises he was used to – conversations humming behind doors, people starting their days, even the traffic on roads – those he couldn't hear and he was trying. He shivered, as did the gargoyles. Nobody said a thing for a minute, and Sam's skin broke into goosebumps.

The only normal sound was Hoy Poy's worried yap. The neighbour's shivering pug raced out of his house. 'She won't wake up! Won't wake up!' he barked.

Then Nick stopped fighting. He sat up and looked around, the distant expression gone from his face. He groaned and fell in a heap, his gaze suddenly alert and darting from Bladder to Wheedle to Spigot and back again. Sam realised Nick was going to have some nasty bruises and maybe some breaks from fighting three gargoyles.

Spigot fell on his tail feathers next to Nick and let out a relieved shriek.

'What's happening?' Wheedle asked.

'I don't know,' said Sam, 'but I think that sound is calling everyone down there.'

Spigot garbled.

Wheedle gulped.

'What did he say?' Sam asked.

'Towards the sea,' Bladder replied.

An icy wind chilled him. Maggie had warned him about waves and a wet witches' song, and now here they were. *Watch them drown?*

He shuddered. Another cold gust blew at him, and he remembered he was wearing his pyjamas. No time to worry about that.

'You need to find Daniel and get Nick inside. I've got to follow them.' Sam pointed towards the mob.

Bladder nodded at Sam. 'Spigot, Wheedle, you put Nick back to bed.'

'Check Beatrice too. And Michelle and Richard,' Sam added.

'Nugget?' Wheedle cried out and looked to the house. 'Did she ... ?'

'Fast asleep in my bed when I last saw her,' Sam said.

The stone bull exhaled. 'Oh, thank—'

Sam frowned. 'The song didn't bother her at all.'

'Lucky her,' Bladder said. 'It's not particularly pleasant.'

Spigot screeched

'True,' Wheedle agreed. 'If I hadn't already been awake, I don't think it would have got me up.'

'It woke me, but I think it's horrible,' Sam said. He stopped himself. 'But the humans seem to find it irresistible.'

'*Young* humans,' Wheedle amended.

Yes, that had struck Sam too. 'We've got to find out what those kids are doing.'

'Right! You've gotta call Daniel.' Bladder pointed at Wheedle. 'Let him know we think those kids are heading to water. Useless bird-brain is probably watching the weather or expecting a tsunami to hit.'

Wheedle shook his horns. 'So were the rest of us, Bladder.'

Bladder harrumphed.

Hoy Poy's whimper came from the neighbour's house.

Sam looked up at the noise. 'Go see if Mrs Roberts is all right too, and give Hoy Poy a treat. Tell him to stay off the street.'

Spigot squawked.

Bladder stopped and sighed. 'You're not coming, Spigot. Whoever goes down there's probably gonna get smashed, but I'm used to it.'

Sam nodded. 'Bladder's right. If you're watching my family, I'll feel much better.'

'Less talk, more run,' Bladder said. 'Climb on.'

Sam clambered on to Bladder's back and the pair galloped after the crowd. Sam peered back to see Spigot gently lift Nick from the ground and limp him back into the house. Then Bladder turned the corner, and Sam could no longer see his home. He listened to the hard click of stone footfalls running over asphalt and the horrible high notes that seemed to be drawing the children away. As they got closer to the crowd, the song got louder again.

When Sam and Bladder broached the top of the next hill, they could see all the way to the shore.

'Oh no,' Bladder said.

Sam groaned.

The song was definitely a call to the sea. At the very head of the crowd, distant children were descending the blue-green steps leading to Brighton's cobbled beach and wading into the water.

Sam saw heads disappear under the waves.

'They'll drown,' Bladder said.

Sam nodded. He couldn't say a thing. He thought he was going to be sick. Maggie had warned him.

And the hideous sound went on and on and on.

Sam studied the crowd. It moved with consistent tread towards its doom.

Sam swallowed the acid tears that gathered behind his eyes. He wiped his nose on his sleeve and wondered how many children were walking to their deaths.

Bladder kept running. He knocked into a few kids as he dashed among them. Some fell, going down hard, but they got back up again and shuffled forward. Bladder pushed on, getting between kids, darting and jumping over their heads to get in front of them. Sam didn't know why. They couldn't hold back this crowd any more than they could hold back the sea itself. Maybe one or two people, but there were thousands. And three gargoyles had struggled to hold Nick down. What could Bladder and Sam do against thousands, or tens of thousands?

'If we can stop that horrible noise', Bladder said, as if he knew Sam's fears, 'we might be able to save most of them.'

Sam was glad Bladder was thinking clearly, but to do that they had to find where the sound was coming from.

It felt strange looking at those young, lifeless faces. As if they'd drowned already. Sam wondered why there were no adults. Like Wheedle said, it was just 'young humans'.

Sam gulped. '"Eat the *children*, swallow them down."'

'What?' Bladder asked as he headed for the shore, following the high crooning notes.

'It's the ...' Sam saw a dark-haired boy shuffling southwards like all the other zombies. 'Wilfred! Bladder, stop, I think I saw Wilfred', Sam cried as they raced by him.

'We've got a better chance of saving him if we can stop the sound.'

They hit Kings Road, the street that ran parallel to the shore, but the racket was coming from further out. Bladder raced towards the beach.

'It sounds like it's out at sea a bit. Let's get to the end of Brighton Pier. It must be coming from there,' Bladder said, and bunched his hind legs before launching himself up, hurdling over the locked gate and racing along the wooden boards.

The pier creaked and complained; it bent and blamed under the weight of the gargoyle. The clamouring song grew no nearer. Sam watched over the railing to see children in endless rows pushing into the water. If they didn't drown, they would freeze, all of them barefoot and in thin pyjamas and nighties, not a dressing gown among them. He wept to see a boy with a baby in his arms step up to his chest into winter-wild water.

Bladder came to a stop and Sam slipped from his back. There was no one at the end of the pier. The rides hung with salt from the air and were covered in tarpaulins and ropes. Only a few lights remained on for security. A racket came from further out, further than Sam could see.

There were no adults about, not one. No one who could help him stop even a few of the children, and they kept on walking into the water. How could they press on against the freezing waters? They couldn't be awake. At least he could hope they didn't feel anything.

Bladder headed to the rail and put his paws up on the metal. His face twisted in a defeated grimace.

He stood for a few moments staring over the waves. Sam called above the noise, wanting Daniel. His throat hurt as the salt from sea and tears mixed and burned his screams.

Winter clouds greyed the sky.

'Sam!' Bladder yelled, breaking through his thoughts. 'Look over there.'

Sam peered down at the water.

The sea was churning, full of active fish life, and among them ...

'Look there, Sam, a shark.'

'Is it eating ... ?' Sam's chest hurt from the cold pressing in on him. He hadn't been aware how thin his pyjamas were, but the early morning wind bit, its teeth as strong as any ogre's. 'We've got to stop anyone else going in,' Sam said.

'Oh my.' Bladder's voice sounded hollow and distant.

'Now, Bladder!' He climbed on to the stone lion without asking, and Bladder ran back to the shore.

Even close to the beach, the water churned. Sam squinted. His eyes were good in the dark. But this was dark, plus movement, plus a lot of water. He couldn't make out any one thing.

A boy's head bobbed out of the foam. His black, vacant eyes peered at the shore. Sam's fingers prickled. More high notes sallied in over the water and poked him, and the pins and needles were not just uncomfortable, they were painful.

Bladder flew over the railing, then in quick strides lobbed on to the crowded beach. The mesmerised children continued to shuffle silently in the dark, the reflection of lamps and lines on the water giving them ghostly silhouettes. Bladder pushed through the kid-covered shore. And as many stepped into the water, others came along Kings Road to fill the space behind them.

A large silver fish flipped out of the water and back in again, reflecting streetlight.

'Do you think the animals're here because of the song too?' Bladder asked.

Sam watched the children walk mechanically into the water. The fish slid and glided amongst the waves. 'If they've been called here, it's not to do the same thing as the kids.' Sam watched the shark fins. He didn't want to guess what the song was telling the fish to do.

Sam saw another shark fin circle the water ahead of the walkers.

He looked back at the lost faces bearing down on Bladder on the beach. They eddied around the lion gargoyle and his passenger.

Sam watched the other defenceless children at the shoreline. A boy ducked underwater. When he came up again, his nose had extended. Sam blinked. It had grown very long and smooth.

'Sam!' Bladder said.

Sam tore his stare away from the long-nosed boy.

'Look at that,' Bladder said.

A small child lay in the water, forced forward by the next group of walkers. She pushed her arms into the cold sea in a smooth breaststroke. Sam saw her turn in the water, and where her arm should have been, a fin grew. The boy next to her slid under the waves and then stood again, his water-darkened hair clinging to his skin. A lump rose on his back, not a solid lump, a sleek and fine ...

Bladder saw it too, and pointed to the boy. 'That a ... shark's fin?'

'They're all changing,' Sam answered.

Children dipped into the water and their pyjamas became scales. Blue scales, red scales, rainbow scales. Polka dots spattered to the natural dots of trout. Pink nighties became salmon. Larger children turned to larger fish, tiny children into schools of whiting. A boy over six foot tall slid into the water, which rippled underneath him. Sam followed the wake of the ripple; when it was not too far out a furred seal's face erupted from the waves and moved further out to sea, the strange noise calling them on.

'They're not drowning,' Bladder said.

'They're turning into sea creatures,' Sam replied.

'But they're not drowning. Which means someone might be able to fix it.'

Sam had no idea who he was going to find that could turn anyone back into a human.

Bladder retreated from the sea's attempts to slip between stones to lick at his paws. 'I don't think I wanna touch that water though,' he said, the mob sliding around him. 'Who knows what's in it.'

65

CHAPTER 6

Daniel alighted on the top of the Royal Albion Hotel. The noise had faded, but it had not completely died down.

Sam, Bladder and Yonah sat with the angel and stared around at the twin towns of Brighton and Hove. Even at a distance – and Sam was used to listening to distances – there were not enough of the right sounds, and too many of the wrong ones. The streets so far were mostly empty and the clock tower said it was well after 10 a.m. The few people who woke were doing so sluggishly, into a nightmare. He couldn't hear specifics, except the sound of the occasional door slam and voices thick with terror sobbing out names. Many phones echoed as the ringing went on and on and no one replied. The majority of doors remained closed. And the shore became less and less of a fish stew as the children-turned-sea-creatures swam further out.

'How far did the song reach?' Sam asked.

'Yonah travelled far and wide', Daniel, said. 'All the way to Worthing that way and Peacehaven the other. It doesn't go too far inland, though. She got up past Stanmer Park, and told me most of the families up there are behaving normally. Of the houses in the danger zone, though, most children are gone. A few little ones were trapped in cots, like Beatrice. The ones left behind have gone back to sleep. Probably exhausted by their night's exertions. But it's Monday', he added. 'and a lot of adults are still asleep. The parents of older kids won't realise – they'll think they've overslept and the kids have gone off to school. 'It's a clever song. Tempts the children out of bed and knocks the adults right out.'

'A symphony for everyone', Bladder scoffed.

'You couldn't find where it was coming from?' Sam asked.

The angel shook his head.

'It's coming from over there.' Bladder pointed beyond the pier.

'It seems to carry on the wind, changing direction. For us anyway.' Yonah cheeped to support Daniel.

Sam winced as a hysterical voice – he couldn't tell if it was a man or a woman – shrieked out 'Bram! Abraham!' but no one replied.

'The Kavanaghs haven't woken up yet?' Bladder asked.

Daniel shook his head. 'Like most of the adults. Nick was out flat on his face, he'd drooled a huge grey patch on to his pillow. But he's all healed.' Daniel held out his hands to show the source of the healing. 'Michelle and Richard, Beatrice as well, hardly moving.'

'And ... ?' Bladder asked.

'Wheedle, Spigot and Nugget are fine. Wheedle may have helped himself to your stash of chocolate. Stress eating, he said.'

Sam shrugged. He was more concerned about the scene before him. 'We have to follow the song, to find out where the kids have gone,' he said.

'Let's get going, then. Can't sit here all day,' Bladder replied, and headed for the footpath.

They listened; the sound lilted distantly in the air. Sam could barely hear it.

Daniel grabbed Sam and flew him towards the ground. It was so odd to do that in the middle of town on a weekday morning, but the main road, normally chock-full of commuters and buses bursting with schoolkids, sat silent and empty. Grey seas churned towards the town; the wind set the ashy skies boiling above.

Sam looked at Brighton Pier. A half-shaved, unbrushed man shuffled towards one of the food stands. 'I'm so late,' he muttered. He yawned a few times. He stopped and stared at the other stands, and looked around. Sam could guess what he was thinking. *If I'm late, where's everyone else?* When no one approached him, after a few moments he sat down and nodded off.

Bladder raced across the street. There were no cars to run him down and the only people looking were an old couple treading at a sprightly pace down the footpath.

Sam stared at them. The few other people he saw shuffled along staring at their feet. The woman gawked at Bladder and Sam, shook her head and trundled on. Sam heard her whisper, 'Do you think they're with the Christmas show?'

The old man, the first person Sam had seen with any energy, looked at her with a frown and then clicked on his hearing aid as he walked past Sam.

The gargoyle flumped down on the footpath. 'Being able to run around without scaring anyone's quite odd.'

A woman came hurtling out of a hotel door and called, 'Margery? Margery?'

'Tell me again what Maggie said,' Daniel said. 'Describe everything for me.'

Sam described the sound and how Beatrice had behaved. Bladder added pointers on Nick's response. Then, of course, what happened in the water, when the children all turned into sea creatures.

'Maggie said the wet witches sang a spell about the sea and then the kids all ended up in it,' Sam concluded.

'Bet you Maggie's doing it. Banshees sing too, you know,' Bladder said.

'I don't think so,' Sam said. 'I've only heard her use her singing voice once, but it makes people miserable, not behave like that.'

Both Daniel and Bladder opened their mouths, but more people appeared in the street. Even with a gargoyle in full view, though, they were only interested in Sam. A man came shambling along the front, holding the railing for support. He drew closer and peered up at Sam, a smile almost on his mouth, before studying him closer.

'Have you seen a boy about your age, dark hair? He'll be wearing ...' And then the man stopped. 'I don't know what he'll be wearing.' He staggered up the footpath. He wasn't the only one searching for someone, Sam heard doors banging and confused calls turn into high-pitched yells.

'It's nearly eleven a.m.', Daniel said. 'The parents are waking.'

Bladder used his nose to point at wild-eyed adults staggering into the streets. 'Better make our apologies and go.' He peered out to sea again. 'It's like the pied piper came and whistled the children away. Do you think it's that? The salty version of a pied piper?' Bladder asked.

A woman ambled towards them.

She stopped, groggily peering at Sam. 'Sam', she said. 'Is that you?'

Sam looked at the face and its half-hearted attempt at a smile. It was the owner of the sweet shop in The Lanes. 'Hello, Mrs Williams', he said.

'It's all gone haywire today. I'm not sure where's up and where's down. People on my street seemed to have misplaced their children. It's such a relief to see one in the flesh. Come by the shop later and let me give you a sugar mouse or two.'

'I don't have any money, Mrs Williams.'

'Don't worry about that, I'm just glad to see you. If you're here, it might be a prank? Right? It did scare me though, I called my daughter to make sure my grandchildren were all right.'

'Were they?'

'Oh, yes, she'd taken them off on the school run a couple of hours ago. Everyone was there, she said.'

'Where was that?'

'Molesey,' she said. 'Near Hampton Court Palace. Have you been there?'

Sam shook his head.

'It really is good to see your face, Sam,' Mrs Williams said. 'Come by the shop, I'll give you a big bag of something.' She stared at Bladder. 'Aren't these pieces amazing? I've seen some in The Lanes. They move them around.' She pushed on Bladder. 'So heavy, though – don't know how they do it.'

Daniel and Yonah flew off in one direction to check on something and left Sam and Bladder as a few more people appeared, screamed and disappeared up the streets.

They watched for a while, until Bladder looked up, listening. 'The sound's stopped.'

Sam listened too. Yes, it had gone. Just wind and human voices filled the air. Something else had changed as well. A man wandered past Sam and Bladder and shook his head as if waking himself. Shops began to open, and in a few minutes there seemed to be police officers everywhere, many scrambling to put on their uniforms properly as they ran on to the streets. Soon, cars came out of side streets and the road along the beach looked as packed as normal.

The people on the streets were growing more alert, Sam realised. Traffic started to build too, but the drivers

71

weren't watching the roads as well as they could. Too often people looked at him, called out and had to slam on their brakes for fear of hitting pedestrians. Others screamed at each other.

'Let's get out of sight a bit?' Bladder suggested.

Sam heard a click across the street as someone's TV went on and he could saw a flickering screen through a window. He scurried towards it as people called to him: 'John', 'Waleed', 'Sonny'. Only one woman gasped to see the stone lion running behind him.

Although Sam couldn't make out the pictures on the television, he could hear it. He huddled down by Bladder's side, using him to shield him from people's eyes and as a windbreak. It didn't help much; Sam was freezing. His fingers had turned blue. He bet his lips had too.

A news reporter's voice said, 'Just in. It appears there has been a mass disappearance of children in Sussex. The central city of Brighton seems most affected, but losses have reached as far as Goring-by-Sea to the west and Newhaven to the east. Areas north of Brighton seem unaffected. All the missing children are seventeen and younger, and some are babies. The police are baffled. Evidence suggests the children left willingly. There have been no signs of forced entry recorded, and in many cases the front door was left wide open. A secondary effect that has MI5 officials concerned is the apparent drugging or sedating of many adults in the area. Even childless adults have succumbed to what professionals are describing as a "mass narcolepsy". People are mentioning signs of grogginess, over-sleeping and difficulty in focusing. The town, most famous for its holiday ...'

Bladder peered up. 'Incoming!' he yelled as Daniel and Yonah landed on the footpath. Sam huddled close to Daniel, trying to warm himself in the angel's wings.

Bladder looked at Daniel's dour face. 'What?'

'Was Wilfred at home?' Sam asked.

'No. You might be right; it was him in the crowd. The shifters were just as affected as everyone else. We checked on Hazel and Amira. They're all gone. All the puppies. Mrs Kintamani rang 'Thrope Control, calling in the big guns. It's obviously supernatural in nature.

Yonah looked as dejected as Daniel.

'There's something you should ...' Daniel started.

A noise smothered his voice. A jam had halted the flow of traffic and angry people were pouring from their vehicles, filling the street. Open fighting began. A man still in his pyjamas punched a driver in the face; another man jumped out of his car and used a cricket bat to smash someone's windscreen.

'Nope, definitely not sleepy any more', Bladder said.

'Yonah', Daniel said.

The dove cooed and took to the street. She did nothing more than fly over the conflict and it settled. The woman with the smashed-up windscreen got out of the car. The man with the bat flung it to the ground and fell on to her shoulder sobbing. Two men stopped yelling and fell into a hug. Instead of letting their separate frustrations explode again, they shared their common grief.

'Recite the poem, Sam,' Daniel asked.

Sam shuddered. His voice cracked as he spoke.

'The sea, the sea, the hungry sea,
Send out your damp reply to me,
Eat the children, swallow them down,
Silence their breath. We'll watch them drown.'

'Someone stole their breath. Stole their lungs too. They've become fish. Turning them into fish would take a huge amount of magic,' Bladder said.

'But they didn't drown,' Daniel said. 'The song mentioned drowning.'

'It's a metaphor,' Bladder replied.

Sam felt sick.

Bladder continued. 'But why turn them to fish?'

A cold as chilly as the Atlantic swept over Sam. *We'll watch them drown.* Metaphor or not, the thought made him shudder.

At last, the streets were truly filled with people. They banged into each other, searched for places their children might have visited, knocked on shop doors. Many sobbed out loud.

A man stumbled by in his dressing gown. He stopped Sam. The man's feet were bare and his toes had turned a shocking blue.

'Son! Son!' he called after Sam. 'Where are the children? Where are the other children?'

When Sam didn't answer, the man grabbed him by his pyjama top.

Bladder pushed his huge, heavy body between them, growling with the deep threat of the lion he resembled. The dressing-gowned man backed off, then, like all the other terrified adults, he sobbed.

Bladder's head jerked. He stared at the water once more. 'Sam, look at that.'

The water was bubbling again. It was full of fish.

'They've come back.' Sam pelted towards the steps and on to the beach, paddling into the icy water so his pyjama trousers were wet to the knee and he could barely feel his toes. Small fish cruised along the shore. Further out, the larger creatures swam and slid over each other. Even a whale popped up and blew a stream of water into the air.

'The song's stopped an' they've come back. Do you think it's stopped for good?' Bladder asked. 'If we can find some magic to turn them back ...'

Yonah alighted on Sam's shoulder and Daniel soared over the water. Under him, light reflected, and a dolphin jumped up, skimming the angel's belly with its silver snout.

The dolphin turned and chirped at Sam and Bladder.

'I want a closer look at that dolphin,' Sam said.

Sam took off back towards the Brighton Pier entrance. Someone had done their job and unlocked the gates, but there were no customers and most of the kiosks remained shut. Sam followed the barrier along the edge; the schools, shoals, floats, fleets, companies, clusters, pods, herds and flocks of sea creatures followed alongside, the mammals in the group barking, yelping and hooting up to him. Daniel carried Bladder to the pier and dropped his heavy stone body on to the planks.

Sam studied the thundering water as he raced towards the end of the pier, where the angel, the dove and the gargoyle waited, staring over the latticed barrier.

The water churned as here and there shapes broke the surface. Silver-metalled fish, grey-furred seals, a black slick-backed shark and a little whale side by side. Most of the creatures of the deep in one place, wriggling over each other. The water eddied and flowed with thousands of them clustering around the pier's supports.

'What are they doing?' Sam asked.

Bladder sidled up next to him with his forepaws on the railing. 'You'd think with all that food about, the shark would have gone crazy.'

A shark's wide mouth surfaced over the water and Sam saw myriad teeth inside its head. The fish about it swam away, but the shark did not bite after them.

'Hey! Hey! Up here, sharky?' Bladder called.

Many of the creatures looked, not just the shark. Sam studied their expressions; there was something odd about them. He'd only been around six months, but he felt he should know what made the shark's face look wrong, what made the seal's face look strange. There were humans inside those sea creatures, he knew, and somehow there was something very human about their faces still. What was it?

The sea creatures peered at him with deliberate, intelligent expressions. Then they all slipped back under the waves.

The water hubbled and bubbled again, troubling him.

Then three heads burst the surface. Yes, the dolphins. The three slithery, silver creatures burbled, their chuckling voices talking directly at him. The one in the middle looked between Sam and Daniel, Daniel and Sam again and again, chortling at them both.

Sam whispered to Bladder. 'I can see there's something odd about them, but what is it?'

Bladder grinned. 'They have human eyes.'

The three dolphins continued gabbling at him. They barked and chatted as if they were expecting him to understand, but he didn't. He understood birds and dogs; why couldn't he understand other creatures? Unless the strange song's magic had muffled that gift.

Three sets of eyes. Human eyes, he knew, with pupils and irises. Two dark brown sets, one honey-coloured.

'Hazel?' he yelled. The dolphin with honey-coloured eyes shrieked back at him. She flipped out of the water and head over tail, splashing the pier.

The other two had to be Amira and Wilfred.

'Wilfred?' he called. The dolphin chuckled and nodded its shiny grey head. 'Amira?' The other dolphin nodded too.

'Well, at least we know exactly where your friends are,' Daniel said. 'And they're still thinking like humans.'

'For now,' Bladder said.

CHAPTER 7

'I've got to find Maggie,' Sam said. 'She'll know what to do. If it's the wet witches, she'll stop them.'

'Yes, of course she will,' Bladder said, 'and what'll she charge you to put it back the way it was?'

Daniel sighed. 'It's true. She'll help you, but she'll probably ask you to build an army to do the work, and once they have finished helping you, that army will look forward to eating humans. If she has a strong enough army, they won't need to hide any more – they could come out of the shadows and fight back. At the moment, humans are far too strong for them to be openly destructive.'

'Well, what can I do to help them?' Sam gestured at the sea creatures.

'I wouldn't make Maggie the first person I asked,' Bladder replied.

Daniel agreed. 'Let's try to do this ourselves first, with no magic help. So, what can we do right now?'

Sam watched the sea creatures. They were grouped in their species, and the water rocked and waved as the bigger creatures cruised below. The dolphins circled the legs of the pier and came back to stare at him, willing him to tell them something.

Sam leaned over the barrier. 'Can everyone understand me?'

Every sea creature near the water's surface turned to him, then paused before many of them dived back under.

'Maybe not,' Daniel said.

Sam exhaled, disappointed.

'Wait, look,' Bladder said.

More heads popped up and seals further out nudged schools of fish. Their glittering heads broke the surface, gasped as they stared at him. Sam knew they couldn't breathe above water, so they were going without for a few seconds to look at him. From Brighton Pier to the Palace Pier, crowds of sea creatures stared back at him.

'I'd take that as a sign,' Bladder said.

Sam raised his voice so he could be heard above the wind. 'I need you to stay here. Between the piers. We'll try to figure out how to get you home. On two legs.'

He guessed his words didn't carry far, but the fact he could tell them anything felt reassuring.

The creatures who could make a noise hooted and bellowed, chittered and roared. Those ones who couldn't – fish mainly – opened and shut their mouths. So many, in fact, it created a bubbling sound. A seal floated up behind the dolphins and waved a fin at him. Sam wondered if he knew it from school. Wilfred, Amira and Hazel jumped out of the water, creating celebratory splashes.

'They seem safe enough. Still here and not eating each other,' Sam said.

'They'll get hungry soon,' Bladder said.

'Books!' Daniel said. 'We need some books.'

'Seriously?' Bladder asked. 'Is this really the best time to start a reading club, Egghead?'

Daniel ignored the gargoyle and flew off into the wintry grey sky.

He returned after a few minutes, carrying a large leather-bound book. Gold words stamped on its cover read *The Book of Water*.

Daniel handed it to Sam. The cover fell open, and Sam flicked through the first few pages. The first one, the flyleaf, was blank. The next page was a painting of a trio of beautiful girls motioning a young man into a lake. The man was looking at the girls with the same lost and blank expression Sam remembered on the faces of the kids as they'd walked into the water. The song did that. Sam decided he didn't like the picture at all. He stood up and looked over the side of the pier. The three dolphins were bobbing around each other in the water. He held out the book.

'What's out there in the water? Who was singing that song?' Sam asked. 'Is it ladies like these ones?'

All three dolphins looked at the pages and then

around at the hundreds of splattering fish, schools of identical herring, identical cod, identical salmon, tiny silver whiting. They didn't reply.

'Perhaps they don't know either. They can't have swum too far out before the song stopped,' Daniel said.

'What else does the book say?' Bladder asked.

Sam slid back down to the decking and turned the next page. At least it had a contents page. It listed 'Large Saltwater Monsters' first: 'Behemoth', 'Cetis', 'Charybdis', 'Giant Octopus', 'Kraken', 'Leviathan', 'Morgawr', 'Nessie', 'Scylla', 'Tamingila', 'Yacumama'. Sam turned the page. There were four times as many names in the next few pages. He didn't understand how they were grouped.

'Move on from monsters. We should look for something that can perform great magic,' Daniel said.

Bladder fake coughed into a paw. 'Fairy dust.'

'You still think Maggie caused this?' Sam asked.

'She's been handing it around like it's a bag of sweeties. That poor little fairy I met, she'd torn his wings off just to get the stuff,' Bladder said.

They stared at him. 'That sounded almost sympathetic,' Daniel said.

Bladder muttered. 'Why has everyone got this impression that I have no sympathy for anyone else? Just because I'm not a sentimental sop ...' He stopped and belched. Sam thought it smelt like eggs again, maybe with vegetables in it.

Bladder swallowed. 'Doesn't necessarily have to be Maggie. Could be someone who's got into her stash. Wet witches, like she said.'

'This is huge magic. Magic that has affected tens of thousands of children,' Daniel said. 'How much fairy dust would you need to change this many children –' he waved his marble-white arm in the direction of the sea – 'into sea creatures? Billions of thousands of fairy wings. This isn't Maggie's doing, or one of her cronies'. This is either true fairy magic, or something else entirely. And fairies have never been known to steal children en masse. So this is likely to be something else.'

Sam couldn't help a little smile. He'd begun to wonder about Maggie too. He didn't want to believe it, but Bladder had been convincing. It was comforting to hear Daniel's certainty that this wasn't her work. He turned again to get to the next section of the book, which was entitled 'Smaller Saltwater Monsters (incl. Sea Imps and Wet Witches)'. It listed 'Fish People', 'Rusalka', 'Selkies', 'Shen', 'Sirens', 'Umibōzu', and so on. The legend at the bottom told him that the ones marked with a blue egg symbol were hatched. That meant they were made in The Hole. The first twenty on the page he was looking at were blue-egged.

'How do sea monster hatchlings get out to sea?' Sam asked.

'They swim,' Bladder replied.

'From The Hole? There's no water.'

'Some have legs and make a run for the sea entrance. Their breeds can't normally get to The Hole to fetch 'em and ogres find them particularly yummy.'

Sam remembered watching a documentary on turtles and how the babies had to make their way to the water without any help. Seagulls picked them off, but a few lucky ones survived.

'What about the ones without legs?' Daniel asked.

Bladder pretended to throw something. 'They get lobbed in like a basketball.'

'And they don't get eaten?'

'Thunderguts kept strict tallies on 'em. If they were underweight, they got thrown in the water, and ogres were only allowed a certain amount per batch. Otherwise ...' Bladder pulled a face. 'Not a pleasant topic, shall we keep reading?'

A short list at the end was titled 'Benevolent Saltwater Creatures'. It was short, mentioning only four species: 'Merpeople', 'Nereids', 'Tritons' and 'Yacuruna'. 'Merpeople' was marked with a silver forward slash. Sam looked at the legend. The slash meant 'Users of magic'.

He looked to see who else had a silver forward slash. None of the larger sea monsters did, but the rusalka, selkies and sirens did. 'I'll start with the sea imps and witches first. They have users of magic among them. I'll skip the benevolent creatures for now. I'm guessing no one kindly is going to have done this.' He flipped to the first silver-slashed page and read aloud: '"Rusalka can be saltwater- or freshwater-based creatures. The two different environs do not greatly alter their natures (see notes on page 172). Rusalka have a singular magic; they can change their appearance to become beautiful in a way that suits the taste of their prey. This magic ..."'

'Nup,' Bladder said. 'Moving on.'

'Nup?' Sam asked. 'What do you mean, "nup"?'

'Well, the magic going on here –' Bladder gestured at the water – 'is about changing the children, not the monsters changing themselves, and a rusalka's magic is not what you need to get all the children here. Not unless she turned herself into an ice-cream van to lure them to sea. And we know that weren't it.'

'She could have—'

'It was related to that noise somehow. Let's not waste time.'

Sam turned to the page entitled 'Selkies'. It started straight into their magic skills. '"Selkies are a type of water 'thrope, able to change from seals to humans and back again." Nup', Sam said. 'Not selkies.'

Bladder chortled. 'That's my boy. What's next?'

'Sirens.' Sam gulped at the very first sentence. '"A siren has a magical voice that draws the hearer to a watery grave, calling human victims into the sea to drown."'

'That noise you heard, Sam', Daniel said.

'It wasn't beautiful, though.'

'Not to you, but you don't have human hearing. Maybe you heard it the way you did because you're part gargoyle. Read on.'

Sam continued. '"Thelxinoe has been queen of the sirens since the early 1500s. Many of her sisters have held this title, and each of the sirens will take the throne for a period of time. Since sirens are immortal – unless they choose to die or are killed – this system seems most fair to them. It is estimated that sirens have sung hundreds of thousands of humans to a watery grave with their beautiful voices. Sirens can alter their song to suit their prey, which gives them the ability to specify a target of their choice, calling only to men at times, only to women, only to children at others, should they wish."'

'Sounds like our lot,' Bladder said.

Sam read on. 'Those not summoned by the siren call are still affected by its magic. The song will stupefy them, keeping them asleep so the sirens can take their prey without interference as their victims head towards certain death. Towns have been nearly emptied of residents, and those who remain have no idea where the missing have gone.'

'We may have found our culprits,' Daniel said.

'"Whole crews have walked off ships (*Mary Celeste*, USS *Cyclops*) and entire villages have been called into the sea. When a love interest eludes her, a siren can focus her song so powerfully that even inland areas are not safe. One of Molpe's desired targets was so terrified of her he moved to an inland town in northern Canada (Anjikuni Lake). Even this did not save him, or those he hid among. Sirens may call one person (Owain Glyndwr, Harold Holt) or many (the entire Ninth Spanish Legion). Sirens are relentless."'

'Relentless? Oh, great,' Bladder said.

'But everyone's been turned into sea creatures,' Daniel said. 'Is there anything about that in the book?'

There was another paragraph on other disappearances attributed to sirens, but nothing about any power other than their glorious voices.

'So sirens could explain how they ended up in the water, but not how they turned into all these sea creatures. And look at this.' Sam pointed to a handwritten note at the side of the page. It had almost completely faded. '"There are only two of the original sirens left, 1997." Maybe other things about sirens have changed too. Maybe they've got bigger magic somehow ...'

Bladder and Daniel looked doubtful.

Sam peered between the latticing of the barrier. The dolphins were staring at him again. He waved, and dorsal fins waved back at him and circled the seals.

'What other magic-wielding creatures are there?' Daniel asked.

'Only the merpeople.'

'Read it,' Bladder said.

'"Merpeople, often confused with rusalka, are in truth more like fairies. Merpeople are nature creatures. They are predominantly benevolent, but if they are crossed they can be exacting, callous and vengeful. They can be intensely dangerous, although it is rare for merpeople to war with each other and they prefer to stay out of the politics of other sea monsters and witches. Merpeople are fish-herds and farmers and wary of land dwellers, often attacking first and querying afterwards. The Merrow of Great Britain are a highly educated and peace-loving merpeople. They re-established the University at Atlantis in 967 AD, which still teaches philosophy, mathematics, art, magic and science.'

'It doesn't sound like they would have had anything to do with this,' Daniel said.

A sudden shrill note pierced the air.

'Oh, no,' Bladder said.

More sounds followed, grating and grinding in Sam's ears. The song had started again.

'Oh, no,' Bladder repeated, and pointed.

One of the tiniest whiting flapped out of the water, putting a sudden distance between itself and the others as it headed to open water. Its brothers and sisters flickered after it. A herring, silver and slick, looked at the shark and disappeared under the waves. The shark turned its concerned blue eyes towards the fish, then to Sam. Sam read begging in its eyes. A salmon flew over Hazel's back and she caught it in her mouth to stop it swimming after the others. It struggled to escape, but she held tight. Its eyes changed as it panicked between her teeth, irises growing bigger and bigger, the slimy gold eating up the whites around it, becoming expressionless. It gasped in the air, so Hazel let it go with a panicked squeak. Sam saw two seals and a smaller dolphin stare at him with bland grey and black stares. As each set of eyes changed, the owner would skitter away and disappear into the water. Sam noticed the song increasing in volume.

Hazel swam under the waves, trying to herd back as many fish as she could. Sam saw her fin glinting as she worried the whiting, but they fled around her, their scales sparkling like Beatrice's stars. A school of herring flooded away beyond her, racing after the smaller fish as they darted out to darker water.

Amira squeaked at Sam, and even without words, he understood her tone. It meant 'hurry'. She was afraid.

'They're not human any more,' Daniel said. 'Siren song can't do that.'

'Looks like it can,' Bladder said.

Sam couldn't see the little whiting at all, the babies, but he could see many other fish as they left. The few remaining watched him with wide stares, every single set of eyes on him still human. Their mouths may have gasped and panted like fish, but those eyes pleaded with him to do something. He was their only chance.

'I've got to get a boat. Something. We've got to follow them,' Sam said.

'You cant,' Bladder said. 'It's magic. It's dangerous. What can you do against all that?'

'I have to go, Bladder. I don't know what I'm supposed to do, but the way to help them all is out there.'

Bladder swore. Sam sneezed.

Daniel peered at Sam in his pyjamas. 'Sam, you're freezing.'

CHAPTER 8

'Are you OK?' Sam asked the dolphins.

The three turned their heads, swam away from the pier and out to the open water, then they turned and swam back. Hazel's nose pointed out to sea.

'We know. We have to follow the little ones', Sam said.

Bladder shuddered. From the water behind Wilfred, a large cod raised its head. As it did, its eyes turned black and silver and it headed towards the song. Three other cod took off after it. A pair of seals gave high barks, pursuing them. At first trying to herd them back, and then following them underwater where Sam could no longer see them.

Amira hooted urgently at Sam.

'We've just got to get some things.'

Hazel pointed a fin at Wilfred's back.

'He'll freeze if he gets in the water with just pyjamas,' Bladder replied. 'We're waiting for the flying dust brush to return with some stuff.'

Amira cocked her head, doglike.

'I mean Daniel, that angel.'

Amira focused on Bladder. She nodded, but she circled below them, agitating the water.

Sam stared at the waves. He didn't like the prospect of going out to deep sea. Bladder was right, he didn't know what was out there, and though it boiled with the fish beneath him, out there it looked flat and empty and lonely all the way to the horizon.

He'd learned about horizons; beyond them the world went on forever.

Sam felt a bit of sick hit the back of his throat. He could breathe underwater, but he couldn't swim. In fact, he would sink to the bottom like a rock. If he followed the creatures he could end up walking the seabed forever, and it would be wet and dark.

Daniel returned with Sam's clothes and two large bags of food.

'Did you get the food from my house too?' Sam asked.

'We have other sources for that. We couldn't go scrounging around in your kitchen. Your family is awake.'

'Are they all right?'

Daniel smiled. 'They're fine. A little worried about you. Yonah left them four feathers. One each for Nick, Michelle, Richard and Beatrice so they can feel at peace in the middle of all this chaos. A quick whisper that you're safe and sound and they settled.'

'Heading out to meet up with who knows what,' Bladder grumped. 'Yeah, very safe and sound.'

'What about the rest of our pack?' Bladder asked.

'Wheedle, Spigot and Nugget are fine.'

The hackles on Bladder's back settled a little.

'Nugget's been a little teary and Wheedle wanted to come down to help you, but we insisted he needed to watch the house,' Daniel went on. He yanked out a padded rain jacket and a pair of wellies from between the feathers near his left arm.

Bladder's expression darkened again. 'What kind of storage system do you have under them wings?' he asked. 'I'm always amazed by what you pull out. You got a fridge in there?'

Sam pulled on his jacket and relaxed into the warmth that gathered near his body. He looked at his hands; they were going pink again. What a relief!

Daniel seemed keen to appease Bladder. 'We could put more wardings up at the house, just to be safe.'

'Not that the ones you've put on have done any good,' Bladder said.

Sam cringed when he saw Daniel's mournful face. He knew how long and hard Daniel had worked on the wardings. 'They weren't meant to lock you inside,' Daniel said. 'No one would find you if they came looking for the house. It was just meant to ...'

Bladder winced. 'You know what a mean temper I have, don't take it to heart. Everyone knows you're doing what you can.'

Sam and Yonah shared a glance. Bladder was apologising again.

'Bladder, are you feeling all right?' Sam asked.

'Heartburn, dodgy tummy. Yes, absolutely fine!' Bladder snapped.

'Come on, everyone. We don't have time for this. We need a boat and Sam needs food and water', Daniel said. 'Who knows how long we'll be out there.'

'We? You're coming too?' Sam asked.

'You can't go alone', Daniel replied.

'Who said he would be alone?' Bladder asked. 'Perfectly good gargoyle here.'

Yonah gave a cooing laugh.

'You can't come, Bladder, you're too heavy – you'll weigh down the craft, slow Sam down', Daniel said. 'The boat might even sink.'

'Then we're gonna need a bigger boat.'

'It's not ...'

'And ballast, every good sailor needs ballast', Bladder retorted. 'Whatever! He's not going without me.'

Sam was sure Daniel was right, but thinking Bladder would be along with him did make him feel better. 'Anyway, why don't we decide when we find a boat', Sam said. 'We don't know what's available.

'We will find Sam a boat', Daniel said. His wings slumped. 'One big enough for you both.'

'What do I do?' Bladder asked.

'Apart from argue? Maybe find him some wet weather gear. There's a place for fishing gear along the beach. We don't need you heading back to the street and scaring people.'

'Don't worry about that. They're going crazy up there. I'm more scared of them than they'll ever be of me.'

'I want Yonah to stay behind and watch my family,' Sam said.

Yonah tweeted and shook her tiny white head.

'If she stays and something happens, she can come and find you so you can help them,' Sam said to the angel.

Daniel gave a considered nod. 'All right.'

Yonah's feathers prickled.

'Besides, you'll be able to have a bit more time with Spigot,' Bladder said, then sniggered.

Daniel stood. 'Half an hour,' he said.

'What do I do?' Sam asked.

'You stay here and figure out anything these last few fishies can tell you. And tell them to stop looking so delicious,' Bladder said. 'They make my tummy rumbly. What's in that bag Feathers brought? Any sandwiches?'

Sam wondered when Bladder had started seeing anything without sugar as worth eating.

'Now let's get you some waterproofs.' The stone lion thumped off down the wooden surface of the pier.

Sam tried to talk with the shifters again, but got no more useful information out of them. Their eyes were still human, as were most of the bigger sea creatures'. The whiting had all fled, as had the herring. The larger cod and trout remained. Sam remembered seeing toddlers turn into whiting. Little children had become larger fish. The older teens were the bigger animals. It had something to do with age. The longer someone had been human, the later they were becoming full sea creatures, although there were some exceptions.

'I am coming. We just need a boat', Sam told the dolphins.

They calmed a bit, although all those eyes looked worried when the seals returned alone. Sam gathered that the cod had got away from them and disappeared into the sea. The remaining creatures looked at each other nervously.

A few of them pushed forward. They stared at him.

'Do I know you?' Sam asked.

The shark nodded.

'From school?'

Sam listed friends from class. No response. Then he looked at the shark's size; it was bigger than the dolphins, so older? He listed Nick's friends' names: Sophia, Millie, Blake. Three of the sea lions nodded. Others barked at him too as he guessed his way through other older students. It seemed they just wanted to hear their names. He comforted them, promised them he would do his best to get them back to themselves soon.

Daniel came gliding into the middle of them, his feet landing solidly on the water. He pulled a large tin dinghy behind him with Bladder plopped in the middle, a set of waterproof overalls beside him. The boat settled into the water deeply, but not as deeply as the half a tonne of stone lion should have made it go. Daniel had painted glowing blessings along the side of the boat, taking some of the weight with a miracle.

Bladder had his foot in his mouth. He spat it out when he saw Sam.

'Blasted angel dropped me in the boat; just dropped me. I hit a seat and my leg broke off.' Bladder glared at Daniel. 'That hurt!'

'Sorry,' Daniel replied as Bladder put his shoulder to his leg and the parts sizzled together. He flexed his paw to make sure it worked.

'Made of rock. Breakable. Remember? I've been broken several times now. I don't know how long I can take it. One more and ...' Bladder gagged and rolled his eyes to show them what might happen if he broke one more time.

In the nook of the prow – if a dinghy can be said to have a prow – sat a large plastic keg with a tap. Water, Sam guessed.

Bladder curled into a U-shape and pressed a big cushion against his belly. Daniel flitted up to Sam and chucked down the food bags.

'Oi! Are you aiming at me?' Bladder asked.

Daniel smiled, picked up Sam and hovered with him for a moment. The sea lions and dolphins gasped. Sam realised even magicked children couldn't see Daniel. Except Wilfred, who watched with bright eyes.

'Bye, Yonah,' Sam said. 'Go home to Spigot and tell him everything, then he can tell Wheedle. Look after everyone for me.'

Daniel lowered Sam into the boat, leaning him against Bladder and the cushion.

'Blanket over there when you need it, Sam,' Bladder said.

Daniel threw out ropes with hoops knotted into them. Wilfred watched the angel and came dashing forward as the rope hit the water, sliding his lithe body through it. Amira and Hazel took the other two.

Daniel reached into the water and touched Wilfred's head. The dolphin gave a happy yap. 'Two days at the most,' the angel said.

'Two days for what?' Sam asked.

'Till the dolphins change completely,' Daniel whispered.

'How can you tell?' Bladder retorted.

'Angels can tell how long a human has left. Although that usually means ... you know ...'

'Death!' Bladder said.

'This will feel something like it,' Daniel replied. 'It is a form of losing your body.'

'We'll stop it,' Sam said.

'If we can,' Daniel added. 'The song is very powerful. It's hard to tell what it's doing to them.'

Sam studied the water. He had thought it looked lonely, but now he knew he was wrong. It teemed with life. Sea lions and seals skipped beside him. The shark and whale calf moved the water before the boat, creating a wake that helped the dolphins swim faster. The fish swam behind like a long silver tail. Daniel sat at the stern, his great wings open in a white sail that caught all the breeze as the boat glided along. Bladder licked Sam with his rough tongue as the cold wind blew over them, but Sam was in a knot of warmth. The nose of the boat cut through the sharpest of the wind.

It was only once they were far out that Sam realised how noisy the land was: the sound of cars and strained voices faded. The echoes of wind moving between buildings became distant. The air crooned gently over the water, and only splashing and the occasional voice of a sea creature replied to it. Away from the distracting shore it became a melody. He was sure the sea lions were humming, but softly, softly underneath it all, he could hear the sirens' song. It was new, and he did not like it any more than the one from the previous night (had it really only been last night?). This one didn't cause him any pain and he could even make out its message. It was a calling, a gentle summons filled with longing and frustration.

It grew louder as they travelled out.

Sam woke to a clear night sky, and the boat had stopped. Maybe those two things had woken him. He could no longer see any land, nor the reflected glow of street lights. The moon was a thoughtful slim smile in the air above, the sky was clear, which made it much colder. He was fine in his coat, but when he reached out, his fingers told him how cold the air had become. The water lapped at the boat, and he heard the constant splash of living creatures breaching the surface. He leaned over the side to see the shark's blue eyes watching him.

'Have we arrived somewhere important?' Sam asked.

The shark struggled to move its head side to side, its whole body swaying against it, and it hit a few fish on either side with its movement. As it swayed, Sam heard its tummy gurgle. 'You're hungry?'

The shark opened and closed its mouth.

'Can't imagine something that shape and size can nod.' Daniel whispered, and Sam understood why. The serenity of the ocean made it hard to speak. That, and the fact Bladder was still in stone form and dormant.

'If that means "yes", do it again,' Sam said.

The shark opened its terrifying mouth. It would have been impossible to count its teeth. Sam looked through the groceries. The awful, artificial sound of opening a plastic bag broke the holy quiet. Bladder was awake in seconds.

'Food? Now?' he asked, one paw rubbing at his eyes.

'The shark's hungry.' Sam stared at Bladder. 'And you're not.'

'Gargoyles don't need to eat. As much as I might like your choccies, I can go without.'

The shark's tummy rumbled again.

Sam didn't know what children-turned-fish-creatures ate, so he opened a packet of crisps. 'These?'

The shark moved closer, blanketed by a school of sleeping shapes hidden in the water. Sam poured the whole bag into the shark's mouth. It gnashed, and crumbs flew across the water. Tiny, round mouths appeared, kissing the water's surface, sucking down the particles of crisps.

'They're all hungry,' Sam said.

'How long until they eat each other, do you think?'
Bladder asked.

Sam stared at the moving water. Tens of thousands of them under there. Knowing their fellow fish were humans, they couldn't possibly eat each other. Could they?

Sam remembered the whiting, their eyes becoming fishlike, the tiny creatures forgetting what they had once been.

'Why have we stopped?'

The shark put its head to one side; a clumsy action, but when it closed its eyes, Sam understood. 'The dolphins are asleep?'

The shark did its manic version of 'yes', then settled into the waves.

'It's eerie, isn't it?' Bladder asked.

'What?'

'Well, the first time the song stopped they all rushed back to shore. This time, some have and some haven't.'

'Maybe it's not hypnotising them all?'

'Or it's hypnotising them to do something different.'

The song had changed too. It was a lullaby.

'I think it's telling them to slow us down,' Bladder said. 'Why's it doing that?'

Sam didn't know. He was tired too. He didn't think their timing had anything to do with the song. He hoped it didn't. He heard a loud tear; Bladder opening a packet of crisps.

'You need something to eat,' the gargoyle said.

'Maybe I should give the fish some too.'

Sam found himself looking down the throat of the shark again. It had to be the most terrifying way of communicating he'd ever seen.

Sam opened another packet of crisps and threw them on to the waves. The few watching, wakeful fish nibbled at them. Sam took a few mouthfuls for himself and scattered the rest.

A bright light grew above the boat as if the moon were getting bigger, but it was only Yonah landing on Daniel's shoulder. She pecked at Daniel's ear.

Sam sat up, startled. 'Is my family OK?'

'The pack?' Bladder added.

Yonah pulled on the angel's ear.

'You're required somewhere else, Daniel,' Bladder said. 'Go.'

'Are you sure?' the angel asked.

'Now, Daniel! Nothing going on here!'

'We'll return to make sure you are all right,' Daniel said.

'Well, thank you very much,' Bladder said. 'But I don't remember a birdman being available last time Sam needed help. Or the time before that. Come to think of it, what use are you generally?'

Daniel pushed his hair away from his hurt eyes.

'He means we'll be fine until you get back,' Sam said.

Yonah pecked the angel this time, and started hopping from one foot to the other.

'Go! Go!' Sam and Bladder yelled together. The water splashed. Their yells had woken a few more fish.

Daniel fluttered out of the boat, following Yonah, but

he kept looking over his shoulder to see Sam drifting away. Then he was gone.

Daniel had not been gone long when the sky lightened behind them, and Sam noticed the nasty sound again. Uncomfortable and high-pitched.

The dolphins began dragging the little boat through the water.

'They're pulling me towards the song, aren't they? It's louder now.'

'What do you think it means?' Bladder asked.

'Means?' Sam asked.

'They all mean something. If it's sirens, the book said they sing people to their deaths. Obviously, these sea creatures aren't going to drown, but I'm guessing this song means something to them. Look at them. So, who do the sirens plan on killing?'

The sea creatures were moving, but they didn't look any more awake than they had before. Their eyes were glazed, their expressions blank and unblinking like they had been on their walk into the water.

Sam gulped. He didn't know what was going on either.

Wheedle lay on the roof of the Kavanaghs' house, staring at the sliver of the crescent moon smiling at him. His eyes felt like gravel. Nugget cried. Nugget had started crying when Sam left, and Wheedle hadn't slept or turned to stone since. Despite the fact she was weeping, Nugget's eyes were shut; she was asleep, her little tummy rising and falling in rhythm with the breeze. Bladder was right – not solidi-fying and spending quality hours in stone form was taking its toll, but a stone Wheedle was no comfort to Nugget, who slept human-style. Wheedle stared at a dark sky salted with white stars. Something was wrong.

Yonah had left a while before. She'd danced along the rim of the roof before taking off without saying goodbye. Spigot had hidden his head under his wing. Wheedle felt for him, but was too tired to be much use to the stone eagle.

About ten minutes after the dove left, Wheedle had been hit by a pungent and wild smell: fairy dust, and a lot of it. Spigot pulled his head out and squawked at the road. Wheedle cuddled Nugget to his chest with gentle hoofs, patted her as she wailed some more, then trotted over to sit next to Spigot.

The streets were empty, and Wheedle knew there should be no monsters around (unless they were gargoyles), because Daniel had put up all the necessary protections, but the gargoyle stared at every tree nonetheless, trying to detect movement, any unnatural rustling of leaves. What had spooked Yonah? Where was the smell coming from?

He couldn't see anything. A squirrel gnawed at a nut in the tree opposite, its heart burring like a machine. A few nightbirds dived at small creatures scurrying in the shadows between grass and hedge, but nothing large was on the move. The hearts of the sleepers inside the houses thumped slow and steady.

Wheedle realised this was odd. So many children had gone missing that day; more than a few lights should be on and he should have been able to hear the erratic heartbeats of uneasy sleepers tossing in nightmare.

Inside the Kavanagh house it was quiet. They didn't seem to have noticed Sam wasn't home where he should be. That angel had put some heavy juju on them so Richard, Michelle, Nick and Beatrice slept.

Wheedle saw something drifting between houses. It looked like mist, then it swirled in the light of lamps. It was fairy dust, drawn to the glow like moths.

'I don't like this, Spigot,' Wheedle said.

The bird shook his head; neither did he. He leaned against Wheedle's leg and the bull felt Yonah's borrowed peace settle him. 'That dove is rubbing off on you,' Wheedle whispered.

Spigot turned away. Wheedle winced. It hadn't been a criticism.

Nugget stared up at him, shifted between his hoofs, wept in his ear and shuddered. She didn't have the vocabulary to explain what frightened her.

Wheedle lay back down on the roof and closed his eyes but could not get back to sleep.

The noise of the angel soaring towards them through the dawning sky disturbed Nugget, making her cry louder. Wheedle felt foggier than before. Broken sleep wasn't good for anyone, especially a gargoyle who needed something deeper. The stone bull groaned.

Nugget yeeped as the angel hovered overhead, spreading noon-bright light across the rooftops. The quieter, quicker flap of Yonah followed, and soon both white beings sat next to the gargoyles. Nugget shuffled towards Daniel and the angel picked her up. Instantly, she fell asleep in his hand, sucking on one talon. Wheedle could have cried. *What am I doing wrong?*

'Has anything happened since Yonah left?' Daniel asked.

'Nothing,' Wheedle replied.

Yonah chirruped something while Nugget dozed.

'That's good. Yonah came and got me because she said she saw fairy dust last night. Has it gone now?' Daniel peered across the street.

'Where's Sam?' Wheedle asked.

'Still at sea.'

'You what? You left him there alone?'

Daniel blinked. 'Yonah seemed to think this problem needed tending to more urgently.'

'You shouldn't have left Sam to come back.'

Yonah cocked her head. Even Wheedle got the tone of her look. *Really?* the gesture said.

'Is he all right?' Wheedle asked.

'He was fine. They were asleep on a calm sea.' Daniel turned and studied the gargoyle's face. 'You look awful, Wheedle.'

'Tell me about it.' Wheedle wondered when Sam would get back. He'd have to ask Sam about Beatrice. Nugget behaved more like a human baby than a new gargoyle. Maybe that was why she seemed better around Sam. Or maybe she just loved Sam more. Wheedle understood that.

'Yonah flew over Brighton before she got to me. She said that while this street is silent the rest of the town is more ... disturbed. People upset about their missing children, as one would expect. The Kavanaghs slept through? Sam's not back. That should make them a bit edgy, even with Yonah's feathers.'

'I thought it was odd too.' Wheedle smelt the air. In the freshness of a good, ordinary wind the scent of fairy dust had faded, but it wasn't entirely gone. Wheedle listened for the Kavanaghs' heartbeats. They slept on, as did everyone on the street, but sleepers stirred inside houses on the corners and further away. 'The dust knows this is Sam's place somehow, doesn't it?'

'It looks like Yonah's right, the Kavanaghs do need help. Sam will be very angry if we don't offer assistance. Maybe the wardings need to be a bit more personal.' Daniel stood and, as if the roof wasn't even there, he plummeted through it into the house. Wheedle jumped, but he was glad to see Daniel's ability to move through solid things was back in full force.

Daniel returned, his head rising out before the rest of him came through the the tiles, then his feet were flat on their surface again.

'Where's the dust from, do you think?' Wheedle asked. 'Titania? Maggie? Other monsters?'

'Who can say?'

'Well, despite what she says to Sam, I think this is Maggie's doing. There's more here than she's lettin' on and Maggie's smarter than anyone gives her credit for. Mustn't underestimate her, I say.'

Daniel nodded. 'You're no doubt right. If so, then she's obviously figured out there is something guarding Sam and his family, so she's looking for ways around it.'

'She won't find one, right?' Wheedle asked. 'You'll stop her, won't you?'

Daniel swung his head sadly. 'As much as is within my power. There are a few things that we can do to improve Sam's chances, but after that, it's up to him.'

'Like what?' Wheedle asked. 'You should go get Sam back. You should get Bladder.'

'They have an important job to do right now, and my job is to provide Sam all the assistance he needs. Your job is to watch over this family.' Daniel pointed down through the roof, to where the Kavanaghs slept. 'Just let me know what happens. They should be OK now. Even when they're out of doors, the big monsters won't want anything to do with them.'

Daniel put Nugget on the tiles. She woke straight away and wailed. Wheedle sighed. Then Yonah and Daniel left again. The gravel on Nugget's surface where she'd lain in the angel's hand looked pitted with holes. Wheedle wondered if it hurt.

Finally, the sky lightened near the horizon. Before anyone woke up, Wheedle decided to travel from rooftop to rooftop, Nugget sitting on his head and holding on to his horns.

They listened to everything. The area was full of people behaving oddly. For a start, it was Tuesday and everyone was wandering around like it was Saturday. No one went to work or school. Wheedle heard the constant buzz of telephones and sad, angry voices talking to people a long way away. The smell of fairy dust had travelled a great distance – Wheedle scented it coming from multiple directions, and it gathered in the Kavanaghs' street.

Wheedle and Nugget went back towards it. The stone bull stopped on the footpath and looked up to study the protective sigils. Not one would protect them from the dust. Supernatural creatures, yes; monsters, yes; maybe even fairies themselves; but dust was not a creature, and the only other angelic sigil that might do something was just a general blessing, hardly specific enough to help. It only added power to the others.

Daniel was right; whoever was doing this was clever. Or desperate. If monsters couldn't find Sam, then maybe the dust could, and someone had used a lot of it. Wheedle shuddered at the thought of how many fairies had been hunted and how many had sacrificed wings to the collection.

Morning came and crayoned the sky pink and red and orange. Sam had never seen such a sunrise; there were no clouds to obscure the vibrancy. It was beautiful, but Daniel was gone.

The boat pitched side to side.

'Hey, settle. You're going to throw us out,' Bladder called to the sea creatures.

The fish squirmed around the boat, and the dolphins tried swimming faster.

'I don't think it's them,' Sam said. 'Look out there.'

The waves grew in the distance too. Ahead of them, billowing water cruised in the direction of the boat. There was no change in the wind when the water began heaving, and the shock of the cold Atlantic water sprayed over Sam and chilled him. The water tossed about. A large wave came at them and forced the boat backwards, dragging the dolphins with it. As it passed, the dolphins had to right themselves and try swimming forwards again.

The sky overhead appeared still and calm.

The swell built to storm waves and yet there was no storm. The sky showed no change; if anything it was turning a muted soft blue, as beautiful as a winter sky can be.

Sam wrapped his arms around Bladder and eyed the sky. 'Where's the clouds? Should be something up there.'

'Don't like this,' Bladder said, and pushed his claws into the bottom of the boat, feeling for something to hold on to. Sam held tighter to the gargoyle's neck.

The waves built quick and ferocious, and Sam pulled a waterproof poncho out of its bag, covering himself and Bladder as the water rode up and down, sometimes slapping the boat on to the surface of the water with a skull-vibrating shudder. The boy and gargoyle took turns screaming.

The smaller fish and the shark disappeared into the depths and the dolphins tried to pull the boat along, but the swell jerked them about and they jolted back as they fought the waves. They were causing a lot of shaking. As

Sam struggled to the front of the boat and waved at the dolphins, a cold upsurge of water slapped his face.

'Let go! Let go of them!' Sam screamed at the water. Waves grabbed the dolphins and hauled them backwards, out of their ropes. Wilfred, Amira and Hazel protested in high squeaks.

The trio stared at him, terrified. Then an upsurge butted between the sea creatures and Sam, throwing the dolphins one way and the boat the other.

Another roller of freezing water pushed Sam backwards into the boat and into Bladder's paws. The gargoyle threw the poncho over Sam and held him.

The waves blatted. Bladder screamed. Under cover, near Sam's ear, he said, 'Can sirens do this kinda magic? It's a trap, and we got sucked into it.'

Bladder pinned the boy down and created a tent that filled quickly with the damp, warm smell of boy and drains. It was not a great smell, but it kept the force of the wind waves away from them, and Bladder's weight kept them from capsizing.

Sam's biggest worry was not that he would drown. He knew water wouldn't kill him. But he would sink to the bottom and it would be dark down there, even darker than The Hole. At least The Hole was lit by sallow light. He peeked out from the cover. Where was the sea taking them?

'Where are we?' Sam asked.

Bladder clenched his claws on the braces of the boat. 'Let's worry about that when the waves have stopped.'

'Why did Daniel have to leave?' Sam asked.

The waves continued churning, faster than before, pulling at the heavy vessel.

Then it all stopped.

Sam lifted his head. He heard the water lapping at the boat. He could hear his own heart beating wildly, but no other. There was no sign of the sea creatures who had pulled them – his shifter friends had gone – and there was no angel to fly him and Bladder away from here if another storm appeared and ...

'No land anywhere,' Bladder said, as if completing Sam's thought. The gargoyle looked up. 'What's that?' he asked.

Sam could hear the distant movement of life under them, fish turning fins and maybe something bigger, another shark or a seal. It was getting closer. 'Maybe the dolphins have managed to follow us,' he said.

'No, not that. Singing. Beautiful singing,' Bladder said.

Bladder and Sam exchanged a glance. They were both thinking the same thing: *sirens*.

Bladder growled in the direction of the noise. Sam guessed it hurt the gargoyle's ears. It hurt Sam's.

Bladder roared. He opened his mouth and Sam could see a red flash from inside. Maybe his heart burned. Bladder always complained it did.

Waves hit the side of the boat and Sam looked up. He heard a tail hit the water.

'It's the dolphins. They've found us,' Sam said.

'Could be. Or could be sirens.'

Sam scrambled to the side of the boat, hoping to see the faces of three friendly grey-backed dolphins. Instead, he saw a woman's face. A beautiful face.

Her bright orange hair trailed in the water behind her, wrapped through with pearls and ribbons of seaweed. She reached a hand towards him.

A large wave smacked him into the sea.

CHAPTER 9

Bladder's face rippled and distorted through the lens of water and shrank as Sam sank like a gargoyle. Shooting downwards, rock heavy and solid, he twisted to look at his captors, but couldn't focus through the whirling sea. Two, no, three faces; one a lovely girl, her expression all surprise as he slipped from their hands. Sam wasn't drowning or struggling like a human. That threw them, which was good, but it was hard to be glad about it as the sunlight faded away. Only the swishing of tails in the water told him his kidnappers had followed him into the darkness.

When he hit bottom, Sam glanced up first, but when he couldn't see his captors in the darkness he peered around. The blackness of The Hole was nothing compared to the murkiness underwater. Sam attempted to run, but the water pushed back at him and he had no idea which way to go.

He stumbled across a rock, and a fish erupted from the dirt, glowing like a small sun.

Bioluminescence. He'd read about that in science class.

He followed as fast as he could, but it darted away and its small light receded, leaving him alone.

Then another circle of light came towards him.

Sam moved forward to meet it.

'There he is', a voice bubbled ahead.

Sam turned, the push of water slowing all his movements. Arms caught him and dragged him along, faster than he could go by himself.

He sailed at great speed. Glowing creatures came out of rocks and sandy holes to peer at him as he floated past them.

Bladder lurched to the side of the boat and stared into the water until Sam's shrinking, panicked face disappeared.

'Sam?'

All he saw was the glint of scales and a girl's face.

Sirens!

Bladder flung himself into the water and dropped towards the retreating light.

The sounds of the new world drowned out the noises above, and there were many of them. It wasn't like the echoes of sewers. In those, all Bladder heard was the slosh of water resounding off concrete, and the clicking of his own paws against the bricking. The ocean broadcast with more life. The distance rumbled with the sound of two huge hearts pounding. Closer were smaller hearts, and they vibrated the water, creating a steady dance. He could hear all their heartbeats as if the water not only amplified them but conducted them, turning them to a tribal orchestra.

Below him, four hearts beat, one of them familiar, fast and worried. Sam's heart. Bladder lost the fading glow, but the drumming was strong enough to lead him.

As he sank and the water blackened, he noticed the creatures around him growing brighter, casting their own light, like underwater angels. A few fish and an eel moved in his wake and shone.

When the gargoyle hit the bottom, he could just make out the outline of rocks and things slithering in the dark. Something struck at him, trying to sink fangs into his leg. A chip of rump fell away, but the wounded creature slid back into the dark. With a broken tooth, Bladder hoped. He gulped. He could cope with things that bit, but *what else was down here?*

Bladder stopped to listen. Pattering heartbeats all around, playing musically. The loudest of them all, Sam's heart, carried to him. He followed its call through black water.

A slick-tailed girl slipped in front of Sam, a glowing eel curled around her neck.

He guessed she was a siren. He understood why sailors were drawn into the sea by them: even Maggie wasn't as lovely with all her glamour. The girl glowed, looking angelic. It was the most deceitful magic he had ever seen.

She moved closer to him. 'You sank so fast; I haven't had time to give you Breath. Do you need Breath?'

Sam stared at her. 'Breath? You mean for me to breathe? No, I'm good underwater.'

She raised her eyebrows in an expression that Sam recognised as disbelief.

He realised her desire to let him breathe meant they didn't mean to kill him. At least there was that.

Then a black cover dropped over his face, four strong arms bound him and he felt himself dragged again along the ocean bed.

Bladder was close enough to see the tailed creatures tie Sam up. Glowing fish and eels shone around them like multiple moons, but the gargoyle was slow compared to the shimmering creatures with long tails, and they carried Sam away before Bladder reached them.

He stood on the sea floor where Sam had been and sighed, except it came out as a large bubble. A flurrying dark shape approached and Bladder flinched as something large and shadowy slipped in front of him. He recognised the shape. Wilfred, Amira and Hazel had turned to something similar.

'Hello,' the dolphin said.

Bladder jumped. He hadn't understood the sea-changed shifters, so he'd expected he wouldn't understand anything else underwater either. 'Hello.'

'You look a little lost. What is something of your type doing here? We don't see many statues in this part of the sea. Are you from Atlantis?'

Bladder found it hard to shake his head, the water put up so much resistance. 'No', he said.

'Well, you should visit. They'd love you.'

Bladder gave a strained smile. 'My friend's been nabbed and I saw 'em drag him off that way.'

'Ah, yes, the palace guards. He must be in a lot of trouble to be taken by them. They can be nasty if they think you're a threat.'

Bladder grimaced. 'Palace guards? They'd be takin' him to the palace then?'

'Sure, it's only ten minutes that way.'

'Ten minutes? I'm on it.' Bladder walked in the direction of the dolphin's nose.

The dolphin studied the gargoyle's legs. 'At that pace, though, maybe a couple of hours. And you really shouldn't go without an invitation.'

Bladder tried to run, but it didn't make him any faster. A couple of hours? What could happen to Sam in a couple of hours?

Sam couldn't see, but his other senses kicked in, and what he noticed most was the warmth of the water. Up in the boat, he'd sat bundled up in his coat and waterproof leggings, but still the wind had licked his face with an icy tongue. He'd spent most of his time rubbing his nose, and he was thicker skinned than the average human. When he fell out he'd felt the shock of freezing water as he sank, but he'd been so worried about his abductors he hadn't spotted the change in temperature.

But, bound and blinded, he had time to notice these things, and the water was warm. Certainly not what he expected the sea to feel like, especially at such a depth (he'd learned in science that it was cold and wet). The other thing he spotted through the fabric of his head bag was a growing luminescence. The colours became stronger and brighter, and he could just make out the outline of a set of doors or a gate with lights bordering a path towards it. He couldn't sniff – that would give him a noseful of water – but he knew it must take a lot of magic to keep lights shining under the sea. Also, there were voices, lots of voices.

Sam clenched his fists. Wherever he was, he was surrounded by underwater people. More sirens?

In front of the gate, someone yanked the cover from his head and the strong arms let him go. He dropped to his knees on the sand and golden swirls coiled around him.

The girl swam forward and called for the guards. An armed man with a fish tail waved to her. He opened the gate and pointed his spear at Sam. The half-fish, half-girl swam forward and Sam's escorts forced him inside.

'Marée, child of Eulimene, welcome', the guard said. 'The queen awaits your arrival. You have brought the traitor?'

Bladder pushed on through the water. He was exhausted. It was like rolling a boulder uphill. He glared at the smug fish that flittered by him, using their aquatically efficient tails to taunt him with their speed.

'Whatcha doin'?' called a choir of small silver fish.

'I've gotta get to the palace,' Bladder said.

'Ooooh,' the fish chorused. 'Why you going to the palace?'

'I have to find a friend. He's been taken there.'

'Do you have an invitation?' they sang together.

'No.'

'Oooooh,' the fish repeated. 'You're not going very fast.'

'Thanks for pointing that out to me, I hadn't realised.' Bladder rolled his eyes. Even that felt difficult underwater. 'Still, it's a matter of life or death. I think.'

He'd obviously offended the small fish. They shot away in the direction he wanted to go. He growled.

He leaned on a rock and tried to pant, making more bubbles. The silver fish returned, followed by a dozen or so flat, wide bodies: stingrays.

The largest ray lurched forward. 'The little guys say you're off to the palace, said it was life or death but you're not making good time.'

'Not in the slightest.'

'Well, me an' the boys thought we could help you out.'

Bladder studied the ray. 'You could? Seriously?'

'Yeah, you look heavy, but we can relay you there. Save you a bit of time.'

'You'd do that for me?'

'Why not?' the ray asked. 'Life or death, right?'

'Yeah, it really is.'

In this way, Bladder managed to surf towards the palace. He was glad he had four legs – he had to crouch or the water pushed at him – but the rays made as steady a surface of themselves as they could.

'We don't have an invitation, so we'll leave you here,' said the largest ray. 'The palace gate is just beyond those rocks.'

Bladder turned to the glowing pearl gates. 'Thank you. Thank you so much.'

'Your funeral. I wouldn't go in if I didn't have an invitation. Think it may be death or death.'

'Bit of a thrill seeker, that one,' another ray added.

Soon the seabed rose to greet Sam and his escort. The terrain was nothing like the rocky grey world where he'd sunk; this was a world of living stone. Rocks had been carefully positioned and covered in seaweed and anemones, sea cucumbers and polyps, which octopus gardeners tended.

His guards dragged Sam towards a door. On either side coral growth filled the water, growing up and up to create walls. The door itself was made of pearls and barnacles. A trident-carrying sentry stood on either side. As they saw the group, they opened the gates.

A squid swam to greet them. 'Her Majesty awaits you in her chambers, Marée, child of Eulimene, and ... it.' The squid glared at Sam.

'Thanks,' Sam replied.

The squid raised its non-existent eyebrows, its big eyes assessing Sam with unblinking curiosity. 'It has manners at least.'

'Come on,' Marée said. 'We can't keep the queen waiting.'

Sam agreed it wasn't a good idea. In his experience, queens could get quite testy, and there were a lot of guards around with stabby, pointy tridents.

On the other hand, he didn't get the impression the queen was going to offer him tea and cake.

'I want to walk,' Sam said.

A guard pointed his spear at Sam.

'I'm not a traitor, whatever you say,' Sam said. 'And you've seen me walk – I can hardly run.'

Marée, child of Eulimene, nodded. 'This is true. Untie him.'

'But, my lady ...' a guard started.

'I am sure if he turns out to be lying you can deal with him.'

The guard sliced through Sam's ties, making sure to whisk the sharp blade very close to his nose.

Marée, child of Eulimene, watched him with a fierce and furrowed face. 'What are you? You're not human. You breathe underwater and your ears don't hurt?' Her hair floated around her face. 'You sink, yet do not feel the water pressure? What creature are you?'

Sam struggled against his remaining bonds. 'I am human, but I am also part gargoyle.'

'What is a gargoyle? And why do you serve the sirens?'

Bladder stared at the gate. It was being watched over by two angry-looking guards. He wasn't going through there. The wall was nice and high, but he couldn't swim and if he tried to climb, he'd be seen. Bladder looked for a nice dark section of wall, maybe shielded by more of those large sea boulders.

Sam had no chance to answer. Another door opened and he was forced inside the throne room.

At the far end, the queen sat on a throne the size of a dining table. She was larger than an angel, and sunlight pouring in from the sky created a halo around her. Her crown was made of shells and starfish, and a trio of blue pearl ropes hung from her neck. Her tail stretched beyond the foot of her throne and was the colour of the sky at sunset, glorious pinks and oranges. It changed with the light.

She was attending to a seal. The seal's snout was trapped in a plastic ring holder and the poor beast looked thin and dishevelled; not at all like the sleek, shiny creatures Sam had seen swimming near the pier. The queen pulled off the plastic, stroking the animal's fur as she did and speaking in a soft, soothing voice. The seal did a grateful, celebratory turn in the water, bowed and thanked Her Majesty before speeding away.

The queen looked down the floor straight at Sam. 'You have fetched him, Marée? Well done, good servant. Come forward, boy,' she said.

Sam stepped towards her, feeling heavy as he pushed against the water.

Marée swam next to him, but stopped when she came to where two more trident-wielding guards stood before the throne. Sam wondered how long it would be before they poked their weapons into him. Marée bowed and stared at Sam, bobbing her head downwards. It took him a second to realise she wanted him to do the same thing. Sam bowed.

'Queen Amphitrite', Marée said, 'I present to you the traitor.'

'Easy, Marée, child of Eulimene. He is not of our kind. He may be the enemy, but he may not be treacherous.'

Sam gave a twisted smile.

'What is your name, boy?'

'Samuel Kavanagh', Sam said.

'Well, Samuel, child of Kavanagh. You are not in the grip of the sirens' spell and yet you let those poor bound creatures take you to them. What errand do the sirens have for you?'

'I'm not on an errand for the sirens. I thought *you* were sirens', Sam said.

One of the guards hit him across the face, the force slowed by the water. It still hurt.

'What! Do I look like a siren?' The queen stood upright on her tail, looking taller, and she clenched her fists.

'I don't know what sirens look like', Sam replied. 'The book didn't have any pictures.'

The queen dropped back to her throne. The frown on her face softened and she laughed, causing bubbles to burst out and float up past the glowing fish. 'Ah, you do not mean it as an insult. Well, for future reference, sirens have bird bodies and scaly feet. Mermaids, on the other hand, look like this.' She gestured at her tail.

'Really? Bird bodies? Don't they live underwater?'

'Not so much underwater as close to it, on the surface. They like the water well enough, but don't need to be in it or under it all the time. They are more like sea birds than sea creatures. They'll get their legs wet, but little else, which is why we don't have as many battles with them as we could. *You* are more a sea creature than they, and it appears you are more innocent than we have been led to believe. If you don't know what a siren looks like, you can hardly be working for them.'

'It may be a trap,' said a merman hovering next to Amphitrite's throne.

The queen smiled, and Sam thought she looked a little like Michelle. She studied Sam's face. 'I don't think so, Viceroy. Let the child of Kavanagh approach.'

Sam's progress was slow, but the queen waited. Up close, she looked bigger and brighter.

She put out one grand hand around him – it covered his back – and pulled him gently towards her.

'You have not given him the Breath, child of Eulimene?'

'No, Your Majesty,' Marée said. 'He breathes on his own.'

'Do you do this by magic, child of Kavanagh?'

'No, Your Majesty. Or, maybe. It's not a magic I have control of. I've always been like this. Although I didn't know about being about to withstand water pressure until just now. I'm part gargoyle.'

'But you look human.'

'I'm a bit that too.'

The queen turned to the merman. 'What are the qualities of a gargoyle, Viceroy?'

The viceroy replied, and his voice had the sing-song tone of someone presenting memorised words. 'A drylander. Stone-skinned, able to petrify at whim. Statue-like and heavy. Can stare at the sun and exist underwater without difficulty. Hatched in The Hole. Of impkind, but records have shown them to be harmless, even friendly on occasion. During the Waves of Athens, it is known that the Gargara of Athens aided in the rescuing of eleven mermaids thrown ashore when one of Poseidon's tidal waves ...'

'No. You. Don't!' a muffled voice said.

A bundle of mer-guards moved at a laborious pace into the throne room. They stabbed at something solid in their midst and a few squealed when their tails got pricked in the melee.

'What is going on?' the queen asked.

'An invader, Majesty. It dug under the wall and nothing we do seems to stop it. We have slowed it only. Away! Away! Before the beast attacks you!'

'Leave. Sam. Alone', the thing covered in mer-guards said. 'Don't. Worry. Sam. I'll. Save. You'. It took a struggling footstep with every word.

The guards stabbed at it some more.

'Bladder?' Sam called.

'You know the invader, child of Kavanagh?'

'It's Bladder. He's part of my pack. He was in the boat with me.'

'Desist from stabbing the creature, Captain. I believe it may be justified in its assault. We did kidnap its kin.'

It took a while for the guards to slide off Bladder. One

gave a last thump at the stone lion's head with the blunt end of a spear and a perky stone ear fell off. It sank to the sandy ground.

'Ow!' Bladder said.

The mer-guards stared at each other and turned their spears around ready to attack him again.

'I said "desist", Captain,' Queen Amphitrite breathed.

The troop retreated with sneers and pouts as Bladder collected his fallen ear and returned it to its proper place on his head. Even underwater, the ear sizzled, making those in attendance jump.

'What is this, Viceroy?' the queen asked.

'This, I believe, ma'am, is a fully hatched gargoyle.'

'They have no history of violence towards merkind?'

'None whatsoever, Majesty. To werewolves and vampires, yes, but their few interactions with us have always been well-intentioned.'

'Do you mean harm to us now, gargoyle?'

Bladder glared at the queen and made his way towards Sam. 'If he's in one piece and I can have him back, I *may* consider lettin' you off with a warning.'

The queen laughed. 'They are loyal and brave, that is true enough. I would rather be friends with you, Sir Bladder, child of Kavanagh.'

'I'm not ...' Bladder started. He looked around. It didn't seem worth explaining. He sniffed Sam and sneezed out a noseful of water. Sam rubbed Bladder's mane.

The queen returned her gaze to Sam. 'Although monsterkind, your species is shown to be friend to the sea.

It is just as occasional that humankind is shown to be friend to the sea. But it is proof it is possible, and the mer accept all such offerings. Are you friend to the sea, children of Kavanagh?'

'I think so, Your Majesty,' Sam said. 'I certainly don't want to hurt it. I just want to get the other children back.'

'Then you are both welcome here. And I apologise, Sir Bladder, for causing you so much grief. We feared for our own and believed this child of Kavanagh was the cause of our fear.'

Bladder grimaced. 'Sam wouldn't hurt a fly.'

'I see the truth of that. We thought he was with the sirens: he appeared a human child and yet their song did not call to him. Know he is safe and we want you on your way soon.' The queen stared at her tail and flicked it a few times. 'Sir Bladder and Sam, children of Kavanagh, the young ones you speak of are transforming into sea creatures, and the sirens continue to sing them to deeper waters. Some are near the end of their transformation. If it is completed, they will never be human again, even in mind.'

'What? Ever?' Sam asked.

'You still have a small window in which you can turn them back and have them return to their true selves, but they must be close to land when they make the change. Else they will drown.'

'I just want to find the sirens and convince them to turn them back to humans.'

'It was not the sirens that changed your friends, Samuel. It was I that changed them.'

Sam and Bladder stared at each other and turned back to the queen. 'You did? Why did you do that?'

One of the guards glared at Sam and lowered his trident ever so slightly. Bladder growled.

'The sirens called them to the water. Had they entered and remained human, they would surely have died. It was the only way to save them all,' Queen Amphitrite said.

'Oh, thank you, thank you so much,' Sam said.

The queen's expression hardened. 'It was kindly meant, yes – we would not have so many children drown – but many have already forgotten their human side and have little time to remember it.' As Sam smiled and opened his mouth to speak, she lifted her hand. 'You must know, Samuel, I am not inclined to remedy this. Our seas are so often depleted by humans, it seems fit to me that humans replenish them.'

Sam hung his head. He understood. If she would not undo her magic, the children would stay fish forever.

'But the sirens?' the viceroy said.

The queen pulled Sam close again. 'Yes, the viceroy reminds me that the sirens must have some dark purpose for stealing human children, as well as calling you to them. And though it would be good for me to keep our waters full, I am also not in the habit of assisting sirens. They are not like gargoyles or humans; there is no record of a siren assisting a merperson. Is that right, Viceroy?'

'None, Your Majesty. And mayhap this theft will prove evil for us also.'

'Yes, well considered. Then, child of Kavanagh, for this reason alone I will consider helping you, but only if you can cause the sirens to discontinue their horrendous song. If you can, I will allow the children to return to their original forms when you have them all near dry land. But by my reckoning you have no more than a day to complete the task before those who have changed already are unable to return to their former shape. Even more will have changed while you have been here.'

Sam bowed low. 'Thank you, Your Majesty. Thank you, so much.'

'I will also gift you something else. If I did not, I would not be sincere in my word.'

Sam looked at her, wondering what else she could give him. Maybe a dolphin to get him back to the boat would be useful.

'I will give you the ability to swim. Touch my tail, Samuel, child of Kavanagh. Touch my tail, Sir Bladder.'

Bladder peered at the queen's tail and put out a paw. 'Looks slimy.'

'Bladder!' Sam said.

Sam reached out too, and they both touched the beautiful tail of the sea queen. Sam's hand tingled as a charge went through him, and he saw Bladder's eyes and mouth open in surprise. Sam felt himself rise, floating up and away from the queen. She grabbed his foot. Bladder tried to swim back to him but his tail continued to rise.

'Marée, child of Eulimene, you will guide this human-gargoyle back to his craft?'

'Yes, Majesty.'

'I do not expect to see you again, Samuel, child of Kavanagh, nor you, Sir Bladder. I would wish you the best, but if you fail, my waters will teem with life. If you succeed, I will have frustrated the sirens. I win either way.'

'There may be other consequences, Majesty,' the viceroy said.

'Perhaps, but they are in Sam's hands now.' Queen Amphitrite released Sam's foot and he floated again. He moved his arms, mimicking Marée and her guards who swam beside him, doing his best to catch up to the rising gargoyle swearing above him.

CHAPTER 10

Nugget cried. Nugget didn't stop crying. Wheedle didn't want to pat her – every time he did, a bit more of her pelt disintegrated – but he crooned and sang to her and shuffled as close as he could possibly get without touching her crumbly coat. And still Nugget. Wouldn't. Stop. Crying.

Wheedle groaned; he was so scared for her and he didn't know what to do.

'Does it hurt, Nugget?'

Nugget's sudden silence came and her dissolving skin shuddered. She peered at the street, shrinking back underneath Wheedle's belly. Stone powder floated off her into the wintry air.

When he saw what had made her so quiet, Wheedle wished Nugget would cry again. 'Spigot,' Wheedle hissed. 'Spigot!'

Spigot shook himself out of solid stoniness, opened one bright eye and stood up on his thick stone legs. The eagle leaned against Wheedle's other side and they all looked down.

The fairy dust was back, circling the lights, hovering in the trees, sliding in from the road towards all the doors along their street. Wheedle leaned over the roof and watched dust coil up the Kavanaghs' steps. He took a quick look up and down the pavement. There were no people, just like the previous night. Wheedle was sure the dust was keeping them asleep. Though sad voices rang out from the far distance, the only human noises in the Kavanaghs' street were snores.

'Can you watch Nugget for me?' Wheedle asked.

Spigot squawked.

Wheedle descended the front wall of the house and shivered as he jumped hoof-deep into swirling powder. By the time he landed, the dust had reached the Kavanaghs' door and begun edging around the hinges and between the door and the frame. The finest dust had got in when nothing else could. Wheedle stood for a moment on the Kavanaghs' doorstep and listened. Inside, Nick gave a snore, then a choked cough. Until that noise, the dust had been sliding under every door along the street that Wheedle could see. But as Nick coughed again, all the dust in the street changed direction, like a wind had caught it.

Wheedle winced. *As if it heard the boy.*

It swept away from the other houses and converged outside the Kavanaghs' house, thick as a sandstorm. It hung there for a moment before roaring forward and hitting the front of the house. Wheedle closed his eyes, scrunched them, and buried his head in his forelegs. The dust pushed over him, flew through his stone fur, caught in his ears and brushed along his tail. When he no longer felt it pour across his back, he looked up and saw the last of it pushing inside through every gap it could. Door, window, vents, cracks.

That can't be good.

He waited, wondering what to do next. He tried the door handle. It was locked, so he couldn't get in without breaking the door down.

Then the sounds began. Rising sounds, the sounds of humans getting out of bed, muffled feet, muffled movements.

That's definitely bad, Wheedle thought.

The door opened and Richard walked out, followed by Nick and then Michelle, who carried Beatrice in her arms. The quartet were blank-eyed and deliberate, striding towards the street.

Wheedle knew he couldn't let them go. He grabbed at Michelle's foot and she tripped. Beatrice flew out of her arms and Wheedle caught the baby deftly enough, but when he put her down she began crawling towards the road. Wheedle grabbed at the baby's nappy and held her close. She went limp. Michelle picked herself up, stared blankly at Wheedle and walked towards him. It reminded him of a fish's unblinking stare and he shuddered. Behind her, Nick and Richard continued their shuffle into the street. Wheedle knew he couldn't stop them by himself, and even if Spigot came down from the roof, now there were three grown humans versus two gargoyles. Nick alone had been hard enough to subdue when Bladder had been there to help.

Michelle reached for Beatrice.

'No, you don't,' the gargoyle said, and ran for the house, shutting the door behind him. Dust swirled around him. It weaved around Beatrice and she struggled to break his grip, but Wheedle held on to her.

The knob turned and Wheedle stretched up and flicked the lock.

Michelle knocked.

'Sorry, no one home,' Wheedle yelled, and retreated further inside, into the kitchen. The dust sat on a thin layer across the floor as Wheedle jumped on to the dining table. The old oak thing complained under his weight. The dust slid back towards the front door.

Michelle stopped knocking and Beatrice relaxed in his forelegs She peered around blearily, as if she'd just woken.

'Spigot, come down,' Wheedle called out, hoping the stone bird was listening.

Spigot's stone face looked in from the kitchen's French doors. Nugget was hanging from his beak. Wheedle unlocked the back door and let them in. Bits of gravel dropped from the little gargoyle on to the back step. Wheedle winced.

'I need to follow Sam's family. You stay here and look after these two.'

The eagle complained.

'No time.' Wheedle placed Beatrice into Spigot's wings and Nugget reached for her too. The stone bull headed for the front door. His eyes felt gritty.

Wheedle scanned the street. Richard, Michelle and Nick were three houses away, lurching down the other side of the road, the fairy dust half leading, half carrying them. Wheedle wondered where they could be going when they stopped at a drain.

Not there. Not The Hole, he thought. *No, they can't!*

They did.

Richard slid his legs between the bars and the metal turned to vapour. Michelle looked back at the house and frowned.

'Yes, yes,' Wheedle called. 'Beatrice is in there. Come home.' He started across the street towards them.

Michelle stepped into the drain, losing substance for a brief moment.

Wheedle ran towards them and heard ogre voices rise from below. Nick crouched on the street, by the drain. Wheedle grabbed at his pyjama collar, but a claw reaching from below yanked hard on Nick's leg. Wheedle pushed his feet into the ground, fixing himself to it. If he held on long enough, maybe the yanker would give up. But three more solid tugs, Nick's collar ripping, sent the boy tumbling through the drain and disappearing into the dark below. All Wheedle could see when he looked down was a gentle circular glow shining from Nick's forehead, which lit his eyes.

Wheedle could make out ogreish voices.

'Yuck, what is them? I fought we was gettin' us some humans.'

'Quick, put the bag over 'em. Let's get 'em to Her Maggisty.'

Wheedle moved forward, sniffing at the drain and listening as heavy footsteps receded and the ogres' conversation faded.

Wheedle did not want to be seen. There were thousands of monsters ahead: he could tell that by the huge sound, the endless conversations and the rumbly deep throats roaring out. The noise was huge, far bigger than it had been when he, Spigot and Bladder had last encountered a large crowd of monsters there. It made sense though; the last time had been in an open field. Here the ogres and boggarts, bogies and imps were holed up in the yawning dome of the Great Cavern, with all its echoes and acoustics. Wheedle slid out of the tunnel mouth and straight up the wall, not even looking to see who might be watching. He needed to get up high, to see if he could spot where the Kavanaghs had been taken. He did not stop climbing until he got to the entrance of his pack's long-abandoned burrow. It'd been months since he'd been here. It sat empty except for a layer of ordinary dust and faded chocolate wrappers.

Sound rose from the cavern floor. Voices, squawks, screams, howls, the rustling and pounding of small and huge feet, the rattling of chains. Wheedle, his ears alert, peered out of the burrow door and looked down.

He could see nothing of importance, except the huge mountains of sighs piled all over the cavern floor having become taller and wider because no ogre king had appeared to breathe on them and hatch them to life. The pounding feet of the surviving ogres and trolls caused small avalanches to ripple down the stacks, but the hillocks remained high enough to clog Wheedle's view. A huge pile of beans blocked his line of sight to where he knew Ogre King Thunderguts's stone throne sat on the dais.

The ledge outside the burrow was bare, so Wheedle stepped out. Nervous faces peered out of holes and dens across the way. Small heads with blinking peepers and big heads with glowing eyes stared at the base of the cavern. No one was interested in one gargoyle running about. If he had to guess, Wheedle would say that Maggie had ordered them all back to the Great Cavern, but they hated the smell of the place. It didn't smell of death so much any more, but it was stale and dormant, lifeless. The place was half full; many of the bigger monsters had been killed off when Sam destroyed the sword, and Wheedle knew pixies, brownies, boggarts, bogies and leprechauns didn't take up as much space. There were no gargoyles though. They would be happy to stay away from this place forever. Most other species of monsterkind had returned, although not all. Maybe others were hiding down in their own caverns.

Stealing the Kavanaghs, getting all the monsters back to The Hole – Wheedle supposed only Sam was missing from Maggie's collection.

As he scurried around, following the ledge that circumscribed the wall of the cavern, he swung his head back and forth, checking burrows to make sure nothing could dash out and push him down to a shattering death. And he kept an eye on the floor, trying to see the throne. If Maggie was anywhere, she was there.

The dais came in to view, but only a lump of an ogre stood next to the throne. He recognised Nasty Nan the Goblin dusting the seat, but there was no Maggie.

Something else caught Wheedle's attention.

Next to the dais was a large solid box, the size of Sam's bedroom, but squarer. On top of it, smack in the middle, sat an upright barrel. He dashed around to the other side of the ledge so he could get a closer look. If it was empty, it might be a good place to hide. It was hard to see; there were yet more egg piles in the way, and he couldn't get a better view. A trio of boggarts sat on the tier below him.

Wheedle heard crying. Soft crying. In The Hole? Crying? Was it a trap? He listened some more. It came from a few tiers down, quite close to the ground, just behind the throne. There was more than one crier. Richard? Nick? Michelle? All three?

Wheedle ran along the top tier until he was behind the stone throne. There was movement on the floor around the dais, but he still couldn't see Maggie, just a lot of scarpering pixies, lumbering ogres and a few clumps of brownies, witches, trolls and the like.

The wall below him was a patchwork of dirt covered with dark burrows. A lot of boggarts had lived there once and, he guessed, still did. He hoped Maggie wasn't inside one of these burrows with the Kavanaghs now. If she was, no wonder they were in tears.

He listened to the crying. It was right below him, about halfway between the tier he was on and the floor. He'd have to risk being seen by those below him. There were several ogres lurching around – big fangs, big fists, big feet – and a few smaller monsters and imps scurrying to get out of the way of stomping ogres. But as he studied them, he realised most monsters were sitting with bowed heads. Not a happy bunch at all, and not one of them was watching the walls above.

He crept down to the burrow the crying came from. He couldn't hear voices talking, just snuffling and weeping – maybe more than three people. Maybe the Kavanaghs weren't the only people who'd been captured.

He put his head through the top of the doorway, getting closer to the sobbers in the dark. It didn't look any different to the dozens of other doors peppering the wall around it. He sniffed. He couldn't smell any fairy dust or humans and crept in a little closer. It was dingy inside, but there was movement, and then the crying stopped.

Wheedle didn't have time to scream as a large mitt clamped over his head and pulled him into the burrow.

CHAPTER 11

Sam scrabbled back into the boat. He'd barely noticed his clothes underwater, but as he tried to get aboard, his top and jacket doubled his weight. Still, he managed it.

As Sam plunged over the rim of the boat, making it bend and bounce, Bladder's claws scraped the side of the hull. Despite his new swimming skills, the gargoyle was too heavy to haul himself back over. Marée swam out of the way as the mer-guards shoved the gargoyle's back half into the craft. It rocked and pitched as Bladder tripped towards the other side. He threw up a glut of seawater and then collapsed, groaning.

In the distance, Sam saw the school of children heading back to the boat; seal noises and whale tunes called out through the air. He could also hear the horrible grating of the siren song. As the dolphins approached him, Sam shuddered, knowing his friends were in the grip of its spell.

He could hear the refrain, discordant and uncomfortable. It made his ears hurt and he had to stop listening.

'Be wary, Samuel, child of Kavanagh. They come, but until the song stops, they are not your friends', Marée said. 'And remember, it is not their fault.'

Sam studied the sea creatures' faces. Though they might have been in thrall to the sirens, their eyes were still human, but as he looked across the muddled and mixed school of animals, he realised it was smaller than before. Some were changing, he guessed, becoming true aquatic beasts and leaving. He didn't have much time.

On the horizon, the sun hung pale and soft. *Dusk*, Sam thought. Which meant he'd already lost half a day. He had until the following morning to get the fish back to shore.

Marée said nothing else as the boat pulled away, though her head bobbed above the waves and she put one hand up in farewell. Sam waved in return and Bladder threw up again before struggling to help the dolphins slip on their harnesses.

Sam sat back in the boat, leaning against Bladder's side, feeling a low thrum through the gargoyle and trying not to worry about what might happen next. He was wet and cold; that was enough to be going on with.

Time passed too quickly. The sun sank below the horizon and a gentle moon eased into the sky as Sam's friends pulled him towards the sirens. As they travelled, more of the group fled ahead and away. The larger fishes' eyes changed colour, the sea-sheeny irises swamping the human colours. Even one of the seals, who Sam had only seen a few times popping up above the waves, turned and studied him with a bewildered frown as its eyes transformed to a total dark brown. It took a terrified look at the shark and swam off with a high-pitched bark. The troupe thinned down the further they travelled, and the most concerned look came from the shark. Sam understood what it must be thinking. If it changed, all the smaller animals huddling close for safety would be the first on the menu. Sam watched with quiet discomfort and listened to Bladder prattle on about his adventures at the bottom of the sea and all the animals he'd encountered. He wanted to know what Sam had seen. Bladder was trying to distract him, Sam realised. Or perhaps he was trying to distract himself.

They both watched the water creatures and Bladder nosed Sam's face a few times, letting him know he understood, that he hadn't forgotten how worried Sam felt.

Sam thought about what was ahead. 'I wonder what they want.'

'The sirens?' Bladder said.

'Even Queen Amphitrite didn't know.'

'She knew enough to be frightened.' Bladder whacked his newly mended ear. 'Blow! I was trying to keep your mind off it. No point worrying until we get there.'

'What iz it?' a gruff goblin voice asked the faces silhouetted above Wheedle.

The stone bull struggled, but the creature leaned its weight on him. He could do little more than wiggle. Long goblin fingers were wrapped around his snout and he couldn't even protest.

'Iz a gumgoyle,' a sniffly voice answered. It was a deep voice, but it sounded like it had been crying.

'We don't haz to kill it, does we?' Gruff asked.

'What? No!' Sniffly answered. 'Iz gumgoyle, I said.'

A smaller voice, high and nervous, spoke up. 'I heard the little prince what Her Maggisty is looking for is all in with gumgoyles. If they hang about with him, they might be awful dangerous.'

'So we do haz to kill it?' Gruff asked. Wheedle did his best to break out of Gruff's grip, but the goblin leaned even harder. Wheedle wanted to come up for air as if he needed to breathe. 'I don't wanna haz to kill it.'

'Oi, let me have a closer look, I carn see nuffin' in the dark,' Sniffly said. Wheedle recognised the voice, but he couldn't place it.

A few of the crowd whimpered. They sounded as snotty and wet at Sniffly.

Like they'd all been crying.

'Take yer hand away, Buzzbrain, let me 'ave a good look,' Sniffly said, and a large muddy-brown ogre eye came right up to Wheedle's face.

'What if he screams?' Buzzbrain asked, his gruff voice getting heavy with snot. 'If he screams, they might finds us.'

'If he screams,' Small-high said, 'drop him and thatta be the end of it.'

'But I ...' Buzzbrain stopped talking as if someone had grabbed his mouth too.

'You doan 'ave to let 'im know you won't kill 'em. It's about soundin' threatnin', Sniffles said. 'You unnerstand me, gumgoyle?' he asked.

Wheedle couldn't nod; Buzzbrain was holding him too tightly. He blinked lots, hoping the sniffling ogre knew what he meant.

'Loosen up a little bit, Buzz,' Sniffles said again.

The goblin eased up, taking his claw off Wheedle's snout.

'I won't scream,' Wheedle said. 'I don't want you to have to threaten me.'

'Thaz a relief,' Buzzbrain said.

'An' you won't tell the uvvers weeze in 'ere?' Sniffles asked.

'Others?'

'The Old Ones. They doan fink much of us newer monsters.'

The ogre studied Wheedle's face. He rubbed a finger along the stone bull's nose. 'Hey, I know this gumgoyle.'

Sniffles leaned over Wheedle, and Wheedle recognised him. The young ogre had grown a bit but he still had a soft face, so oddly sweet compared to other ogres, the 'Old Ones', as he called them. Buzzbrain the goblin peered at Wheedle with a grimace and tear-red eyes.

'He's one of the ones we met at that first gathering. 'Member?' the goblin said.

Wheedle recognised the goblin too. It had given him a chest-crushing hug in the field where Maggie had called together the huge monster mob. He hadn't remembered the goblin's name was Buzzbrain. Come to think of it, he didn't think anyone had told him. Sniffles, though – he'd told them his name.

'Cob?' Wheedle asked.

The young ogre jumped. 'Iz you ... Bladder?'

'No, that's my pack mate. I'm Wheedle.'

'You know 'im?' Buzzbrain asked Cob.

'Yeah, he's a friend. You *are* a friend, right?' Cob asked.

Wheedle nodded. If it got him out of there, he'd be their friend.

'Don't say that word out loud,' a high-pitched voice said. Wheedle turned his head and saw an assortment of pixies settled against the back wall. 'If they hear "friend" or "like" or "hug" or any o' them words, we're mincemeat.' The pixie wagged a warning finger at the ogre. 'We keep tellin' ya.'

'Well, you stops sayin' them too,' Cob said. 'Wheedle, what you doin' lookin' in our burrow? Good fing for us iz you? Good fing for you iz us.'

'I heard crying.'

The group went quiet.

Cob whispered, 'Does you fink anyone else iz heard us?'

Wheedle shook his head. 'Only if they have gargoyle ears. Gargoyles hear very well. It keeps us out of the ogres' way. Generally.'

'Ain't seen too many gargoyles for a long, long time. Not until you and Bladder,' Cob replied.

Wheedle squinted around the room. The faces were neither menacing nor sneaky, neither vicious nor spiteful – not the way a room full of imps and larger monsters would normally look. These faces were worried, wary, fearful. And dirty as if they had been rubbing blubbing eyes with grubby hands, which, Wheedle guessed, was exactly what they'd been doing.

'Why were you all crying?' he asked.

'They want us to take humans', Cob answered.

'So ... so ... so they can eat them', Buzzbrain added.

'I don't wanna', a little goblin said, and burst into tears.

Cob put his arm around the goblin. 'There, there, Prickles, weeze jus' stay 'ere where they can't find us, 'ey?'

Prickles rubbed his nose on his sleeve. 'They'll find us eventual-like, and then we'll have to hurt people. Bombottom almos' broke my arm when I dint bring him nuffin' last time.'

'What about the pixies?' Wheedle turned to them. 'You're not being sent to eat humans, are you?' he asked.

'Babies! They want us to get babies.' The pixies burst into wails.

'Hush, hush, everyone', Cob said.

'What are they doing while you do all the hunting?' Wheedle asked.

'Her Maggisty says she's gotta protect the big'uns – the real ogres an' trolls an' goblins – until the little prince makes more of them. We're expandible.'

'Expendable', Prickles corrected.

'Thazzit. She says there's something wrong wivvus, but we can do menial tasks while the Old Ones prepare for war.'

'I caught a fairy for her', a pixie said. 'It was awful. It cried and begged me to let it go.'

'So what did you do?' Wheedle asked.

'I let it go,' the pixie replied. 'I couldn't hurt it. Or hand it in. She takes their wings for the fairy dust and then the Old Ones eat what's left. Poor little blighters. When we chased them on the field it wor fun, but then we saw what happened after. I wouldn't want anyone doin' that to me.'

The crowd of young monsters shook their heads and spoke over the top of each other. 'Oh, no, I woont. You woont iver, woot you? Not me. Me neeva.'

Wheedle let them all agree that they wouldn't enjoy being caught and eaten and let the unhappy brood settle before he spoke again. 'You don't know anything about three humans being caught together recently?' he asked.

'Her Maggisty sent the Old Ones to capture three full-growns and a baby,' a boggart said. 'Said they were pacifically wanted, not for num-nums, but because they are His Soon-to-be Royal Harness's pets. If he lives here, he'll want 'em for walkies or summat.'

'They're not his pets,' Wheedle said. 'They're his family. He loves them. I managed to keep the baby upstairs, but the other three ...'

The group stared, their mouths open so every fang was exposed. Wheedle recognised something like hunger on their faces. 'I'm made of stone,' he said. 'I'm not edible.'

'You said ...' Cob started, then dropped his voice. 'He *loves* 'em?'

'Yes, he loves us too,' Wheedle added. 'His pack. We're very important to him ...'

'How many people does His Future Kingling ... *love*?'

Wheedle thought about it. 'Well, there's the four of us gargoyles. His family – not just the ones he lives with, there's some in Ireland too and quite a few in London. He's got friends, close ones and ones he knows at school. Come to think of it, I don't think I know how many people he loves. Lots.'

'An' some of them is monsters?'

'Monsters? What? Oh, you mean us gargoyles? I've been with Sam so long, I don't think of myself as a monster any more. No offence.'

The boggart put a finger on Wheedle's nose. 'I bet that's –' his voice dropped – 'nice.'

At least the water's still flat, Sam thought. And every now and then a wave came to push him towards the sirens a little faster. Sam guessed Amphitrite was helping in more ways than she had promised. He would have to do something to show the sea queen his appreciation. He wondered if she liked chocolates.

The sky grew darker, which meant evening had settled in.

Sam pondered their direction. Queen Amphitrite had established without a doubt it was sirens who were singing, but were they really calling the sea creatures to bring him to them? Maybe they meant to drown him or eat him.

Too many maybes. He'd deal with them when he got there. He couldn't just go home and leave thousands of children to turn into sea creatures forever, but he had no idea what he could do or say to the sirens to get them to stop singing.

Bladder nudged through the food bags, found a sandwich and sat back with it in his paws, nibbling slowly. 'Tum's a bit sensitive.' The gargoyle stretched his forelegs then his back legs and looked better than he had in ages. Few shadows blurred his face, and the moon made him look a lovely soft grey, like a wild rabbit. He took up position on the other side of Sam, trying to keep as much wind off him as possible. Sam was dry, but getting colder, which meant they were approaching what Michelle called the 'wee hours'. The cold didn't bother him; what bothered him was the idea he was running out of time. He only had till morning to get the children home.

'Rocks,' Bladder said, breaking through his pondering.

Great grizzled boulders loomed up out of the water, peering miserably at them and quietening the small crew. They looked unearthly sticking out of the sea, a small collection of stones in the middle of nowhere.

'We're here,' Bladder said. 'Wherever here is.' The dolphins slid out from their ropes and the boat skimmed on a current over the water towards the outcrop.

The rocks poked out of a circle of coral, a bowl of salt water in the greater sea. It was full of whiting and other small fish whose scales caught the moonlight. A few larger fish were swimming at the edge of the atoll, tails flapping with excitement. Sam guessed these were the smaller children who'd swum away in the process of forgetting they'd been human once.

As soon as the boat hit the coral, the singing stopped and the dolphins and fish behind him made an awful racket in the water. The song no longer bound them, and the poor animals tried to drag the boat away. Sam pulled the ropes into the boat to stop the dolphins from looping themselves in them again. He looked down to see Amira, Hazel and Wilfred's eyes widen, their expressions clear and human. Sam was glad to see their eyes unchanged, as human as ever. They chittered angrily at him and nosed the side of the boat, pushing it away from the rocks.

The dolphins and other creatures carried on flapping outside the rocky shelf, but they could not swim past the rocks; it was too shallow for their large bodies. The tiny fish inside raced to the middle of the lagoon, away from what, in nature, would have been their predators. Sam shuddered to think what would happen if he couldn't get them back to the shore.

Wilfred pushed Sam's boat away from the outcrop of stone and positioned himself between the shelf and the boat.

'Don't worry', Sam soothed, 'I know what's ahead. I have to talk to them. If you don't let me, I can't save you.'

Wilfred checked Sam's face, possibly to see if Sam was under a spell. Behind him, Hazel hooted in warning, and Sam waved at her. 'It's all right, I want to meet up with the sirens. That's why I came. I knew what you were doing and you're not responsible. I would have come by myself, if I had to.'

The dolphins exchanged guilty glances.

Even Bladder stood up and spoke to them. 'You've been under a spell. It ain't your fault.'

Sam nodded. 'I have to ask the sirens to stop singing at you so you can go back to Brighton.'

'Sounds like they've stopped already,' Bladder said.

'You're right.' Sam turned from Wilfred to address all of the animals. 'Go home. Go home now! You'll turn human as you get to shore. If you don't, you'll remain this way forever.'

A few of the creatures nodded and swam off, but many others watched the tiny fish inside the atoll and stayed close. The shifters swam nearer to the boat. A sea lion barked in query, but as it yapped Sam saw its eyes darken, the whites thinning back to outlines; it would lose its humanity soon.

'Don't look now, but we got company,' Bladder said.

Even the brave shark shuffled back towards deeper water. Sam flinched to see thin scratches of blood muddying its back, where it had scraped against the coral. The dolphins retreated and watched him from the waves. Sam turned to see two shadows shuffling to the tops of the rocks, their dark shapes leaning over him.

'Not the most attractive group,' Bladder said, and gagged.

The sirens were ugly, and they were just as Queen Amphitrite had described. They had bird bodies, with legs that reminded Sam of Baba Yaga's half-plucked chicken drumstick thighs, and their feet looked diseased, like they had a nasty kind of scaly, flaky skin problem. One used a claw to scratch harshly at the other foot. *That has to hurt,* Sam thought. The sirens' faces weren't unpleasant. They were very normal-looking human faces. One looked ancient, but the other looked no older than Michelle. Still, Sam found his glance returning to those awful avian bodies.

Sam clambered from the boat into the shallow pool inside the coral ring. Bladder climbed after him.

Wheedle stared at the boggart that had just come into the burrow waving its long arms about and complaining.

'What exactly made you throw up?' Cob asked the boggart.

'Them human pets,' it said. 'Looking at 'em made my tum-tum so squishy awful I couldn't do it no more. Doan know why His Future Kingliness wants 'em. Ugly, they iz. Deformed.'

Wheedle shuddered. What had the kidnappers done to the Kavanaghs?

'They wuz so awful they put them in that box and chucked a blankie over 'em. Even the Old Ones can't stand looking at them.'

Wheedle felt his own tum-tum turn squishy.

'Go on, have a look. Everyone else is,' the boggart said. 'But I'm staying here now. Bombottom is putting together another hunting party.'

The monsters groaned.

Wheedle's legs shook as he climbed down the wall towards the huge box next to the dais. He studied the barrel on top. He'd seen it when he'd come in, and wondered what it was for. Now he watched as a flock of pixies – some old, some new – passed small buckets of water up to the barrel and filled it bit by bit. It looked about the size of a large bin.

Maybe it's for the Kavanaghs. Bladder had told him and Spigot about Sam going wobbly when he ran out of drinking water. That meant Maggie wanted the Kavanaghs alive, which had to be a good thing.

Wheedle carried on down the wall and the barrel moved out of view as he passed a shivering group of brownies. He sidled by some younger trolls, trying to look tough and dangerous like the Old Ones, but when he stepped on a set of toes, the troll squeaked and scooted away.

He couldn't believe it. A troll? Backing away from him, a gargoyle? The trolls might have been young and small, but they were still capable of cracking his head.

Everyone else avoided looking at him. The Old Ones were too busy – there weren't as many as there used to be (thanks to the souls from the sword) – and the younger ones were avoiding bringing too much attention to themselves.

He stepped into the crowd. Not one foot, fist or even a verbal insult hit him. The crowd seemed nervous and wary.

Pixies lined the sides of the cavern. The closer he moved to the throne, the larger the creatures became. First pixies, then leprechauns rolling dice.

Wheedle gulped as leprechauns gave way to goblins, all of them packed in like a market crowd. Ogres at the edge of the dais were trading slabs of meat, trolls and witches haggled over wriggling bags of ... what? Wheedle didn't like to think. A few shuffled past him, but no one paid him much attention.

Suddenly, one of the witches' bags burst open and a terrified rabbit shot across the dirt, causing high humour amongst the littlest creatures. On the tier above Wheedle's head, older brownies laughed uproariously. A young troll pushed past him, followed its adolescent comrades and raced after the bunny. Wheedle felt sorry for the rabbit; the thousands of hands around it meant there was no escape, but he delighted to see it disappear into an access way to the upper world.

Sitting on the dais was the large ogre Wheedle had spotted earlier. It wasn't the largest Wheedle had ever seen – all of the oldest and largest had gone. Still, it was two storeys tall and crushing something in its huge taloned claws. Wheedle remembered the beast now. It was the huge ogre that Maggie had stood on at the first field gathering: Bombottom. It seemed that the ogre had gained confidence and not a little nastiness since Wheedle had seen him then. He was using a troll as a footstool and slapping any monster that spoke to him. *Maggie must love him*, Wheedle thought.

'Hey, it's a gargoyle', a happy troll's voice said behind him. Wheedle turned to say something, but the troll started licking its toes.

A group of goblins had crowded around the box. It had been covered with a huge coarse blanket.

One of the imps lifted it off. 'Ooh, that *is* ugly.'

'Chuck 'em. Now, let's get out of here,' another said, and the group strolled away, trying hard to not look embarrassed.

It couldn't be the Kavanaghs. The Kavanaghs were lovely. They looked like Sam. They should look delicious to this lot.

Wheedle wondered what could be so horrible that it made anything down here think it was ugly. And vomit. He gulped and lifted the blanket.

The first thing he saw was iron bars. Then the sides of the box, rough wooden planks, and, sitting huddled at the back, were the Kavanaghs: Nick, Richard and Michelle.

They peered back at Wheedle.

Wheedle recognised the dazed, uncomprehending expression that humans always made when seeing a monster's face for the first time. *You poor things*, he thought, *my ugly mug one of the least frightening you're gonna see for a while.*

The next thing that occurred to him was that he would much rather not eat them; they didn't look very appetising. In fact, he had never seen anyone look so unpalatable. He blinked. The idea of eating a human had never occurred to him before, so the idea of NOT eating one was bizarre.

Where Nick's and Richard's hair covered their pale faces, Michelle's was pulled back in a messy ponytail, and Wheedle could see her forehead clearly. A distinct glowing thumbprint shone out. Wheedle grinned. That was it. He recognised Daniel's handiwork. The angel's mark made all the humans look less edible: Wheedle had never thought a human edible in the first place, and he thought the Kavanaghs looked completely disgusting. The angel had blessed them.

Wheedle shifted with discomfort. He'd been so annoyed with Daniel for leaving Sam alone at sea, he'd never thought to consider that the angel, although not at work looking after Sam, would at least be at work looking after his family. Daniel had put a protection mark on them, preventing any monster from finding them delicious. It had worked so well the monsters had covered them with the huge throwover, so they didn't even have to gaze upon them. Even though it was a miserable cage, it was better than being peered at by hungry monsters all day.

On the floor in front of them, the ground was covered in chocolates, sweets, tins of sugary drinks and packets of biscuits. Wheedle guessed the pixies and brownies oversaw feeding the captives. Pixies would feed humans what they thought they liked. Enough little humans had been trapped by sweet lures, it wasn't odd the brownies thought that's all they'd want.

The three Kavanaghs stared at Wheedle.

'Hello,' he said.

'Go away,' Richard replied, and threw something at him. It was a hard-boiled sweet.

'What is it?' Michelle asked. 'It looks like a cow.'

'I'm a gargoyle. Wheedle.'

'Like in Sam's story? *Sam's* Wheedle?' Michelle asked.

'The very same.'

A long silence occurred, during which the Kavanaghs exchanged bewildered glances.

'When we first met Sam, he told us about you. He told the psychologist. Oh', Michelle said. 'I'm in Sam's nightmare'.

Richard pinched himself. 'Nope, I'm awake. I don't want to be, but I am'.

'He said you were a friend', Nick said to Wheedle.

'And I am. We'll get you back home some way, but it's not safe yet. First I have to figure out how to get you out of this cage'. Wheedle peered around. A huge, heavy lock hung to his left on the door. It would take a lot of effort to open it. 'Looks like we may have to come up with a good plan, but if you keep your heads down, no monster will eat you. Daniel has put a protective mark on you'.

'Daniel?' Michelle asked. 'The angel? Sam told us about him too. I didn't believe a word of it'. Michelle put her head against Richard and groaned. 'I'm so stupid'.

Richard patted her. 'It's not like it was very believable'. He turned to Wheedle. 'I'm not even sure I believe it now, and I'm in a cage surrounded by monsters'.

'I wish I didn't believe it', Nick said. 'No offence'.

'None taken', Wheedle replied. 'Our whole strategy for the last few hundred years has been to make you all forget us. Monsters're safer then'.

'Safer?' Richard said. 'Those things out there are hideous and bloodthirsty. Why would they need protection from us?' He blinked at Wheedle. 'Present company excluded', he added.

'Is Sam really part monster?' Nick asked. 'Like them? He told us he was.'

'He's part gargoyle. An' all good. Don't you worry about him. Let's just concern ourselves with you for now.' A cheer went up outside of the cage and Wheedle felt an imp thud against his rump. He'd have to move soon; the mob sounds had increased and the crowd was shuffling forwards.

'We walked here. Just ... walked,' Michelle said. 'We even –' she gulped – 'slipped through the gutter. I remember it all, but it seems so strange.' She stared at him. 'I remember you now. You took Beatrice from me.'

'She's safe and sound at home with Spigot.'

'Thank goodness. Thank you. I can't believe I just left her.'

'Ah, you've been dusted, that's all. Can't blame yourselves for that.'

CHAPTER 12

'Oi, Ugly! Down here!' Bladder splashed about in the water, scaring the small fish to the sides of the pool.

Sam glanced up as the younger-looking of the sirens opened her mouth and grinned around a sharp set of fangs. Then she sang. Bladder screamed, and Sam wailed too. A headache grew in the air, filling the atmosphere with stabs and sharp pain.

The song's not for Bladder or me, Sam thought. The siren stood, stretching out her bird body to its full and hideous length, and she opened her jaw, her song getting stronger. The sea creatures around them moaned. Medium-sized fish threw themselves into the rocky basin. The dolphins battered their bodies against the too-shallow rocky area. Bladder jumped out of the basin into deeper water, swimming between the sea creatures. He tried to grab a dolphin to pull her away from the scratching coral and his magically grippy paws held on to Amira as he pulled her underwater. The other animals crashed the boat into the coral basin, sending silver fish fleeing. The water swelled as the whale calf steamed in from the distance.

'Stop!' Sam yelled as the animals scratched themselves.

Bladder's head bobbed up next to Amira's snout. She was straining herself trying to dislodge him. Wilfred bit his tail. Bladder let go of Amira and pulled on Wilfred's fin just before the dolphin boy flipped into the atoll.

Sam watched the frenzied sea creatures.

'Sam, if the dolphins flip themselves into the shallow area, they won't be able to get out again', Bladder gurgled. 'And that whale's going to crash into us soon.'

Larger fish raced towards the sirens and flung themselves into the coral bowl, boiling around Sam.

Sam twisted towards the sirens and waved his arms. It didn't stop the singing. He felt helpless. He stared up at the sirens, who were focused on him with more interest than on the creatures preparing to batter themselves on the stone. Bladder started back towards the rocks.

'Stop it!' Sam yelled at the younger siren. 'Stop singing! Please!'

He expected her to turn to him, bare her fangs, jump down and put a talon to his throat, something nasty, but she just stopped. Like he'd asked.

'As you wish, little master, but *he* needs to be somewhere I can see him.' She pointed at Bladder. 'No nasty gargoyle tricks. I know how well they climb.'

'I'm going to pull her legs off with my bare claws.'

'Bladder!' Sam warned.

Bladder grumbled, but clambered back into the atoll and glared up at the two sirens. Sam noticed there was blood in the water. The shark swam off. Its expression, Sam could tell, was very disturbed.

The older siren pointed to the boat and giggled. It was rocking and swaying as water settled in its bottom. It had a crack in the side where it had hit coral.

The animals settled too, their whines and moans fading.

Sam's ears delighted in the lovely sounds of waves, the wind and even the weeping chitters of dolphins and other sea creatures. Sad as it was, it was a lovelier song than the sirens'. The flight of larger fish flipped their bodies back into the sea on the other side of the coral wall. The whale blew a stream of water into the air in disgust.

'You are Samuel?' the older siren asked him.

'Are you the queen of the sirens?'

She laughed. 'I am the elder,' she replied. 'I imagine that will do as queen.'

'He does not appear as interesting as she described,' the younger siren said.

'Who described?' Sam asked, but he knew the answer. 'You mean Maggie?'

The sirens' few feathers ruffled.

Bladder groaned. 'I told ya. That lying ...'

'Bladder!' Sam said.

'But she was behind this the whole time,' Bladder raged. 'Tryna convince you some other monsters was out to get you, so you'd rush to her for safety.'

Sam studied the older siren's face. 'And Maggie told you to call the children?'

'She did. She said she would reward us with a child of our own.'

The younger siren ahhed and oohed in a broody hum.

'She says there will be no more sirens without you. You can hatch sighs?'

'A siren is a rare thing,' the older siren said. 'Only once in a few hundred years does someone so avaricious and greedy sigh an egg that hatches into a siren. It becomes precious. Maggie found this one under the great heaps of beads and gave it to us.' She held up a dark stone. It was as big as her fist and beautiful in an awful way. The opposite of mother-of-pearl in colouring, casting dark colour and dark sheen, sucking in the healthy moonlight.

'How can you make it into a siren now the ogre king's dead?' Bladder asked. 'Only they can sigh a bead into being.'

The sirens glared at Bladder. 'Stone tongue speaks lies. Maggie told us the fairy dust and her little prince together can hatch a monster. And she said she would help make this one into a new siren if we called the humans to a watery death. She said it would bring you to her side in grief, and if she also ...'

'Also what?' Bladder moved forward.

Sam felt the seawater drop a degree or two. What else could Maggie do to him?

'She said she could make you bent and twisted, and with a smattering of fairy dust she would hatch us a new sister.'

'It failed, though. You didn't drown the children,' Sam said.

'No, Amphitrite intruded and changed them instead. But then we heard you had come to the water looking for them yourself, and we knew we no longer had need of Maggie's intervention. We sang and they brought you here.'

'So much better; we do not have to wait,' the younger siren said.

'Sam himself doesn't respond to your caterwauling though, does he? He came here freely,' Bladder said. 'So he doesn't have to do what you ask.'

'We could sing your little school of friends into the rocks until one by one they die. Or you could make another little sister for us and we will let them all go.'

Bladder stared at Sam. The air seemed to freeze around him. Sam shook his head. 'I can't help you, even if I wanted to. I need a magic I don't have to hatch a bead. I can't complete the spell.' Sam looked at the damaged boat as the moon cast horrible shapes on the water.

The old siren pulled a tin out from under her wing. 'Of course. You mean this? Fairy dust. With the right song, a fairy can be made willing to give a snifter of wing powder.'

The younger siren cackled. It made Sam tremble.

The older siren continued. 'We know Maggie means only for you to hatch ogres. For war. But we sirens cannot afford the losses; there are so few of us, we only want life.' Her face pulled down into sad lines. 'Please. Do this and we will let you all go.'

Bladder looked at Sam. 'It's just one. One siren for all of these kids', he whispered. 'It doesn't seem so much. There's only two of them.'

Sam nodded. It didn't seem much, but he knew what sirens could do. He would be bringing another cruel monster into the world, and if he did that, he'd feel awful. Also, Marée and Queen Amphitrite would not be happy.

'They don't want war any more 'an we do', Bladder said.

'So they say, but they're monsters.'

'So are we, Sam.'

Sam hung his head and Bladder raised his to the sirens.

'How do we know you will honour your word?' Bladder asked. Sam sighed. It was a good question. He was glad Bladder had come; hearing the sirens' request had chilled all of the sensible questions out of Sam.

'What word?' the older siren asked.

'You said you would let them go if Sam hatched the egg.'

The sirens laughed sadly. 'We will. If that's what you want. If you can turn a bead into a babe, then you are the ogre king. You would be our liege, and we will be your servants.'

'I'm gonna throw up', Bladder said.

Sam felt the same. He wasn't the ogre king; he'd never be the ogre king. The idea was horrible.

'I don't want you calling children to sea again.'

'Never', the old siren said. 'If Your Highness wishes it.'

'In fact, I want you to sing them back to shore, so we don't lose even one of them.'

'Yes, yes,' both the sirens agreed.

The old siren scrabbled down the rock. Sam wondered at her fragility and discomfort, and how the pair got across the water. Perhaps they could charm any sailor to give them transport.

Up close, Sam noticed how intensely she was gazing at the bead.

'There's only two of you left?' he asked.

'Only two,' she echoed. 'All our other sisters gone. And if one of us should ... go.' She glanced back at the other siren briefly, then held out the bead and the tin to Sam. 'Please, sire.'

Bladder raised his eyebrows. Sam understood. Monsters never said 'please' and she'd said it twice.

Sam sighed and took the tin. When he opened it, the fairy dust glowed in the moonlight, sparkling like a collection of stolen stars. He blew it over the egg.

'Come on, no need to watch it happen,' Bladder said, and jumped towards the boat. It lurched, causing it to drift away from the rocky atoll, but he made it. Sam scrabbled after him and as he landed his foot disappeared into the puddle at the bottom of the little craft. The boat was already sinking. The dolphins looped the ropes around themselves again and chirruped at him. Sam hoped they knew where they were going.

He heard the egg crack as the boat pulled away from the rocks and he turned to watch the siren place it gently on a stone. A small arm pushed out of the top, and the dark sides crumbled down. A small girl's face appeared atop a downy dove's body. The little siren was pretty. The other sirens laughed fondly as it reached for them, and the younger one pulled the infant into her arms.

'It don't look right', Bladder said.

'It's a beautiful baby', Sam replied.

'Exactly. Not right.'

Then the infant began to sing. It was lovely, even to Sam's ears.

The sea creatures halted and listened to the sound. It wasn't hypnotising them. Not in the normal siren way, not playing with their minds – it was simply a sweet voice singing a sweet song. Then the other sirens joined with it, singing a going-home song. There were notes in it Sam didn't understand, but overall, it was glorious.

CHAPTER 13

Spigot shrieked at the babies. Beatrice and Nugget were so happy to be with each other that they smooched and stroked each other with tiny hands and claws. It would have been adorable to watch if debris wasn't flying off Nugget's surface and leaving grey piles on the ground. Wheedle had said to look after them, and Spigot knew Wheedle was worried about Nugget. Nugget was falling apart, that's what concerned him, and the silly baby was letting herself get patted to pieces.

She was happy though, happier than she'd been in days, weeks even.

Pebbles of gargoyle pelt peppered the tiles, but Nugget scooted and giggled, rolling on her back and play fighting as Beatrice grabbed her wings. Maybe it wasn't pain that had been making Nugget cry so much; maybe it was loneliness. She had needed a playmate.

Nugget was agile, far more than human baby Beatrice, who crawled and sometimes grabbed chairs and table legs to right herself so she could chase the tiny gargoyle. The pair goo-gooed at each other and Spigot screamed again for them to stop. Grey ash from Nugget spread across the kitchen floor. Poor baby Nugget, letting herself crumble away, all because she wanted to play.

Nugget crawled under a dressing gown lying on the kitchen floor. One of the human adults must have dropped it when the dust took them.

Nugget put her head out and looked at Beatrice. 'Peek-boo', Nugget said. Beatrice fell on her bottom laughing. Nugget thought this was so wonderful, she peek-booed again.

A high sound shrilled through the kitchen. Spigot screeched in alarm as the piercing noise went on and on.

Then it stopped. Spigot exhaled. It wasn't that horrible noise that had made Nick want to fight. And Beatrice wasn't paying it much mind, like it was normal to her. Spigot flustered at the babies. He had to stop Nugget dusting off more of her skin on the dressing gown. Why wouldn't she stop? Spigot shook his wings at her, but the pair giggled again, then they cuddled each other. Beatrice put her wet mouth on Nugget's cheek and it came away ringed in grey. Nugget touched the drool on her face and grinned at Spigot.

The stone eagle wanted to cry. Then the shrill noise began again, stabbing at his head. *What was it?* It was an awful sound, but then he recognised it. He'd heard it many times, often softened by the roof, sure, as he heard it coming up through the house, but occasionally he'd heard the same sound come from Sam's bottom.

Mobile phone. That's what Sam called it.

Spigot trained his eagle eye on the kitchen. On the bench, next to the kettle, sat a black rectangle, just like Sam's phone. It glowed. Spigot squawked at it and took a step closer.

The phone rang.

Spigot took another step towards it.

What were you supposed to do with phones? What did Sam do?

Spigot pecked the phone. The trilling stopped. Then a voice started.

'Hello? Hello? Richard?'

Spigot screeched a greeting at the voice.

'Who is this? Richard? Richard? Is something wrong?'

Spigot cheeped. *You could say that.*

'What's going on?'

Spigot tried to explain, squawking and shrieking for extra emphasis. *Michelle, Nick and Richard have run away. Beatrice is patting Nugget to death. Literally. She's falling apart, and so is everything else. Oh, and Sam has gone out to sea with Bladder and Daniel.* Spigot panted. He felt hopeless. *I need help.*

'Whatever's going on, tell Richard I'm coming,' the voice said. There was a click. The voice went away.

Spigot felt a bit of relief, although he had told the voice Richard had gone off, so who did she think he would be telling? Ooh, *maybe the human at the other end can take Beatrice. That might help Nugget from completely disintegrating.* At least there was that.

Spigot turned. The babies lay together, sleeping on the dressing gown. Nugget slept without whimpering, her forepaw over Beatrice's shoulder. Both babies had thumbs stuck in their mouths.

Spigot leaned over them. If Nugget's wings hadn't been so chipped and her stone skin so cracked and powdery, it would have been a sweet scene.

Spigot nestled on the floor next to them and watched the babies as they dreamed.

The boat stayed afloat another hour, but it got increasingly difficult to drag. Sam could see the strain on the faces of the dolphins as they pulled the waterlogged vessel.

'It'd be easier to swim,' Bladder said.

Despite the sea queen's gift, Sam was a bit nervous about slipping into the water, but he'd have to soon, and so would Bladder. The gargoyle's bulk made the boat sink quicker and move slower.

Hazel and Wilfred slid alongside the boat and chittered. Their happy noises comforted him. He patted Hazel and she slipped her fin into his hand.

'I think she's telling you to get on,' Bladder said. 'An' it looks like I'm swimming home,' he moaned. 'How many sea miles do you think it is?'

Sam slid into the water, holding Wilfred's fin in one hand and Hazel's in the other. His chest clenched in the freezing sea and he felt relieved to get some heat from the dolphins, although he could feel them shivering too. He wondered how they had coped for so long.

'I could swim with you,' he said to Bladder.

'Don't be silly, you gotta get this lot back to land.' As Bladder spoke, the whale calf bumped the other side of the boat.

'I think that's your ride,' Sam said through chattering teeth.

Bladder shuddered, and put a tentative paw on the calf's back. It held. He put on another, and the whale let out a spout of water, which crashed down on Bladder's head.

'Oh, this is going to be soooo pleasant,' Bladder said. He looked shaky on the whale's back, and slumped his belly on to the grey, shiny skin of the great beast.

The whale crested forward.

'Great, just great,' Bladder said.

A mist covered the sea, which meant Sam could not see where they were going, and he had to trust the sirens' song was taking the sea creatures in the right direction, not leaving them stranded.

The shimmer of fish curved with the waves and slowly Sam's grip on Hazel and Wilfred began slipping. Both of their smooth dolphin backs were getting smaller. They still shone a lovely pearl grey but they were smaller, their dorsal fins barely poking out of their backs and their pectoral fins growing longer, slimmer, the ends of them splaying out and splashing about. Sam looked over his shoulder to see their tails beginning to split in two.

Their transformation back into human shape had begun, but Sam knew they weren't close enough to land. It was too soon. He looked around and took in the rest of the creatures: the sharks, the seals, the other dolphins. Most of them still appeared the same, but they were shrinking, becoming more kid-sized. The rest of the crowd clustered together as the littler fish – the cod, the herring, the trout and the tiny minnows – suddenly began to grow. Some of their eyes still gazed ahead, fish-blank, and only the song kept them with the group. A salmon stared at Sam. A little brown and very human nose poked out of its scaly face.

Bladder rode the whale calf's back, his eyes wide and his jaw hanging open. The whale under him had shrunk enough to pull the gargoyle's forepaws together; his ride wasn't going to last long and Sam guessed Bladder was judging how far he'd have left to swim.

'What's that?' Bladder called out.

Sam peered up and squinted. He felt so cold, he couldn't focus. He'd lost his wellies, and he wondered if the cold would kill him soon. He'd heard it could.

Two shining white eyes glared at him over the dark water.

'I hope that's not some sort of sea monster,' Bladder said. 'Did the book say anything about creatures with glowing eyes?'

Sam had been looking for information on magic, not huge monsters with bright eyes. It could have been a scylla, or Nessie. He had no idea. He wondered how big it was and what kind of appetite it had. It headed towards them, its eyes staring with unyielding light.

Then he heard human voices, and a third 'eye' shone out. He spluttered as a wave hit him in the face. 'It's not a monster, it's a boat.'

The humans aboard yelled at each other and Sam heard the churn of machinery. It was on a definite course to meet them.

'What sort of boat goes out at night?' Bladder asked. 'Won't be a pleasure ride.'

The boat came out of the darkness, no longer disguised by waves and distance. It was hard to see what type it was – it was boat-shaped all right, but with a huge metal arm leaning over the side and dragging a sheet alongside it.

Bladder yelled. 'You gotta be kidding me! It's a trawler. I've seen movies, Sam, that's a trawler!'

'What's a trawler?' Sam yelled back over the sound of engines pushing towards them.

A seal screamed.

'A fishing trawler, Sam. They catch fish.'

The larger creatures moved out of the way of the metal monster bearing down on them, but the smaller fish, mesmerised by the sirens' song and maintaining the course the song sent them on, kept swimming in its direction.

The net, for Sam could see it was a net, pulled through the water, scooping up the helpless whiting, salmon, herring and trout. A seal trying to herd the fish away got tangled up with the bundle, along with a dolphin. Sam thought it might be Amira. The net lifted out of the water, whiting and other small fish falling free of the trap.

'Sam, they'll drown!' Bladder shouted.

'Drown?'

'Fish can't breathe out of water. Look at them!'

Sam saw the hundreds of fish-children gasping as they rose into the night air.

'Captain, there's something out there,' a voice called. The huge torchlight landed on Bladder astride his shrinking whale.

'Get me to that boat,' Sam told Wilfred and Hazel. His hands were so cold, he wondered if they'd stick.

Bladder was right beside him as he got to the side of the boat. It looked so high. Sam put one hand on the bulkhead and pulled himself out of the water. Wet and in the full blast of the winter wind, he was even colder out of the waves. He looked at the fish in the net, thrashing so hard they slammed into each other. Bladder ran up the side of the boat.

'Sam? Are you all right, Sam?' Bladder came back towards him. 'How are you so blue?'

Sam shook so hard, he couldn't speak.

'How were you able to survive at the bottom of the ocean but not here? Mermaid magic? Must be. Where's that blasted angel when we need him?'

Sam wanted to let go and drop to the water. He didn't have the energy for this. 'Save the fish,' was all he could manage.

'You first, then fish.' Bladder grabbed him by his soaking anorak and dragged him to the top of the boat.

'What the ... ?' screamed one of the boatmen as Bladder threw the shaking Sam on to the deck.

'Let my fish go!' Bladder yelled.

'Captain!' another screamed.

The captain – Sam could tell by his hat – ran forward, holding a long rod with a hook at the end. He waved it in Bladder's face. 'Where'd you come from?'

'Out of the water, you twit! Let the fish go!'

'Back! Back!' the captain yelled.

Bladder lunged forward, grabbed the hook in his mouth and snapped the rod in two. Two more crew members came at him with fishing rods. One had a filleting knife in her hand. Bladder roared and bit down on the woman's wrist. She screamed and the knife skidded towards Sam.

Sam stood. He shook so hard he couldn't get the words out. 'Let. Fish. Go.'

'It's a kid', the woman yelled.

Bladder backed away from the crew, yelling 'Yah, yah!' at them, and clambered towards the swinging net. Sam watched. Some of the fish weren't flapping as much. Sam grabbed the knife.

'Where in the world did the boy come from?'

Whether it was panic, being out of the water or something else, Sam found the sudden energy to follow Bladder towards the net. He jumped out towards it, causing it to swing and sway, allowing a few more fish to fall to the safety of the water below. The full net lurched and waved over the water. As Sam swung back towards the boat, a crew member tried to grab him.

'No, you don't!' Bladder yelled and barrelled into the man, pitching him into the water.

Sam caught hold of the net and used it like a ladder, clenching the knife between his teeth like he'd seen in a movie. He hoped he didn't slip. The knife was very sharp.

'Hurry, Sam!' Bladder called out.

'Get that boy off the net!' the captain yelled.

'Captain! Ben's in the water! And there's a shark!'

The captain swore. The crew forgot Sam and went to work trying to get their crew member to safety. Sam thought that was a good idea. The shark wouldn't hurt Ben, but without a couple of warm dolphins lending him a bit of warmth, the water could freeze him to death.

Sam scrambled to the top of the net. The fish were opening and closing their mouths, trying to breathe air that was useless to them. He saw their begging expressions.

He sat astride the metal arm holding the net and began cutting ropes. They looked thick. He hacked and the fish panted. As the first rope thinned down, his frozen fingers got sorer and sorer. He slipped, slicing his thumb. He couldn't stop though and his blood, bright red in the cold air, fell on to the gasping fish. Just a couple more strands to cut and he could move on to the other rope.

The first rope dropped as it broke through, but Sam never got to the second one.

The net opened, spilling all the fish into the water, and the seals and dolphins swarmed forwards to help them. Ben, the crewman in the water, screamed as the larger creatures moved towards him.

Sam watched as the fish fell. He felt a moment of relief, until the bar, which had been held down by the weight of hundreds of fish, catapulted him into the air, above the deck, over the head of a yelling gargoyle.

He closed his eyes. He was so cold, so very, very cold. As the last of his warmth left his body, Sam closed his eyes.

CHAPTER 14

Sam opened his eyes. He was flying. He looked at the sea below and the boat moving further away, with its bewildered crew pulling Ben on to the deck. A few paces from them a stone lion climbed on to the boat railing, ready to fling itself back in the water in the direction of a whale calf watching him with bright blue eyes. The size of the school of mismatched fish and sea creatures was huge. It looked magical from above.

And he felt warm.

'How are you?' a familiar voice asked.

'Daniel?'

'It's taken ages to find you. You aren't fitted with a GPS and if you don't call for me, you are very hard to locate.' The angel sighed. 'Thank goodness that gargoyle had a good whinge. Although we will have words about him calling me a "blasted angel".'

'I thought I was going to die.'

'You very nearly did. In fact, it's miraculous you withstood the cold so long. That's got to be a little of the gargoyle toughness Bladder keeps bragging about.'

Above the herd, Sam could make out distant lights. The whole of the Sussex coastline, he guessed. It was still too far away. He wondered at the changes he had seen. Queen Amphitrite had said the children needed to be close to shore when they began to change. He'd never thought to ask what 'close' meant to her. If the changes took place too soon, some of these fish would turn into very small children, toddlers even, and many of them, maybe most, couldn't swim. Even a hundred metres from shore would be a death sentence. He hoped the changes would slow down.

'We've got to move faster,' Sam said.

'Tell them.' Daniel dropped closer to the waves.

Sam shuddered. He wouldn't resist if Daniel let him go, but the thought of the freezing water made him close his eyes as he prepared for the shock.

The angel did not release him. Instead he held Sam closer, warming him from his nose to his toes, and hovered above a cluster of the larger animals. Sam repeated his instruction to Wilfred, Amira, Hazel, the whale calf and a bob of seals.

Wilfred let out a high-pitched song that reminded Sam of laughter, and many of the fish nodded. Sam noted many eyes were fully human, no longer the blank black inside eye sockets. Blue, brown and green irises stared up at him. A grey nurse shark herded a school of trout as the silvery fish flicked their tails and got a move on. In the middle of the group, one trout stood out; its luminescent scales had become pink skin, but it was swimming as quickly as the others.

'I can smell land', said the shark. The shark looked pleased to be able to speak again, its toothy grin spreading across its wide face. It still had the blank eyes of a predator, which made the whole expression far creepier than the fish around it liked.

Sam was glad the shark was happy, but wary of every sign of returning humanity. 'Faster, faster', he said.

The dolphins chuckled again, above water and under, and the unwieldy flock of sea beasts did their best to keep up the pace. The stingrays struggled with the growing minnows, and a bed of eels, far more sleepy and idle than Sam liked, slithered about, collecting the small fish falling behind or drifting from their group. Each strong member looked after the weak. Maybe they would have bullied each other if this had been the playground, but they all seemed to understand that this was life and death. Sam wondered which ones were kids from school. He'd never be able to tell; there were thousands of children swimming with him.

Then Sam saw the flutter of lights become more distinct and the shore took shape, and a structure grew out of the sea: the top of the i360. He had no sense of how far away it was, but at least he could see it.

Hazel stared at him, her dolphin eyes beginning to take on more of the golden cast of the girl he knew.

They were already going as quickly as they could, so Sam bit down on the urge to yell 'Faster!' once more.

Little fish became bigger, so they were moving with more speed towards the tower, their fins stretching and hinting that they would soon be legs. The creatures bumped into each other, slowing their progress. A growing minnow stared at Sam with happy brown eyes. He didn't know whether to worry or be glad.

'We're going to have to stretch out, so we'll all be able to climb out on the shore at the same time,' he yelled down to them.

Wilfred hooted in his dolphin voice again, and the line strained outwards. Some creatures struggled in the water. A few eels slid up to seals and shuffled them over, a stingray pushed at a shark until it shifted to widen the line, and Bladder was talking to his steadily shrinking whale. The whale gave a flick of its tail and headed north-east, putting distance between Bladder and Sam as it led away salmon, trout and various other fish.

When Sam could see Brighton Pier and make out the grey outlines of buildings propped against each other along the coastline, he almost whooped. A wave lapped up at him and licked his bare feet, but it did not swallow his cheer.

'I'll find you, Sam, don't worry,' Bladder's voice called back to him, and the gargoyle's whale sailed away, the line of fish life and water mammals spreading thinner and thinner.

The ones large enough to have a wake pulled smaller ones at a faster speed than they could manage by themselves, and soon the buildings went from being a blur of grey shapes against a dark blue sky to having height and definition. Sam was higher up and had gargoyle vision and could see better than most, he knew, but he was relieved to make out the ironwork on the front of the French-style buildings.

'Help! Help!' a child's voice called out. The school of trout, most of them still fish-shaped, fled in a sudden dash closer to the beach, leaving a girl with dark, curly hair thrashing about in the waves. Then the waves covered her, lapping over her sinking head.

Wilfred slipped out from where he swam under Sam and dived. Sam watched the boy-shaped silver sliver dash off into the water. Wilfred had legs and arms, but each ended with a fin, and he swam with animal speed into the sea. A few seconds later, Wilfred's grey snout appeared, the little girl's face next to his. She gasped and spluttered.

Another child choked. His arms flailed above the surface, clad in blue pyjamas instead of fur or scales. A seal dived at the boy and let him grab its neck.

Sam felt relief when he saw a pebbled beach appearing through the cloudy air. He urged the group on. The great swell of animals, creatures spreading out to his left and his right, all kept pace with Daniel. They surged towards the beach dragging the smaller fish in their rapid wake. Waves pushed from behind as if the sea itself wanted them closer to the shore, and the tide pulled them forward towards Brighton, Hove and the other towns east and west along the coast.

Another small body screamed for assistance. It could have had brown hair, maybe yellow, the sombre morning air and the sea darkened it so much, but a shrinking shark with hazel eyes let the child grab its fin and pushed forward faster to get the little one to safety.

Sam saw the seal with the pyjama-wearing boy riding on its back. The poor thing was shivering in the freezing water and holding his breath every time the seal ducked under the waves. His lips looked bluer each time. There were others well along their way to becoming human, but Sam was relieved to see very few had completely reversed, and those who swam well ferried the strugglers.

Brighton Pier and the clapped-out skeleton of the Palace Pier appeared clearer. A few of the larger creatures coursed ahead, weaving between the posts of both piers. One or two had already flopped on the beach. The tide was coming in, pulling the creatures further and faster than they could have gone just by swimming.

Schools of herring, the half-whale, half-human and a basking shark swam between the piers' posts too. Sam couldn't see Dolphin Wilfred and his human charge anywhere.

As they came within a short distance of the shore, the metamorphosis sped up. A few screams rose, but older children pulled the younger to shore and dragged them to where the water was shallow enough to walk.

Some only changed as they hit Brighton's pebbled beach.

Daniel dropped Sam on to the stones and turned away.

'We've got other fish to fry,' Daniel said. 'Sorry, bad expression.'

'What are you talking ... ?' Sam asked.

'No time,' Daniel replied and flew away.

Sam did not ponder Daniel's leaving for long. The scene in front of him – the great exodus from the ocean and the marvellous transformations – was a great distraction.

A seal stood up in the foamy tide, its body turned into a grey-furred child, while red flared underneath its pelt, flaming up its body. With the change completed, a little boy with dark hair and dark skin stood in his wet, red pyjamas, staring up at the railing above. The rays of morning sun softened the smooth, dark rocks under his bare feet. He shivered and cried.

A bed of eels slithered between the rocks, and arms and legs and heads shot out like one of those shows Sam had seen with plants growing rapidly because the camera used something called 'time lapse' (he had squealed like a dolphin when they had shown it in science). The whale became a human girl and rose out of the water, her pyjamas still grey. Dolphins beached themselves, writhing for a few seconds before they became children rolling around on hard stones. Fish threw themselves at the beach and fell in great silver drops. The newly reverted children threw their arms over their faces to protect themselves from the flapping. Most flipped over once and were children as soon as they set down.

The wind pushed in from the sea, carrying their voices inland.

* * *

There were a few adults up on the street above, walking near the rail. Sam saw one man wearing a tweed trilby hat grab it and squash it to his chest as he let out a garbled scream. This brought everyone else running, but by the time they calmed the old man, reshaped his hat and figured out there was something on the beach of interest, they had missed the sudden evolution of hundreds of sea creatures into humans.

What they saw next wasn't as bizarre as that, but it was fascinating enough. There were children on the beach. Wet, cold, distressed children.

Thousands of them.

Sam felt chilly again. His feet were bare and the beach was wet, but his clothes were dry and his jacket thick. Daniel was right, these children were wet and in thin pyjamas.

'Come on, everyone, up the stairs,' he called.

The adults at the top headed towards them too. Some called names, parents of lost children scanned the crowd.

'Tyson?'

'Carys?'

'Hashem?'

'Boo?'

Sam called out. 'Hazel, Wilfred, Amira.' A few faces looked at him, but none of them were his friends.

Hazel found him within a few seconds, then began her own calling. 'Amira? Wilfred?' Her hair stuck about her face and her teeth chattered, but she smiled when she heard a distant 'ahoy' from Wilfred, who staggered between bawling toddlers and a few bawling teenagers to get to her. Amira followed him, dancing over the rocks on light, agile feet.

Sam was surprised to see that Wilfred hadn't completely reverted yet. His skin glowed dove grey in the sunshine. 'Coming?' Wilfred said to Sam.

'We have to get these kids inside, anywhere. You too,' Sam said. 'The little ones won't know to do it for themselves.'

'This way.' Wilfred gestured east and they trotted off up the beach, collecting a small red-haired child and a bewildered boy who called out, 'Mama? Papa?'

Amira and Hazel scooped up a crying toddler each and headed to the steps.

They weren't the only ones to realise the need. A police helicopter circled the beach as teenagers herded the other frightened children up the steps. Adults at the top took off coats and wrapped them around crying youngsters. Someone yelled to 'put the urn on'.

Sam helped half a dozen squalling kids on to their feet and encouraged them to go up to the street.

When the last of the kids moved to the footpath above, Sam climbed up too, fighting through not only children but hundreds of adults who had rushed down as soon as news spread. Many of them were yet to find who they were looking for, but the police were in the mix, collecting the names of as many children as they could, phoning for parents, backup, hot chocolate. The traffic stopped as the throng of children crammed the footpaths and spilt on to roads. The hotels opened wide their front doors, and guests and staff alike pulled damp kids inside to keep them warm.

The parents came, the police checked ID, and the children cried, or laughed, or tried to get away, and officers cordoned off the roads to make sure no small children left before an adult came to fetch them. Then there were more helpers, volunteers with blankets, with hot chocolate, with iPads, taking details and grouping children by suburbs. A few Brighton bus drivers showed up and offered to take kids to their homes and many of the older kids climbed on board. They sat for a while as other volunteers phoned every home.

Many of the children were too young to remember Mummy or Daddy's phone number, but someone showed up with a printout of the missing children and tried to get the smallest ones to tell their names.

'I was fish', one said to a flustered woman trying to get a straight answer out of the child.

When Sam, Wilfred, Hazel and Amira saw every child had been claimed or pulled indoors, they let themselves be herded inside too.

'What's your name, lad?' someone asked at Sam's elbow.

He turned and realised the man in the argyle sweater was talking to him.

'Samuel Kavanagh', he answered.

The man looked through his iPad and scrolled and scrolled. 'Rebecca, Leroy ... How are you spelling that?'

Sam spelled Kavanagh. The man shook his head.

'Which county are you from? Everyone here seems pretty local.'

Sam gave the man his address, but the helper continued shaking his head. He tapped in a few more words. 'I have a Simon Lawson Cavanagh from Bognor Regis.'

'Not me.'

'Don't worry, we'll get you home. Do you know your number?' the man asked, but disappeared as someone grabbed him to tell him something.

Sam wandered out to the footpath again. If he'd still had shoes, he would've just walked home. He could no longer see his friends in the dense crowd. He hoped their parents had taken them.

A few seagulls let out screeching greetings overhead, and he spotted Yonah staring at him from an iron railing on the hotel's second floor. She said nothing, just pointed her beak upwards to where Bladder peered at him from a sloping roof. The stone lion pointed in the direction of home. Sam nodded. He'd meet him later.

'What are you doing out here?' The man in the argyle jumper had found Sam again. 'Do you have a number for your family?'

Sam patted his pocket, where he would carry his phone. It was instinct, but he was surprised to find its hard outlines under his hand. He pulled out his mobile. It was still dry in his jacket pocket. He couldn't believe it until he saw the obvious angelic thumbprint on the screen.

'Well, that was easy,' the man said. 'You know, I think you're the first one with a phone on him.'

Sam handed it to him, watching elated parents and stupefied children make teary reunions in the hotel's foyer. A young man in a blue uniform and red tie came over with a tray of warm drinks.

'No one is answering. Do you have anyone else I can call?' the man asked. 'There's a missed call on your phone from someone called "GA Colleen".'

Great-Aunt Colleen. 'Yes, call her.'

The man dialled the number. 'Hello, my name is Fayard James. I have a Samuel Kavanagh ...'

The phone burst to life with a barrage of Irish invective. Sam guessed most of it was excitement and relief, and hoped the helpful man didn't understand too much.

'Yes, yes, I'll put him on,' Mr James said, and handed Sam the phone.

'Oh, Samuel, my Samuel, you're all right then?'

'Yes, Great-Aunt Colleen.'

'Where is it they're keeping you?' she asked.

'I'm at the Brighton Front,' Sam said, and named the hotel.

'Tell them to put you in a taxi and send you home. Your Uncle Paddy and I are already at the airport. Are your parents with you? Beatrice? Nick?'

'No, Great-Aunt Colleen.' Sam felt a sea wash of nausea tide up from his belly. 'I don't know where anyone is. Why are you here?'

'I had a rather interesting talk over your father's phone. A lot of squawks and shrieks.'

'Spigot?'

'That's one of your gargoyles then?'

'Yes, Great-Aunt Colleen. But how did you know there was a problem?'

'It's not often a bird chats to me from your father's number. I might not understand what it said, but it was a bit of a giveaway that there was something awful happening. Also, I had a bad feelin', you see, which is why I called your da in the first place.'

The sea never made Sam feel as cold as he did at that moment.

CHAPTER 15

Wheedle couldn't get the Kavanaghs out by himself. He needed help. A lot of help. He left Sam's family with promises to return and the cavern far behind him.

He sniffed his way along the exit tunnel in the direction of home, picking up the scent of the escaped rabbit as he went. The bunny had got itself turned around a few times. Its smell came from everywhere as it headed all over the place. Wheedle might have missed it, if the rabbit hadn't been so tired and intent on digging a burrow for a kip.

He was impressed the bunny had managed to get this far.

Wheedle snuck closer. The half-asleep creature made an occasional scrape at the ground, its fluffy rump sticking out, its ears deep inside the burrow, which meant even a half-tonne gargoyle could sneak up on it.

'Gotcha!' Wheedle said as he grabbed the animal. He almost lost hold as the terrified creature twisted and turned in his hoofs, but eventually Wheedle got a steady grip. 'Don't worry, little one, you're not my idea of a snack.' It was so light and small, the gargoyle wondered why the ogres had any interest in it at all. Perhaps just for the chase. It would explain why they gave up.

Wheedle reached to his full height and looked at the bars. The rabbit wiggled against his chest, hissing and squealing. If the gargoyle had been made of anything but stone, the fierce little creature would have scratched him to shreds, but Wheedle waited until the rabbit gave up, panting and puffing, and settled.

Wheedle carried it with him to the drain opening and lifted it to the outside world. It went rigid as it passed through the bars. As small as its head was, it couldn't go through the gap without monster magic to help it. It calmed as it saw morning light, and Wheedle placed it gently on the pavement outside. As soon as the gargoyle let it go, it raced to the nearest shrubbery, the hum of its bewildered heart quicker than its feet.

'No, that's fine, you're welcome,' Wheedle called after it. 'Don't mention it. My pleasure.'

He pulled himself out, the rest of the bars fading through him like mist.

The day was overcast, an early winter grey, and he stared up and down the street before tiptoeing back to the Kavanagh house.

He heard the sound of flapping wings and Daniel landed.

'The house is all but empty', the angel said.

'Down in The Hole. Maggie's got 'em. We've gotta get 'em out. Where's Sam? If he's still out on the sea, he needs ...'

But the angel was gone.

'Well, that's helpful', Wheedle muttered.

He had no time to think about it, because a taxi pulled up.

He froze, pretending he was a doorstop. Sam jumped out and, as soon as the car door closed, the taxi squealed off.

Wheedle raced to the kerb and snuffled at Sam's face.

Bladder came sprinting up the empty streets towards them both and Wheedle rubbed noses with the stone lion too.

'You're both back', Wheedle said. 'Oh my goodness, do I have a lot to tell you.'

'Not as much as we have to tell you', Bladder replied.

Sam walked up to the door and turned the knob. It was locked. He patted his pockets, then groaned. 'I didn't take keys.'

The door swung open. Spigot stood in the entrance with Beatrice under one wing and Nugget hanging off his neck. 'Squark!' he said.

Nugget hung from the eagle's neck and lobbed herself on to Wheedle's back, and little Beatrice held up a chubby fist to Sam.

'Tham, Tham!'

'Hello, baby.' Sam took her from Spigot and the eagle flopped on the floor.

'I know exactly how you feel', Wheedle said.

192

Sam peered around, listening to the quiet in the rest of the house.

'They're gone,' he said.

'That's what I needed to tell you,' Wheedle replied.

'Well, it sounds like we've all had an adventure,' Bladder said. 'I wondered why Chicken Breath flew off so quickly. He's always going off and abandoning Sam.' Bladder nudged Wheedle. 'I said, "He's always going off and abandoning Sam."'

Wheedle didn't reply. He just stared at Nugget. Bladder understood. She looked worn, like an age-old gargoyle left out for centuries to weather storms and battles. She didn't look like a gargoyle who was only a few months old.

Bladder sighed. 'It's getting worse, isn't it?'

At least Nugget was asleep. Bladder wondered if it was because she was falling apart. The Kavanaghs slept more when they 'came down with something'. Beatrice watched the baby gargoyle on the makeshift bed in the middle of the kitchen floor, but Spigot was doing a wonderful job of distracting her with biscuits and occupying himself at the same time. The pair left a pile of crumbs on the tiles.

Bladder remembered the little siren. Its sweet face. It was small too, like it needed to grow. He wondered if it too would start falling apart.

Sam had been watching Nugget as well. His face creased and twisted in a very human way. 'I'm so sorry, Wheedle,' the boy said.

Bladder put a paw on the boy's knee. 'It's not your fault, Sam. You didn't mean to hatch her and you couldn't have known that ...'

'... she would fall apart', Wheedle finished. He shook his head. 'No, you couldn't, Sam. You can't blame yourself for any of this.'

Sam's face didn't change expression. Bladder felt for him. Sam had enough on his plate without feeling guilty about Nugget.

'Maybe if I had some fairy dust I could do something for Nugget.'

'Well, we need to get the Kavanaghs back. If we achieve that', Bladder said, 'then getting some fairy dust should be simple.' He tried to sound sprightly, but he knew he looked as wretched as the rest of them; even Spigot, who had a beak full of biscuits. Bladder didn't feel like biscuits himself.

'I don't understand', Sam said. 'Maggie promised she'd leave me alone, she said ...'

'She *said* she had nothing to do with the sea calling to the children, but she was behind it all the time', Bladder finished. 'It was a distraction, to pull you away from the house so that she could kidnap the Kavanaghs – or something worse. It was a way to get you to go back to her. First, she tried sugar, now she's trying spice. We should have realised.'

'Sam', Wheedle said. 'She organised to have thousands of kids drowned, just to get at you. If Amphitrite hadn't stepped in, who knows what would have happened. I suspect Maggie meant for you to have no one else at all. Just her.'

Tears wove a path down Sam's face. 'If I hadn't sneezed, she wouldn't have any reason to do this.'

'We have Nugget,' Wheedle said. 'You hadn't sneezed, we wouldn't have Nugget.'

'We won't even have Nugget anyway.'

Bladder rubbed Sam's back with a gentle paw. 'It's not your fault, Sam. Not a bit of it. An' look at you. You should be proud of yourself. You saved every single one of those kids. Every. Single. One. If you can do that, you can save your family. What's three more, hey? I won't have any of this blub-blubbing.'

'But I don't know how we're going to get them back,' Sam said. He put his head in his hands. Beatrice sat at Spigot's feet and threw sparkles across the room at Sam. He didn't hit any of them back.

Bladder desperately tried to find something cheerful to say.

'It'll have to be sneaky,' Wheedle said. 'A night raid.'

'A night raid? In the Great Cavern? Where it's always dark?' Sam asked. 'You need to join a spy agency, you do.'

Bladder winced. It wasn't like Sam to make barbed remarks. That was Bladder's job, but he didn't feel like having a go at Wheedle.

The stone bull put his snout between his hoofs.

'I'm so sorry, Wheedle, that was a mean thing to say,' Sam said.

'No, you're right. It is a stupid idea. We gotta think better. She's failed at drowning the kids, so she'll be desperate. She's got the Kavanaghs to get you down there.

She'll be expecting you, an' there're thousands of monsters working with her. You go to The Hole, you need to go ready to battle. An' there's only four of us.'

'Maybe we can get them to come up here?' Sam said. 'Trick Maggie into bringing them back? I could ...'

'What? Agree to parley with her?' Bladder asked. 'She's a liar and a trickster. She'll say whatever you want to hear, but we know exactly what she wants. She wants you to hatch all those beans, and you know how many there are. Millions. She'll be picky too, piling up all the ogre beads and leaving the rest.'

'But ...' Sam started, and looked at Nugget.

Bladder understood. He remembered the little siren and said, 'I've told you before, the first hatches of any ogre king have been off in some way. I remember the story of Thunderguts. It took him months before he could hatch even one. Your hatches will probably end up being stronger than his.'

'That doesn't help Nugget,' Sam muttered.

'The point is, you will get better at it. It's what Maggie'll believe, and when you do, if you start hatching them for her, it won't just be the death of humanity, it'll be the end of gargoyles. And pixies, and sprites. All the little ones. She don't need us. Even Thunderguts was better than her. He was king of the ogres, but he breathed on anything. He woke all the monsters.'

'What's that noise?' Wheedle asked.

It sounded like a crowd coming up from Brighton. The hum was a long way off, but maybe that's what it was.

'Probably all them parents bringing their kids home,' Bladder said out loud.

Sam heard steps and a clipping come up the Kavanagh steps and someone knocked. From the next garden Hoy Poy barked, and a dog in the distance replied.

Sam ran to open the front door. 'Great-Aunt Colleen! Uncle Paddy!' He hugged the old lady and the not-so-old man.

Great-Aunt Colleen hobbled in, leaning on her walking stick, and headed towards the kitchen. Uncle Paddy came in behind her, carrying two small cases. Sam padded along behind them.

'I'll just pop these here then, shall I?' Uncle Paddy said. 'Where's your ma? You'll be putting on the kettle, won't ... ?'

The old lady did not even blink when she saw the gargoyles, but Uncle Paddy stood in the doorway with his mouth so far open Bladder considered throwing peanuts into it.

'Well, it must be a bit of a to-do if you're willing to be seen up and laughin',' Great-Aunt Colleen said to Bladder.

'You're tellin' me,' he replied.

'Sam, make your uncle a coffee. Make it extra strong. I think he's just lost his marbles.' Great-Aunt Colleen sat at the kitchen table. 'So, you have a story or two to tell, I'm guessing.'

Wheedle sat and listened as Sam and Bladder related their adventures at sea. Their story didn't take as long the *second* time. They only needed to give the old lady the highlights.

But Sam wanted him to go into detail about what had happened to the Kavanaghs. It was what they had to deal with next. Bladder, Sam and the old lady nodded at the right bits and asked him questions to make him go over certain parts, sometimes making him draw things.

While they talked, Wheedle couldn't stop glancing at the man Sam had called Uncle Paddy. Paddy stared blankly at Nugget sleeping on Sam's lap. It gave Wheedle the creeps.

'Well,' Great-Aunt Colleen said once they'd finished up, 'you have two plans then. Either raid the Great Cavern and get caught in the process or offer to parley. You know what she'll want you to do to get your family back, so that seems an awful option too, but it might be your only choice.'

Wheedle worked hard to follow the conversation. He could hear a parade. It sounded like a parade, anyway. A great lot of people marching. He pinched himself to pay attention.

'... and increase her army,' Sam was saying. 'She has a huge army.'

'An' you don't.' Great-Aunt Colleen sipped her tea. 'Looks to me, we have to come up with a plan that doesn't involve you needing an army too.'

'Gargoyles,' said Uncle Paddy, and drooled in his coffee.

Wheedle whispered to Bladder, 'I think we've broken him. We better send him home. If he can't handle gargoyles, he's gonna be completely useless for what comes next.'

Bladder grinned. 'Actually, I'm enjoying the effect myself. It's been ages since a human's looked at me like that.' He glanced at the window again. 'That crowd sounds close.'

For the second time in an hour someone knocked on the front door.

Great-Aunt Colleen stared at the dribbling man. 'Paddy, go and see who it is now.'

Uncle Paddy staggered up the stairs, taking a good look at the group in the kitchen as he left. 'Ahh,' was all he said.

Great-Aunt Colleen studied the sad faces around her. 'It seems we need to be putting our heads together and coming up with a better idea, right?'

Another knock, and Wheedle heard creaking hinges.

'Paddy, who is it?' Great-Aunt Colleen asked.

They heard a thump; the sound of a body hitting the floor.

'What is wrong with that boy?' The old lady sighed.

CHAPTER 16

Sam dashed to the door to help his uncle. The poor man lay in a dazed heap half in and half out of the house. Pairs of hands were lifting him and propping him up against the jamb.

There were lots of hands.

There were lots of hands because there was a huge crowd covering every bit of concrete and green outside the house. The street was filled, and Sam knew most of them. He hadn't realised he knew that many creatures before. Hoy Poy came wandering out of his side path, looked at the strange mob and went yelping back indoors.

Amira, Hazel and Wilfred stood at the top of the steps, but more shifters covered the footpath and street behind them and gazed at him. He knew the smiling Kintamanis, Kokonis and Salukis, but many more wild-haired people nodded at him. He thought he recognised the Labrador twins from school, and a group of officious adults in uniforms. 'Thrope controllers. The ones who'd arrested the man who'd pretended to be Sam's real father. To the left of the steps, a dishevelled group of people with dogs lingered. Sam recognised Russell and his corgi Kylie amongst them. All of them, dog and human, had an angelic thumbprint on their foreheads. Wheedle had told him his family members each had one, to make them unappetising to monsters. A few thousand small fairies waited behind them, blocking the road, the opposite footpath and the park beyond, weaving about the trees and sitting between their leaves. Sam saw Daniel peeking from between the branches of a beech tree. To the right of the path, two dozen gargoyles had appeared. Some were grey and gravelly, some marbleised, while others looked like they had been made of clay and fired in a kiln. Many had distorted human faces on animal bodies, or the other way around, or they were a mix of different animals. A lot looked rather like Nugget: bat-winged, monkey-faced, dog-bodied. A trio were standing in front of the others, gaping at the group headed by Russell. They looked uncomfortable. Sam could see the words 'humans' and 'looking at us' spread from stone mouth to stone mouth. Behind them a pair of white-winged angels and a small, rosy cherub hovered and grinned at Sam.

'Seems to me you do have an army', Great-Aunt Colleen said from behind him.

Sam turned to his shifter friends. 'Hazel?' he asked. 'What's going on?'

'Ask Wilfred. He said he got some message you needed help.' She leaned forward and tapped her nose. 'A divine one, he said. Your angel visited him, he said. We've been asked to believe an awful lot in the last few months, so here we are. All the shifters came. Dogs, cats, badgers. Even a few rabbits, but they don't like fighting.'

A nervous-looking young man stepped forward. 'I'm Reuben. You saved me from Woermann's orb. We owe you, Sam.'

'Well said, bunny boy,' someone called.

Sam looked around for Wilfred, who was sitting on a step scratching at an ear. 'Wilfred?'

'I'd just got out of the car at home and Daniel showed up to say your family are missing. Dad can't see him, but I told him what was going on. I don't think anyone would have believed me yesterday, but all the kids had just turned back from being fish and we'd all seen you chat with a siren. Dad just accepted everything I said. Also, Mrs Maltese from next door could see him too. Anyway, Daniel said you were desperate and I told Dad, who told everyone else, so here we are ...' Wilfred motioned his free hand at the mob. 'Please tell them you need help; some of them still think I'm bonkers.'

'I definitely do, but did Daniel tell you what *kind* of help I need?'

'Said your parents were taken by monsters into some underground lair and you could use a few people to get them back,' Wilfred's dad, D.I. Kintamani, replied.

'Oh, that's where he was goin',' Wheedle said.

'There's really a Daniel?' D.I. Kintamani asked.

'Yep, big, beautiful and incredibly annoying', Bladder said.

'Wow!'

Sam peered at the crowd. 'I hope we don't have to fight, but having a lot of people behind me to fetch my family back would be great.'

'If that's what you need.' D.I. Kintamani saluted him.

'Thank you very much', Sam replied.

'Now we know the problem, how can we help?'

A fairy pushed forward. 'Why'd monsters take your family?'

Sam glanced at the fairy. 'I think they want to use them to blackmail me into doing something horrible.'

'With all the dust that hag Maggie's been stealing from us?'

The few members of the crowd who could see the fairy studied him. He turned to them all and showed them the tiny stumps of wings. A few people 'ouched'.

'Please, sir, your consideration, sir.' The fairy turned to Bladder. 'We fairies all want to help because we heard some gargoyles needed aid. As one of them did me a great service, we would like to repay it.'

'A gargoyle did you a service?' Bladder asked.

'Yes, sir; you did. At the Great Meadow Hunt. My name is Milkthistle.' He reached to his shoulder and touched the stumps peeking over. 'They are coming back, and I might have had none at all, because I'd be dead if you hadn't saved me from being eaten.' The fairy turned to the mob of tinies. 'Hid me in his mouth, he did. I thought *he* was going to eat me himself, but he kept me safe and let me go when we were out of sight of the Great Hunt. On that night, I said I would give you a boon, sir.'

'I thought that was a type of chocolate,' Bladder replied.

The fairies giggled.

'The ogres are hunting fairies,' Sam said. 'Aren't you worried they might catch you?'

'They stalk us individually. Each of us has only a little magic; together we are quite formidable.'

Sam understood fairy magic. It was potent stuff. Maybe they could just whisk his family out of The Hole.

The fairies made up the majority of the throng, and they looked furious. They might not scare the older monsters, but Sam thought they might send the young monsters into a panic.

Kylie dashed through the middle of the crowd and up the steps. 'We homeless have-nots and hobos, we merry bunch of bums, we flat-broke few, we too offer our service to the cause. Some of our masters and mistresses have gone missing, and no more,' Kylie yapped. 'No more!'

'Well said, pup.' D.I. Kintamani replied.

The shifters, 'thropes and dogs howled in agreement. Everyone else looked around, not understanding the dogs and wild-looking humans. They had no idea what had set them off. Kylie raced back to Russell for an ear rub.

'Are you sure you want to be here?' Sam asked Russell, who stood at the head of his group.

'We heard that Michelle has gone missing, and she's been good to us at the shelter. Also, no one's seen or heard of that strange redhead since you said you'd meet with her. We just want to help.' He stared about the crowd. 'Only, um, what kind of help do you need?'

His group hummed and hemmed in agreement. 'We got a note saying to come here, if we wanted to help,' a woman in a dirty great overcoat said. 'That we might even see some magical beings.'

'You may have to fight,' Sam said.

Russell held up a stick.

'In The Hole. It's full of monsters.'

Russell looked around the gathering. 'Then it looks like Nutty Nellie's stories aren't so nutty after all.'

'Yeah.' The woman in the overcoat grinned. 'Look at these ones.' She pointed as a lumpy, reddish-brown brick of a gargoyle lumbered forward.

Sam heard happy screeches from Spigot as he scuttled down the steps, pushing his way through the gathering and crowing as he danced.

'Gouttière!' Bladder shouted, and rubbed noses with the gargoyle.

'Ah, the Brighton air does you good, *mon ami*,' the gargoyle said. 'You are, how you say? Cheerful?'

'Sam, I have to introduce you to our good friend Gouttière,' Bladder said. 'Wheedle! Wheedle! Come out!'

While Wheedle dragged himself out of the house, Sam looked back through the doorway. He noticed that Uncle Paddy was gone, but Great-Aunt Colleen remained, watching from the entry with Beatrice and Nugget playing behind her swollen ankles.

The reddish-brown gargoyle bowed low. 'I am Gouttière, once a pack member with Spigot, Bladder and Wheedle. These are my new pack: Égout, Aigle and Plomberie. And 'ere are many other gargoyles.'

Sam's attention was caught by something at the back of the crowd. Daniel was struggling to move forward; there were so many people between him and Sam, he had to push his way through them. His face was urgent with intent.

'Thank you for coming', Sam said to Gouttière. 'We need everyone we can get.'

'We 'ave come because our angels told us there was a need, and until we got 'ere, we thought we would be 'appy to 'elp, but we cannot go to The 'Ole and fight, if that is what you want. That place is dangerous enough to gargoyles when we are trying to stay out of trouble. We are *très, très* sorry, little man, but now we go 'ome.'

The little cherub had been grinning at Gouttière, but the bright smile dimmed. 'No, you can't', she said, touching the gargoyle's shoulder. 'You have to fight for Samuel.' She said Sam's name so the last two syllables sounded out *you-well*.

Égout stepped forward now and shook his head. 'We break easily and our fighting skills, they are not good. We come because we thought we could 'elp. We are no use to you, little man.'

'*Nous sommes désolés.* We are truly sorry, little man',

Gouttière said. 'We are sorry, most especially to you, *mes amis*.' He dipped his head at Bladder, Wheedle and Spigot, and promptly turned tail, shouldering his way back through the crowd. The other gargoyles followed.

Russell, Kylie and the humans around them (the homeless people were the only true humans present, Sam realised) watched the gargoyles with mouths so wide open, Sam could see the pink of their throats.

Daniel had managed to slink through the crowd at last, and he grabbed Sam's arm. 'You mustn't let the gargoyles leave.'

'Why?'

'To be truly complete, a gargoyle must learn sacrifice. Though they are monsters and made from sighs, they are meant for noble purpose. If they give in to their better natures, they get a great reward. It's why angels look after them. It's always been why we watch over them. Saving your parents would be the ultimate noble purpose. The other angels are so excited. Some of us have been waiting centuries for an opportunity like this.'

Sam frowned. He wasn't sure he understood.

'Did you never wonder why we needed to take care of them? The first of their kind were made from the living soil of Eden – what was left over by the first humans. You know how special they are. They have hearts. They're blessed.'

'How?'

'Sam, trust me,' Daniel said. 'Anyway, it's The Hole. You need as many bodies down there that know the lay of the land as possible. Look at the size of this group. Don't let your experts go.' The angel threw an arm in the direction of the crowd.

Sam looked at them all. They were a few thousand, and none of them would know how to reach the Great Cavern without guides. Then he wouldn't just have to save his parents, he might be spending months searching for missing fairies in pitch-black chambers.

Sam ran after the gargoyles.

'Win them back, Sam,' Daniel called.

A wild courage surged from Daniel and into him, and Sam ran for the end of the street, Bladder at his heels. Shifters, 'thropes and fairies tried to ask him questions, but he ran on, hoping he could find the right words to say.

'Back off. Let the boy do what he thinks is necessary.' Great-Aunt Colleen hobbled down the step, helped by Russell and Nutty Nellie. Kylie and a few other small dogs scrambled through the group repeating her commands.

The mob all turned back to her with questions about Sam's needs, weaponry, tactics and so on. Sam peered back to see her handling it and pointing at crowd members to represent their species. *She makes a great general*, Sam thought.

The large pack had stopped at the end of the road. They'd been jittery enough with Russell and the other wanderers looking at them, but there were even more people at the crossroads as crowds of parents and their newly returned children continued to make their way back from the beach. The French gargoyles huddled in the shadows, wondering what to do.

'It will take us days to get back to the ferry with all these people everywhere,' Sam heard Plomberie say. 'It was quiet when we arrived. Where did all these people come from?'

'An' now, we are this 'uge group. We cannot avoid being seen,' Égout added.

'Then we will split up again,' Gouttière replied. 'We are less likely to be seen. Small packs. *Oui?*'

Sam opened his mouth, but a stronger voice came from over his shoulder. 'You're not monsters. You're not!' Bladder called.

Gouttière turned to him. 'You have forgotten about the way monsters are formed then, *mon ami.*'

'No, I haven't, and you're not monsters in the same sense as ogres and trolls,' Bladder replied.

'We are made of sighs. We might be considered the lowest of the low, but we are still monsters.'

'We have hearts.' Bladder put a paw to his chest. He breathed out a 'whoof!'.

Sam guessed the weight of such a confession took a lot of courage.

Each member of the French pack gasped.

'You do not say this out loud!' Gouttière stared at Bladder, then looked at Sam. 'The little man, he knows?'

'He figured it out himself. He says we're beautiful. He says our hearts are beautiful.'

Sam smiled. *Yes, Bladder knows exactly what to say.*

The pack fell silent. They studied Sam's face, to see if they were being mocked.

209

'He does not think we are beautiful,' Égout said.

Bladder chuckled. 'Yes, he does, and many other humans think we are too. Sam showed me on the Webby-Net. There's tonnes of people who take our photos and study us and discuss us in universities as something to be prized, like artwork.'

'This is not true,' Gouttière said. The gargoyle pack harrumphed and boffed. Sam felt the air move over him as the packs' angels set down, serenely smiling at Bladder. The cherub touched the end of his tail. Bladder glowed.

'It is true,' Bladder replied. Some of the gargoyles grimaced or raised eyebrows. Some frowned.

'We are the stones that sing,' Bladder continued. 'At worst, humans think we are quirky and interesting.'

'But some really think we are beautiful? Truly?' Plomberie asked. 'Even though we were 'atched?'

'It doesn't matter if you were hatched,' Bladder said. 'Sam was hatched too, but he has a heart and a human soul.'

The pack oohed.

'It's where you want to belong and who you want to belong to that counts. And, from the very beginning, we were meant to do something more than eat chocolate. Always,' Bladder added. 'I'm learning this.'

'You do not sound like your old self, Bladder,' Gouttière said.

'I don't think I am. I'm changing,' Bladder agreed. 'And I've learned that I'm not as much of a monster as I've been led to believe. Humans are our kind,' Bladder said. 'Humans have hearts and love the sun; we have more in common with them than ogres and trolls or any wet witch.'

Gouttière shook his head. 'It was nice to see you, *mon ami*, but we will let you battle on your own. This is not our war.'

'I do not agree,' Plomberie said. 'Bladder is right. We do have –' she inhaled – '"earts. I want to meet more of these humans who find me beautiful. No one has ever said that to me before.'

'You are beautiful,' Sam said.

'Yes, we think so too.' Hazel, Amira and Wilfred raced to stand next to Sam.

Plomberie's brick colouring reddened more.

Spigot ran into the mix and squawked. He did a dance with wings outstretched. Plomberie gave Spigot a friendly sniff, and then followed him back to Sam's side. A few other gargoyles joined in, and blinked shyly when the shifter children scratched their stone ears.

'Fight for those who love you, do not leave them to the mercy of those who never cared about you,' Bladder said.

In the end, even Gouttière smiled. 'Ah, we shall all end in broken pieces,' he said and stepped towards Sam.

Sam, Daniel, Bladder, Wheedle, the fairy called Milkthistle, a 'Thrope Controller ('*Call me* T.C. *Angelina*'), Russell, Kylie, D.I. Kintamani, Gouttière and Great-Aunt Colleen encircled the Kavanaghs' kitchen table. Wheedle had set up its surface with salt and pepper pots, trivets, tea towels, coasters, egg cups and other bits and pieces he'd found in the kitchen to map out the layout of the Great Cavern.

'This is where Maggie's dais and throne are. This is the cage she's put the Kavanaghs in. There are eight possible entrances to use; the biggest are here, here and here.' The bull-faced gargoyle pointed. 'And I think we should use these burrows here and here to set up watchpoints.'

'So, the first step is to talk to Maggie and if that doesn't work, incapacitate her?' Bladder asked. 'What with?'

'I can prepare a spell, stronger than my day-to-day magics, that will make her incapable of moving until we decide to let her,' Milkthistle said.

'Good, cut the head off the serpent ...' Daniel started.

'What serpent? Nobody said anything about snakes,' Kylie said. 'I don't like snakes.'

'It means if you bring down their leader, an army is likely to scatter. They've got no one to follow,' Great-Aunt Colleen said. 'It's a grand plan. There are fewer of the nasty big ones, our stone friend has said.' She patted Wheedle. 'And with most being small and nervous, they might stampede.'

'It happened before,' Wheedle added. 'A bit dangerous, but if we go in small, separate groups, then we can back up against the walls if they look to be heading in our direction. The winged warriors can fly above them.'

'And stay in the entrance way to your burrow. That way the monsters won't know the size of each group. We may be able to imply numbers, rather than actually ever have to show them,' Daniel added.

Sam nodded. 'They're already frightened of me. A lot of ogres were killed last time I was there, so we can use their fear against them.'

'The only problem will be getting the Kavanaghs out of the cage. It's solid,' Wheedle said.

'What's the cage made of?' T.C. Angelina asked.

'The bars are metal, but the bulk of it is wood. We could cut them out.'

A voice rang out from the door. 'Where's my Samuel? My dear friend?' Sam heard twittering and scuffling along with it.

'What are you?' Uncle Paddy cried out.

'Sam's friend. And this here's my family; I already told 'em tha' out of doors,' the voice said. 'They said ye'd let me in.'

'What does that boy think he's doing? Patrick, go back upstairs,' Great-Aunt Colleen called out. 'And come in, Sam's friend, whoever you are.'

Sam heard the thumping feet of his uncle running back to Nick's room. The man began singing himself a lullaby.

'In here, Dad,' another voice called out.

A bundle of twigs fell into the kitchen and a trio of smaller bundles bounced in after it. 'Dad! Dad! Dad! Are you OK?'

The bundle stood up. 'I be fine, I be fine.'

Sam rushed over. 'One-i'-the-Wood?'

The twig person stood. His face was a collection of fruits and flowers – two grapes for eyes, a pansy for a nose and a smile made from a row of tiny daisies. The body was taller, the legs straighter and greener (and wearing wellington boots), and both hands had twiggy thumbs.

Sam barely recognised him: raspberries, a rose and a leaf had made up One's face last time Sam had seen him, but Sam knew the voice, and he was pleased that One-i'-the-Wood had included two strands of willow for eyebrows. It gave the twig person much more expression.

Behind the grape eyes, three finches fluttered inside his head.

'You got some dreams,' Sam said.

'That I do, that I do,' One said, obviously pleased Sam had noticed. 'All because of 'ee, Sam. Have a closer look.' The twig person leaned forward to let Sam see the finches. 'Settle down, now, fellas,' One said, and the finches perched on a sturdy branch that ran from one of One's ears to the other. 'Ye gave me my first want, Sam: that handsome bird there with the fine red chest is Arthur, and he is my dream to make myself a family. Come on, kids, come and say hello to my friend Sam.'

The three smaller twig people hugged close to One-i'-the-Wood. A leaf, a reed, and a feather made up their different smiles.

'This is my eldest, Two-i'-the-Wood,' One said, gesturing at the twig person closest in height to him. It picked up a woven hat from its head.

The next twig person bowed low. 'I be Three-i'-the-Wood.'

'You must be Four-i'-the-Wood,' Sam said to the small-est twig person.

'Oh, no, I be Daisy,' the twig person said. 'Four ent a girl's name. An' I always has a daisy for a nose, so you can tell.'

'Well, you are very welcome,' Sam said.

'Thank 'ee, thank 'ee, Sam,' One-i'-the-Wood said. 'You see, coming here helps me fill up on my next want. I wanted to see 'ee again, my friend, and be of some help to 'ee. It made me feel life was fuller and more, I don't know, more real somehow, when I helped 'ee last. I wanted to do it again.'

'Well, you couldn't have come at a better time,' Great-Aunt Colleen said. 'Sam needs help getting his family back.'

'Oh, my, the most magnificent of wants ever!' One-i'-the-Wood. 'How absolutely perfect! Now, did I hear 'ee say this family of yours was trapped in wood? Well, no one knows wood better than me an' mine.'

When the plans were set, Sam and the gargoyles took up posts at eight different grates along the kerb on his street. Daniel flitted from group to group, pressing his thumb on to every human, part-human and animal forehead, making them as unappetising as possible to monsterkind. Then the gargoyles helped Sam's army move through the bars, each creature surprised at how it worked (except the fairies, of course. Magic was not odd to them).

'Can you teach me how to do that?' Russell said, Kylie under one arm. 'There's a few nice dry spots all barred up I could use for a good kip.' He looked at Sam hopefully. Sam shook his head apologetically. 'Well, you never know unless you ask.'

It took half an hour to get everyone through. Great-Aunt Colleen remained in the doorway holding Nugget.

Uncle Paddy cuddled Beatrice like a security blanket, his gaze darting from the baby gargoyle to the array of not-quite-humans and mythical creatures jumping into the drains in front of him. Uncle Paddy made a low groaning noise and he wasn't blinking. He stared when Wilfred, Amira and Hazel began arguing with their mums and dads. As the shifter parents transformed into dogs, Sam could see the whites of Uncle Paddy's eyes all the way around. It didn't look healthy. Paddy's mouth dropped open as he watched the kids whining at the pack of dogs that used to be their parents. Sam hoped he would be OK.

'But Sam's the same age as us,' Wilfred was saying.

'He's battle hardened,' Wilfred's dad replied.

'He can climb walls,' Amira's mum said.

Hazel's parents just shook their doggy heads. 'No,' her dad replied.

'We could be some use,' Wilfred said.

The trio looked dejected, and stared at Sam, hoping for support, but he wasn't going to give it. He didn't want his friends facing off against trolls and ogres either. It was bad enough Richard, Michelle and Nick being down there.

'It's all right, my darlin's,' said Great-Aunt Colleen. 'Some of us need to keep the home fires burning. To help those soldiers when they return. You can stay here with me and Paddy. He doesn't seem to hear any words I'm saying to him right this moment, but he'll come back to us for a nice cup of tea and a talking-to, if you give them to him. And you'd be doin' me a favour.'

'Go on,' Wilfred's dad said.

'Spigot, you stay here and look after the babies. It's an important job,' Bladder said.

Spigot squawked.

The stone eagle and the shifter children all looked at Sam as if he'd betrayed them, but finally they hung their heads and followed Great-Aunt Colleen inside.

Sam thought Great-Aunt Colleen would be a bit put out, but she winked at him. 'Grand!' she said. Then she nodded at Sam. 'Come safe home, my lovely boy, I know you'll bring the others with you.'

'Thanks for looking after them all,' D.I. Kintamani barked at Great-Aunt Colleen.

'Good dog,' she said.

Amira's mum laughed.

Sam slipped through the grate, meeting his group underground. He would try talking to Maggie first. Better not to go in with brute force – not an obvious one, anyway – so he'd organised a small group.

Bladder wasn't happy. 'What if she tries to catch you?'

'I expect she will if it goes badly. But if I go in in a large threatening troop, it's a statement of war. I want to avoid that, if at all possible.'

The shifters, 'thropes and even the dogs were not happy Sam refused to take any of them as part of his personal team, but he only wanted the I'-the-Wood family with him and a few fairies. They could break through the cage while Sam talked to Maggie. If he could talk to Maggie first, not let it come to blows, that would be the best thing, he thought.

'He's important to you, sir', Milkthistle had said to Bladder, 'so I will defend him with my life.' The wingless fairy was flanked by two winged comrades who also carried swords as long and sharp as embroidery needles.

As Sam dropped into the tunnel's mouth, he considered his other worries. Once his army had been divided up into eight groups, they hadn't looked as big as a street-full. Even a street-full couldn't contend with a cavern of monsters, could they? And, while the grates were a few feet apart above ground, by the time they fed underground they were leagues away from each other. Until they got to their destination, the teams might as well be worlds apart. Even when they did arrive at the Great Cavern, they'd be at opposite ends.

'It stinks down here', a fairy whined.

Sam ignored the complaints and pushed to the front. 'This way', he said.

He led them through tunnel after tunnel, following the smell of ogres and other monsters towards the Great Cavern. Some ceilings stooped so low that Sam and One had to crawl on hands and knees. Sam wondered what that was about. He'd never had trouble travelling The Hole before. The first time it happened, Milkthistle cast a spell on the opening, commanding it to widen. On Earth or in Faeryland, the dirt would have vanished into the air, but all the fairy's spell did was cause muck to tumble on to the troop in clods and clumps.

'I don't think yer magic works the same down here', One-i'-the-Wood said to the fairy. 'Ye be an awful lot of "yes" and the magic down here be all "noes". I suspect that may be why the going is so hard. The magic knows yer comin'. I'd be careful using yours, until you know how to work it better.'

The fairies muttered amongst themselves and tried little spells behind Sam as they went. There was much complaining, until one of them brought a flower out of nowhere and it blossomed in her hand. The group gave a low cheer.

'Still, be careful,' One-i'-the-Wood counselled.

Sam wondered what else could go wrong. He hoped they didn't have to fight. If One was nervous, it was worth paying attention. He was a very wise twig man and understood many things the fairies didn't.

The fairies lit the way. Sam was glad there were so many others with the humans. They did not have gargoyle eyes to see in this dark.

They trekked in the direction Bladder had suggested, until Sam found himself under another grate near a bricked sewer. He put his hand on the wall. He remembered. This was the wall he had climbed on his first day of life. If he put his head up, there would be a cathedral above and a street where May no longer worked. He remembered Ben, Beth and Henry, and hoped they were well.

'What are we doing?' Two-i'-the-Wood asked, cutting through his memory.

Sam led them the rest of the way, waving them back as he stepped into the Great Cavern, waiting in the shadows to see if he could spot any of the others.

He hoped they all made it without being discovered. If his talk with Maggie failed, maybe the surprise of a few thousand creatures coming out the darkness would scare the monsters. Great-Aunt Colleen, Bladder and One had talked about using the cover of the cavern entrances to suggest they were more than just a few thousand strong. Sam wouldn't have thought of that.

Sam had come through the very back entrance, where the least monster traffic moved. He could see the huge blanket-covered lump holding his family and the gathering of monsters around it, and more surrounding the throne and dais. On top of it sat the water barrel; something was sloshing around up there, maybe a pixie going for a cup of water for Michelle, Nick or Richard. He squinted to see.

Movement distracted him at the far end of the cavern, and he caught sight of Bladder appearing from a distant entrance. He looked tiny, but waved a torch at Sam. Right at the other end of the cavern, where Gouttière and Plomberie's group were meant to enter, Sam saw the glow of a tiny white dove. It was such a long way off. He saw shimmering on the wall opposite Bladder where the homeless people, their dogs and Daniel had emerged. Sam shuddered; Daniel's light was low.

Daniel had explained that with enough humans packed together to sustain their need for love and faith, and angels and cherubs to give them hope, the human group would be able to cope with the collection of monsters in The Hole. And vice versa. A mutual support network, he'd said. Sam could just see the smaller angels at the rear, each with a hand on a human. They weren't glowing too brightly either. Wheedle waved at him from the ledge outside their old burrow. Sam knew that from his perch there Wheedle would be able to see the layout of the entire Hole.

Bladder waved his torch again, letting them know that everyone was present.

It was all going the way they'd organised.

He relaxed a little.

Sam dropped back into the tunnel opening. 'Everyone's here', he said. 'Time to move in, but remember to stick to the plan.'

Sam headed towards the cage and dais, followed by the I'-the-Woods and three nervous fairies. Going in by himself would have been less nerve-racking than taking in the small company. The trio of glowing fairies made him highly visible, and interesting to the monsters. Also, Daniel's ward might protect the fairies from being eaten, but an ogre would not be opposed to tearing off their wings.

And if they had to fight, more than wings would be hurt. Armies clashed and soldiers got hurt. He was grateful everyone was willing to come and help save his family, but he wondered how much it would cost them.

CHAPTER 17

Spigot watched from the doorstep as the others left.

'Come inside,' said the old woman called Great-Aunt Colleen. 'It's cold, you're letting all the heat out.'

Spigot knew about cold. Sam didn't like cold and felt awful when there was too much, so the stone bird hurried inside and closed the door. He couldn't feel the cold himself, but he could still look after others.

Sam's Uncle Paddy had already run upstairs and the three shifter children were making lunch in the kitchen. Spigot hoped they found cake, sweets or something worth eating. Then he thought about his pack. He should put something aside for them.

Beatrice sat in the high chair. Nugget squatted on the table in front of her. Wilfred fed them both, taking turns to put a spoonful of food in Beatrice's mouth and a spoonful in Nugget's mouth.

'Yummy', Wilfred said.

'Nummy', the babies echoed, and giggled at their own cleverness.

Spigot would have giggled too if Nugget wasn't leaving clumps of concrete dust everywhere.

'Would you like something to eat?' Amira asked him.

Spigot didn't feel hungry, but he nodded. He would put it away for Sam, Bladder and Wheedle.

'A sandwich? I've got chicken or roast beef here.'

'For me too, please', Great-Aunt Colleen said. 'Aren't you lovely?'

Spigot peered into the fridge. It didn't look very exciting. Where were the chocolates? Where was the ice cream?

There had been biscuits on the counter earlier, so Spigot examined the bench, looking for more. Hazel opened a cupboard door and he spotted treasure. The stone bird shuffled over. Chocolate – something with a picture of a cake on it – but the writing said 'Cake Mix', which meant not-cake-yet (he'd tried that before; too dry). Then Spigot saw crisps. Two huge bags. Salt and vinegar and ready salted flavour. He grabbed them both and carried them to the middle of the kitchen floor. He'd save those for his pack.

'Oh, no you don't', Great-Aunt Colleen said. 'You take those outside.'

I *wasn't going to eat them*, Spigot shrilled.

'Out you go, out you go', Great-Aunt Colleen said.

Hazel opened the back door.

Maybe just one bag, Spigot thought.

Spigot checked Nugget again. No one was touching her, and although she continued to crumble, leaving small gritty piles on her chair, he couldn't do anything about that. The little gargoyle looked happy. She'd spent so much time crying in the last couple of weeks, Spigot relaxed a little, relieved someone knew how to cheer her.

He wandered into the back garden and sat up in the swing chair.

Yonah, Spigot thought. Food wasn't fun unless you could share it. But Yonah was down in The Hole; she wouldn't hear him.

Then, as if his thought *had* summoned her, Yonah put her head over the eaves.

Spigot's stone heart leaped. She was so light and lovely. He didn't think he'd seen anything so beautiful before. He held up the bag of crisps.

Yonah flew down and joined him on the seat. Spigot ripped at the bag and half the contents fell on the seat, but the dove didn't mind and she nestled next to him on the swing, pecking at the crisps on the cushion and taking turns with Spigot to dip beaks into the bag.

Yonah snuggled closer to Spigot's wing, heating his insides. He always felt warm when she was near. He knew what warm meant when she was around. *It's all going to be all right*, her presence told him.

Milkthistle and the family of I'-the-Woods marched forward, leading Sam's group with such severe and terrifying expressions that many pixies and brownies around them squealed and got out of the way. Each member of his troupe, like his army, was marked with an angel's thumbprint and looked disgustingly unappetising, so trolls, goblins and boggarts backed up too.

Sam strode into the Great Cavern. He marvelled at the size of the bean hills. There were a few brownies near his entrance but as he walked in the direction of the dais, he began to pass clusters of imps. Many turned to watch him. He stood twice the height of the brownies and pixies, and his head showed above the reclining boggarts and young goblins. He was visible to everyone, and the closer he got to the centre of the cavern, the thicker the crowd became. The monsters all remained seated, as if waiting for something.

'Come on,' he said to the I'-the-Woods and the fairies, pushing forwards.

They weaved around a few hillocks of beads, coming closer and closer to the centre. Sam marched as straight as he could, two of the I'-the-Woods on either side of him, the fairies trotting in front so he could watch for any sneaky claws trying to grab one.

His little band stopped an arm's length from the cage. Sam stared at it. Wheedle had told him the Kavanaghs were under that blanket.

'Don't look like no one will stop 'ee,' One said.

One was right. The imps around studied him with interest, but not one moved to attack.

It gave him hope, and across the cavern, angel-light flared.

Sam heard a splash from the barrel on top and a wave of water washed on to the blanket, spreading a dark patch down the side of the cage. He stepped back to look at what made the water spatter, then someone cried out, 'Nick!'

Michelle! Sam lifted the blanket and scrambled underneath.

'Go away!' a trembling man's voice said to him.

'Richard?'

'Sam? Sam? Is that you?' The man clambered towards him and leaned on the bars. 'What are you doing here?'

'It's a trap. Get out, now,' Michelle called from the back of the cage.

Nick lay too quiet on Michelle's lap. He looked dead, his face pale. The easy roses in his cheeks had drained away. Nick still had Daniel's protective sigil, but the Kavanaghs had been there too long and hopelessness had settled in.

A few pixies gathered beside him, huffing and puffing to get under the blanket, squinting beneath Sam's arms at the humans. At least the larger beasts weren't peering in. Richard reached through the bars and pulled Sam's shoulders to his, kissing his face. A pixie yucked but moved closer.

'I've just got to talk to Maggie, then I think she will let us all go,' he said.

'You know her?' Richard asked.

'Of course he knows her, he's been telling us all about this the whole time,' Michelle said. 'We didn't believe him.' Her voice sounded laboured, as if it hurt to speak.

Richard peered around. 'To be quite honest, I still don't believe it.'

If the situation hadn't been so dire, Sam would've laughed. 'It's going to be OK.'

'So, are you really a monster then?' asked Nick. His voice sounded thin. 'I saw you climb a wall. I saw the gargoyles. What are you?'

'I'm Samuel Kavanagh,' Sam said. 'I'm half fairy, half monster, and I have a human soul.'

'A *human* soul?' Michelle asked.

'Maggie stole a soul. She stole what makes me *me*. And she and the ogre king put me into this body.'

Richard rubbed his forehead. 'How do you steal a soul? From another person. Is there a human out there wandering around without a soul?'

'No. Humans *are* souls in a body. They can't live without them. My last body died and now I'm in this one.'

'If'n it's not rude of me, I'd like to suggest you jaw about this later,' One-i'-the-Wood said at Sam's shoulder. 'Let's get this box open, shall we? I think I see a nice grain there.'

'What are you?' Richard asked.

'I be a self-made man,' One said, posing proudly. He tapped on the side of the cage. 'Ah, oak, a goodly wood, a fine wood, a magnificent wood. We'll have you out in a jiffy.'

Michelle left Nick sitting limply on the seat and came forward. Her hand whipped out past One and she grabbed Sam's wrist. 'Whose soul, Sam? Whose soul do you have? Who are you?'

'I'm Samuel Kavanagh,' he said. 'I've always been Samuel Kavanagh.'

Michelle gasped and released his arm.

Sam saw the last of the colour draining from Richard's and Michelle's lips; they looked white as walls.

Nick stared at Sam. 'What does that mean?' he croaked.

One pushed Sam out of the blanket. 'If you want to save these 'uns, my friend, your hard work be out there. Go do it. Me and mine'll stay here and make an opening for yours to get out. If we haveta, we'll make a run for it with them.'

Sam let the blanket fall away. He was out in the Great Cavern again, surrounded by curious monsters.

Time to find Maggie.

Sam looked towards the dais. He still couldn't see whether or not Maggie was there; a solid flank of adolescent ogre bodies blocked his view.

Not one monster had stopped him talking to his family. Not one moved forward to bar his way to the dais. For a good moment he felt a surge of hope, and across the cavern he saw another sudden flare of angel light.

Then a few steps towards the dais and a dark hill swallowed the glow, and when he looked up to the tiers above, he couldn't see Wheedle. The gargoyle had faded back into the shadows, and Sam had no idea which was their old burrow.

He felt alone, guarded only by the three jittery fairies walking before him.

Sam approached the dais, and the monsters shuffled aside, creating a path. He remembered the way the ogres parted to let him through the Ogres' Cavern, all those months ago, forcing him with bullying claws towards the then ogre king, Thunderguts.

This time I chose to come, he thought. *On my own terms.*

Except, he wouldn't have come if Maggie hadn't kidnapped his family. He may not have been forced physically, but the banshee held the Kavanaghs captive.

He hoped she cared for him a little. If he could make her see how much this hurt him, maybe ...

He sighed. She'd lied to him and he'd believed her. She'd distracted him by attempting to drown thousands of children. There was nothing sympathetic in her. He had to figure out what Maggie wanted *most*, what she desired more than creating a horde of monsters.

It was useless appealing to her better nature; she didn't have one.

Sam and his troop trotted straight to the stone platform.

As he got to the fence of bodies around the dais, an ogre stepped aside and Sam saw Maggie resting on the throne, head in chin.

'Sam, you came back to me.' She looked halfway between her young self and her true crone's appearance. Her red hair faded to greyed peach, her face sagged, and she looked a bit like Great-Aunt Colleen. She shuffled towards him.

'Have you come to parley?' she asked.

'Parley?'

'Talk. Is it a conversation you're after having? Or you've brought me a present?' She peered at the fairies. 'It looks like one of your number's already spent some time in our company.'

Milkthistle grumbled.

'I came to get my family back.'

'And what will you do for me if I give them to you?'

'I won't let my army attack you,' Sam replied.

'Oh, he has an army, does he? Three fairies? Save me, save me.' Maggie cackled.

The collection of ogres sniggered as she pointedly counted his small group. One old brute leaned over to snatch at Milkthistle's comrades; the fairies shuffled back against Sam's legs, their tiny swords out and ready. The ogre chuckled but as he examined the tiny trio closer, Daniel's protective sigils began to glow and he gagged.

'Iz not yummy,' he said.

'Help me down, lads,' Maggie commanded.

'Yes, Your Maggisty.' An ogre lifted Maggie gently on to the ground in front of Sam.

'And is this your army now?' she said, peering around the Great Cavern. 'I see a paltry set of fairies, a few flammable twigs messing with my prison-box and one misguided monster boy.' She grinned at Sam. 'Here's my offer. You hatch a few thousand of these eggs, and I'll let you take one of your Kavanaghs home. You can pick which one.'

'No,' Sam said. 'You give the Kavanaghs back to me and I won't destroy the few monsters you have left.' Sam looked to his left. A group of pixies beamed at him, naughty, mischievous but cute. He hoped they ran and hid when the rest of his troops came. The dogs and the shifters had sharp teeth.

Maggie tittered. 'So, let's assume this army could do anything useful. Would you be wanting to risk their lives?' She said the last word like it was a chocolate.

No, I *really wouldn't*, Sam thought, but aloud he said what Bladder and Great-Aunt Colleen had suggested. 'Fairies will continue to be created, humans and their kind will carry on being born, even One-i'-the-Wood can make more children, but you will have no more monsters. Are you willing to let that happen?'

'Doesn't my darlin' boy sound bold? I like this new Sam. He sounds kingly.' She fixed her vivid green gaze on him. 'We'll die out anyway, my darlin'. All you're suggestin' is the slower way. There will be no more monsters, no more imps, no more ogres, leprechauns, boggarts, brownies. No more sirens.' She gave him a sad smile. 'Not even gargoyles. You're liking them the most, I know.'

Sam couldn't help glancing at the nearest pile of beads. He spotted a couple of gravelly grey nuggets, small and irregular. Each one would make another Bladder, Spigot or Wheedle. Maybe he could sneak a few of those away and create more little gargoyles.

He remembered Nugget falling apart. Maybe not.

'You can have as many as you like,' Maggie said, following his gaze.

'No,' Sam said. 'I've made two new monsters, and they've gone wrong. One is dying.' Saying that out aloud about Nugget made his chest hurt.

'And many more will too, but you are the ogre king, Samuel. With the help of a little fairy dust, and you'll get better and better at it, just like Thunderguts did. One day you'll have an army to command.'

'If I'm the king, what will that make you?'

'Your advisor, your viceroy, a banshee ready to take her place in the world. That's power enough. I carried you, Sam. I know what you want, you see, because we're made of the same stuff.'

'I don't think we are.'

'Well, I won't stop until I've proven it to you.'

'Maggie, don't do this. I really do have an army waiting in the tunnels,' Sam said.

'Do you, my darlin'?' She put her arms up and the ogres lifted her back on to the dais. 'Well, then war it will have to be.'

Sam raised his right hand – the signal they'd all agreed to – and Maggie watched him, a smile on her lips. Above them, Wheedle waved a torch and within a few seconds the troops stepped out of the access points, just a little, so their numbers were disguised by darkness.

The monsters peered around. The smaller ones squealed and whined, huddling together. Those near burrows scurried inside, and their eyes peered out from the gloom.

The largest ogre sniggered and licked his lips. 'War.'

The Old Ones – goblins, trolls, ogres – chuckled along with him. Maggie gestured to the exits, inviting Sam's troops in.

'She's not going to negotiate,' one of Milkthistle's comrades said.

'I think you're right,' Sam agreed.

'Plan B?'

Milkthistle put away his sword and pulled out a wand. 'Yah!' the fairy screamed, and Sam saw lightning scorch a trail above his head and hit Maggie in the chest. The banshee stumbled back.

Her ageing face changed.

A wail threaded through the mob of monsters and imps. Sam saw the angels and cherubs brighten in each of the entrances.

It *might work*.

But Maggie's face and body didn't freeze. She didn't diminish; she became younger, her hair brightened to a vibrant red and her eyes a clear green.

In the dim cavern light, the young queen stepped forward and stood above Sam, beautiful and strong. She grinned at the small group of fairies before her, their brave and fierce expressions fading fast.

'Did you really think fairy magic would aid you in my own place?' Maggie asked. 'Especially when I have used so much of your dust for so long? I've learned its power, you silly things.' She pointed at a group of boggarts. 'You! Bind the fairies. Don't damage their wings, we can harvest the dust later.' She turned to Sam, a beautiful grin on her face. 'Please tell me you brought plenty more.'

With shrieks half fear and half anger, Sam's army rushed forward. A polar bear pounced in front of

Milkthistle's fairies and Sam, shielding them with his body and snapping at any hand reaching for them.

A pair of goblins grabbed the white bear and flung it at the oncoming battalion of humans and 'thropes. They scattered as the shifter hit the ground with a high-pitched roar.

Sam heard an answering clatter spread through the Great Cavern as his other troops pulled out their weapons and skirmishes began to break out.

'Oh, well, if we must fight. Just remember, this is for your own good, darlin' boy.' Maggie peered up at the largest ogre in her company. 'Grab him, Bombottom.'

The largest ogre grinned at Sam and leaned for him.

At about the same time an ogre with arms like oak branches turned its interest to Sam, Spigot and Yonah were finishing their crisps. When the bag and seat were clean, they leaned back full and fat-bellied. A pair of pigeons waited shyly at the back of the Kavanaghs' garden, peeking out from a sheltered nest.

Spigot jumped off the seat, remembering to take the empty bag with him, and Yonah rubbed her cheek against his. Spigot shivered with pleasure. He know she meant 'farewell' and watched her fly up and over the house.

Back to The Hole, he thought.

Spigot rapped on the back door. Great-Aunt Colleen opened it. Before he hopped back in, Spigot surveyed the back garden. The pigeons moved closer, and pecked at the ground to find all the bigger bits of crisps. Then they began working through the tiny pieces too.

One cocked its head and cooed at him. It looked like a pretty bird, but it wasn't as beautiful as Yonah.

Inside, the kitchen was quiet. Great-Aunt Colleen sat knitting at the table, her fingers the only things showing the agitation she felt. Spigot understood. It was hard being left behind to do nothing but wait.

Well, he did have one job.

Spigot looked at Great-Aunt Colleen. He squawked.

'I don't know what you're saying, my friend', Great-Aunt Colleen replied.

Spigot karked at her. *I'm looking for Nugget, I'm supposed to be watching over her. Where is she?*

'If I was to take a guess, I'd say you're after your little ward.' Great-Aunt Colleen looked at him with one eye closed. 'She's having a bath with Beatrice.'

Spigot looked around the kitchen. The crumbly mess of grey dust on the kitchen table had been cleared away, as if evidence of Nugget had to be erased. Spigot's stone heart bumped against his insides. It felt odd.

'Aunt Colleen?' The shifter children's voices came high and urgent from above, and Spigot raced for the stairs as fast as his stone legs would take him. Behind him, much slower, the old human woman followed.

Spigot's wings spread themselves wide, useless to him, not adding to his speed. He smelt hot water and rocketed into a room with a bath in it. The floor was wet and he skidded towards the tub, a claw breaking off with a burning crack. Inside the bath, at the base, lay a thick layer of grey. Limestone dust, bits of stone, all the things of which Nugget was made.

They've dissolved Nugget! Spigot clambered into the tub and tried to scrape the residue together, but the sloshing water melted it into a lifeless sludge. Spigot squawked and sobbed. Water ran from his eyes and beak as he tried again, until he collapsed, wailing. *Oh, Nugget, Nugget, I'm so sorry, Nugget.*

'Wow.' Wilfred put his head around the door. 'What a noise. Spigot, Aunt Colleen, you have to see this.'

'Coming, coming,' the old woman said with more than a little irritation.

'In the baby's room,' Hazel called out.

'You have to see this,' Wilfred said again, and disappeared from the doorway.

Wilfred and Hazel were laughing. They did not sound like children who had melted a baby gargoyle in the bathtub.

Spigot scrambled out of the bath and limped towards the sound, picking up his dropped talon and wiping bathwater from his soggy eyes.

'How darling,' Great-Aunt Colleen said as Spigot followed the smell of milk and talcum powder into a bedroom. Amira and Hazel each held a towel-wrapped package. Beatrice peeked out of Hazel's towel.

Spigot thumped closer to look at Amira's towel. Nugget's grey head poked out. ''Pigit,' she said to Spigot, trying out his name. She looked clean and whole. At least her top part did.

'Oh, my,' Great-Aunt Colleen said, studying the baby gargoyle closer.

Spigot drew nearer too. Maybe her bottom half had dropped off in the bath. Still, there was something of her left. Amira lowered Nugget to Spigot so they could see each other, snout to beak.

Spigot shrieked.

'It all came off in the bath,' Amira said. 'Her ... I don't know what you'd call it.' She looked at Spigot for help, but Spigot didn't know. He'd never seen this happen before.

'Outer surface,' suggested Wilfred.

'Shell,' offered Hazel.

The baby gargoyle rubbed her warm, soft nose on Spigot's beak. She was damp from being in a bath, but she wasn't stone any more; she was skin and blood and living smells and ...

'Fur,' Wilfred said.

Fur! Spigot thought.

Bombottom reached for him, and Sam stumbled back into a giggling brood of brownies. The hands and little claws of the waiting imps reached out, and he slapped them away. This slowed him for a step, as did the vibrating ground. Bombottom's heavy, flat feet shook the earth while Sam tried to dodge backwards. A scuffle of pixies and brownies rolled out of his way and he twisted around and sprang forward, racing towards the tunnel he'd entered through. He saw the I'-the-Woods still at the cage, a few leprechauns pulling at them, but they'd thrust their arms into the cage walls and the wood held on to them, protecting them.

Neither of his plans had worked, and there weren't enough warriors in his army to make it a good fight. He'd relied on tactics and fear, not battling it out. Even if the imps didn't participate, any ogre could take on ten adults easily. Maybe evasion and escape were their best options. He looked over his shoulder – not at Bombottom, but at Maggie. What was she doing?

Maggie watched him. The rest of the humans weren't important to her, so they weren't important to the monsters either. Maybe he could distract the beasts long enough to get everyone out.

If I can just stay out of reach of this stupid ogre until One's got the Kavanaghs free, then the others can make a break for it.

A shifter wolf ran at him and put itself between Sam and the ogre, but Bombottom flicked it away and it flipped through the air with a yelp.

Sam ran on, the shaking dirt telling him Bombottom had picked up his pace too. The air was full of screaming magic creatures and humans. Shifters, gargoyles, 'thrope controllers and all the rest of Sam's army piled out of the entrances and were fighting towards him. Bladder threw pixies and brownies left and right and they scattered.

The ogre stayed right behind Sam.

Bam!

The ground shuddered so hard Sam fell forward, thumping into a stone. A leprechaun leaped out from beside it. Something cracked; it gave a high snap and Sam felt the automatic need to nurse his hand, but it was a far-off thought as he bounced up and focused on evading the ogre.

He could only run.

Bombottom growled, the ogre's heavy tread turning solid earth to the rolling deck of a ship. The ground rocked as dirt shook. Sam's army and imps alike fell on to the juddering dirt as they passed. Sam sprinted through a squabble of brownies and dogs, who scurried away as the huge beast cast a shadow over them.

Did he feel fingers at his neck?

Sam stooped to avoid pixies who hadn't joined the fighting, but as he did, one tripped him, and those ogre fingers, each as big as his arm, snatched at his hair. He shot forward, weaving between distracted faces. Goblins fell on fairies, Kylie and Russell's pack jabbed at boggarts with crowbars and walking sticks. Shifters and trolls bit one another. Thrope controllers poked hard goblin skin with sharp knives.

Sam fell again, on to his wounded side. This time the pain was clear, it lit up his arm, and he saw his purple finger. Broken right out of joint.

The air moved behind him, and then Sam was lifted by his head.

'Don't hold him like that!' Through the fingers squeezing at Sam's skull, which muffled his hearing, Sam made out a raging voice. 'You'll kill him. He's not a gargoyle.'

The ogre turned to face the caller, and flung Sam around. If he'd been less solid, the turn would have broken Sam's neck. A stone lion's face peered up at him, its expression set in sad lines.

'Please,' Bladder said. 'Don't hurt him.'

A voice spoke low and soft, but the tone was stone-hard. 'It's best you don't damage my boy.' The ogre twisted again, this time to face Maggie.

'Maggisty?' the great brute said.

'I told you to catch him, but the gargoyle's right, we need him alive. A little battered will not be a problem, but if you don't watch your clumsy claws you'll break him, and his life is worth a thousand of yours.' Maggie's voice was clipped and sharp.

It made Sam sad.

Maggie spoke with her banshee voice and monster faces grew long with grimaces, frowns, tears and sighs.

The fighting slowed. Every eye in the cavern turned their gaze to Maggie, even though she spoke in a whisper. Bombottom's shoulders hunched.

They're terrified of her, Sam thought. He felt a deathly cold go through him.

The quiet grew. Yelling stopped. Shouts of bloodthirsty encouragement ceased. Then even those caught in a fighting frenzy found their attention drawn to the banshee and the boy dangling from the ogre's claw.

Every creature in the Great Cavern turned to watch, and Sam's army shuffled towards him or to the cage with their weapons ready. The threat in Maggie's voice kept them alert. The younger monsters frowned, as concerned for Sam as his friends were. Maggie needed the boy alive and she'd punish anyone who failed at this task. She stood so small compared to the ogres, but her hair blazed, as did her eyes, and there was death in her every word. Sam saw imps desperate to flee in misery – dusty and bruised. They didn't want to be part of this. Many larger monsters held fairies or shifters in their claws. An ogre had the top half of a gargoyle griffin in one hand, the bottom half in the other, a jagged break through its middle. Its bird-face was frozen in a shout.

Maggie spoke quietly, and her audience leaned in to listen. 'Put the boy down.'

'Where?' Bombottom said.

'Here at my feet, Bombottom.'

Bombottom dropped Sam gently into his other claw and in three long strides covered the distance to the dais. He placed Sam in a crumple at Maggie's feet.

Sam landed on his hand again. He howled as pain ignited his arm and he curled into a ball, nursing his head and finger.

Sharp gasps came from the monster crowd.

Ogres looked at Maggie, then Bombottom, as if questioning what might happen to the ogre if the boy was too damaged.

'But she told him to,' a goblin said. 'Didn't she?'

'Hush,' a troll replied.

'Well done, Bombottom,' Maggie said in her other, more normal voice. 'But from now on, all of you, when I say "catch" I mean "catch alive".'

The collective sigh of the monsters and imps rose in the dark air.

'But she never said that before,' the goblin said.

'Hush', a troll said again.

Sam peered up to see relief on Bladder's face, along with the raised sticks and swords of the collection of oddballs who had come to fight for him.

It was such a small group compared to the monsters. They were outnumbered, and every person who had followed Sam was in sight of the dais.

'So *this* is your army, my darlin'?' Maggie smiled.

The crowd had become still, and Sam scanned them. The wolf had shifted back into human shape to help speed the healing of whatever hurt she'd experienced. Many 'thropes stood with blood on their faces. The rest of the animals were wounded too but, apart from the splash of red on the polar bear's back, he could not see blood as it blended with their fur. The angels stood among them, whispering encouragement, and they were fearless, standing ready to battle, and he was in arm's reach. D.I. Kintamani made a war signal in the air. Did he want the 'thropes and shifters to storm the dais, grab him and run the banshee through?

The monsters and imps turned to Maggie and grinned.

'Begin!' she called out over the Great Cavern.

Then the singing started. In Sam's ears, it sounded like train wheels screeching to a halt on rails, but his friends turned to listen, their faces lit with smiles and gentle blushes, as if lost in a delightful memory. Their arms drooped and their weapons clattered or thudded to the dirt.

His army had managed to get close to him in a short time; a few held pixies in their arms, and others kept brownies pinned, but as the dust settled and the song grew, their expressions dulled and their grips loosened, and the imps climbed out. The fairies and the humans, even the shifters and the 'thropes, looked pleased, as if everything were working out as planned. He saw a 'thrope controller smile and gaze at her hand; a pack of shifter dogs licked each other's ears. A shifter bear curled into a ball and hibernated.

The monsters remained unaffected, which included the gargoyles, who looked around, bewildered.

An ogre grabbed a shifter badger and the creature lolled in the brute's arms as if it were being petted. Pixies and brownies ran at humans and their dogs, and pinched and poked them. When that got no reaction, they stole their sticks. Trolls gathered the swords the 'thropes had dropped, and Sam's army grinned as they were disarmed. A trio of goblins lunged after a fleshy-looking shifter pig as the rest of their kind scooped up fairies and carried them towards the dais.

'Arrêtez!' Goutièrre yelled. 'Stop !' His pack threw themselves in front of the herding goblins and were picked up and thrown. The sound of screams was followed by the ugly crunch of breaking rock.

And the fairies giggled in their captors' arms.

Maggie knelt beside Sam. 'I knew you'd do this, Samuel. You want your playthings and your freedom, yet you can't have it all. You've a monster king's responsibility.'

She laughed and kissed him on the cheek. 'But you've shown your true desire: you have a monster's want for power, my darklin' darlin'. Look at them all; you've bewitched almost every up-worlder creature I've heard of. I'm just amazed you haven't a league of merpeople crawling across the dry stone to serve you. I'm not here to rule you, my love. I'm here to serve you, but your true self. And if you look inside that strange body of yours, you'll know you're not the least bit human, and you'll stop this fightin' against your rightful place on the stone throne. I will keep on wrestlin' with you until you remember yourself. You are a monster!' She waved a hand at the crowd in front of them. 'Look at you, you don't have to settle for monster-kind, you can rule everyone. The world. Believe me when I tell you I prepared for ten times this many. I know how strong you are, my babby. I carried you inside me, remember? You almost destroyed me with your need and desire. So powerful are you, that only a siren song could slow you down.'

Sirens, of course, Sam thought. The singing grew louder and Sam looked for the source. He should have recognised it straight away. It grated in his ears.

But they like water, and The Hole is a dry place.

He'd seen water though, hadn't he? Leaking into the blanket covering the Kavanaghs. He looked towards the cage.

From the height of the dais, he could see the barrel Wheedle had described and the heads of the old sirens singing out over the cavern. The little white one he'd breathed to life sat quietly between them.

Bladder stepped forward, ready to leap to the dais. 'Sam, get away from her. Come on down.'

'I don't think so,' Maggie replied. 'Get rid of this lump of nothing for me. He's keeping our king from his true destiny.'

A troupe of pixies crept towards Bladder. The gargoyle scowled and tensed himself, ready to fight.

'Leave him alone,' Sam called.

The pixies stopped. Sam felt warmth, as if Daniel's hand rested on his shoulder. If they thought he was their king, he could override Maggie's orders. The pixies looked to Maggie for confirmation.

She held up a hand and the pixies paused. 'They'll be your devoted servants if you take your throne the way you should have a long time ago, Sam. Otherwise, the sirens will sing your little army to their deaths. Do what you're born for, and you can save them.'

'By making you monsters?'

'It's what you yourself were made to do. Why fight it?'

'Because they kill people.'

Maggie put her forehead to Sam's. 'But you won't know those people, my sweet. Do they really matter?' She reached for his hands and Sam winced. 'Oh, my darlin', you're sufferin'. Let me fix that for you.' She reached into her dress and pulled out a silver tin. Sam recognised it and saw the lovely sparkle of fairy dust as she opened it. She blew it at Sam's face and the magic powder writhed between his lips, the pain becoming distant and vague.

Maggie smiled at him and kissed him on the nose. 'That'll stop you doing anything stupid.'

A goblin dumped a couple of dozen fairies on the edge of the dais in a heap. They rolled over and went to sleep on the stone.

'Maggisty, I ...' The goblin stopped, then it turned and faced the cage. The other monsters halted their activities and looked in the same direction.

Another softer note in the sirens' song began. It sounded lovely even to Sam's ears. Was he succumbing to their song too?

No, he felt foggy because of the fairy dust, but his thoughts were his own.

I'm still myself. I can run if I have to.

Sam looked at Bladder. The gargoyle had been preparing himself to fling pixies about the place, but the pixies hadn't moved since Sam began speaking, and now something else about them changed too. Their eyes widened and became dewy as grins lifted their naughty faces. They stared in the direction of the cage.

Even Maggie gaped at the sound and a sweet smile made her lovely face even lovelier. She leaned against Sam's cheek, humming along with the tune.

Other imps and monsters calmed. Bombottom flumped to the ground with a happy face. The goblins let go of the fairies or cuddled them. The one chasing the pig sat next to the fairy-collectors and they patted each other fondly. Ogres let go of 'thropes and shifters. Brownies and pixies sat on the ground and sighed.

Bladder raced to the dais and put his paws on the edge. 'Let's get you out of here, Sam.'

The sirens' song is affecting everyone, Sam realised. *It seems only Bladder and I are unaffected.*

Although it was hard fighting the sleepiness the dust caused.

Maggie blinked at the melody. Sam realised she was trying to fight it, and it was winning until she reached over to hug him and a cloud of fairy dust unsettled itself from his face and powdered into the air. She breathed in and shook herself.

'What's this, Samuel?' she asked, her eyes still dewy and gentle. 'How are you doing this?'

Sam could hear the grating melody. It annoyed him enough to keep him awake. It meant the sirens were still at work overpowering his army.

Sam watched Maggie fight the good feeling. She seemed halfway to drifting off on the new, lovely counter-melody, succumbing to the song's power.

Maggie shook herself. She groaned with the effort, knelt up and flicked open her silver tin from her dress, taking two pinches. 'What magic is this?' she asked after her head cleared. 'It's banjaxing me. Stop it.'

'*Your* sirens are making it.'

'You're lyin'; you've done somethin'. Why would you do this to your own kind?' Maggie glared at him and stood. She gaped to see so few remained unenchanted.

Pixies settled into games with fairies, brownies shared toffees with 'thropes, boggarts picked fleas from dogs' fur. Thousands sat, humans and monsters together. A troll opened its claw and three fairies fell out, hitting the dust in a deep sleep. A pixie in a hessian jacket took it off and used it to cover the dozers. A crew of brownies pulled together the pieces of Plomberie. Sam heard the sizzles before she sat up in one piece, grinning. Then the brownies started on Égout. Goblins wove the swords they'd taken from 'thropes into a silver tree and bent one into a star, which they sat on top. Shifters sang a carol to the sirens' tune. One, Two, Three and Daisy fell from underneath the blanket of the cage and stared into the dank air above them, seeing dreams, visions, something; maybe all their wants in one place. Even One's dreams nestled quietly on the perch in his head, and his squirrel heart yawned and pulled its tail over itself. Daisy held a circle of oak in her twiggy hands, which had been part of the side of the cage. It would leave a hole big enough for the Kavanaghs to climb through. Except, Sam guessed, his family were still inside, numb from the enchantment.

It could have been a sweet scene, but Daniel and the other angels, who were already staggering as they fluttered and flew to the dais, collapsed to the ground and sent brown dust into the air. Sam groaned at the weighty noise. The heavenly beings were all too sick and pale to move as all real hope had dried up. Whatever was bewitching the humans, it was not good. It sucked their true desires and will out of them. Only Yonah fluttered above their midst, grey and dirty. She took off, flying limply towards an exit.

Yes, get away, Sam thought.

A cry from Wheedle carried to him from somewhere.

'Bombottom, wake up!' Maggie yelled. 'Somebody stop that singing. Someone get more fairy dust! I'm going to need it all to wake this lot.'

The ogre looked at her. 'Huh?'

'I said, "Wake up".' She strode to the edge of the dais and tossed fairy dust at the ogre, which revived him, although he still looked strangely content.

The great lump struggled to his feet.

'Now break that gargoyle,' she said, pointing to Bladder. 'He's keeping Sam from his true destiny. They all are. Destroy his family and we'll be the only pack left for him. Bombottom, you smash them all.' Maggie turned to Sam. 'You'll be better without them.'

'No!' Sam called. 'Bladder. Run. Somebody help him. One? Milkthistle? Wheedle?' He looked at the humans, the shifters, the 'thropes.

Nobody moved.

D.I. Kintamani lay curled up in an ogre's lap in his black dog shape. He peered up at Sam. 'It's going to be all right.' He smiled. 'Bladder's not in danger. We're all friends here.'

CHAPTER 18

What do I do? *What do I do?* Wheedle paced in front of the entrance of the old burrow, peering down at the Great Cavern.

As soon as the sirens started singing, Wheedle recognised the horrible noise; it sounded like metal dragging across rock. He stared around and located it coming from the barrel on top of the Kavanaghs' cage. There they were, just as Sam had described them, two bird-bodied women; one older, one younger, playing with something white in front of them. How had Maggie got them here? Were they being kept prisoner too? Sam had said something about them promising never to sing. They'd been too terrified Sam would never make another siren.

Wheedle scurried along the high tier for a closer look. Silver manacles held their wings and they looked miserable. In the tight barrel, squished against the older sirens' chests, sat the tiny new siren. She was swan-pretty, but her face was sad and she rocked herself in her arms.

Poor little thing, Wheedle thought.

Sam's army had stopped. Many who'd been holding their weapons high dropped their arms. He watched the fairies fall into a deep sleep. Shifters in their animal shapes curled on the ground. Russell and the others in his group just collapsed along with their dogs.

Then a new voice joined, and the monsters stopped too. Wheedle looked back at the barrel and squinted. The small sweet-faced siren was crooning across The Hole.

Wheedle felt the song, felt the jolliness of it, felt it call out for friendship; yet at the same time it expressed loneliness.

It was lovely. It wasn't the same as the older sirens' song, full of manipulation and malice. It was a call to the heart, the soul, and if you didn't have either of those, a call to the very core of the listener. He liked it.

As much as it moved him, he could see it had an even more powerful effect on Maggie's army. The larger beasts sat down giggling, pulling brownies and boggarts into hugs, and the imps let them. Goblins released the fairies they'd been gathering. Ogres and trolls stroked the dogs and shifters. Wheedle marvelled as he watched various monster breeds collect pieces of stone bodies and reassemble the gargoyles they'd just broken.

After the goblins built the sword tree, the pixies danced about it. Its silver shape reminded him of Christmas. Brownies and leprechauns began playing together; dice, gold coins and knuckle bones spilt to the ground. On his tier, a few burrows away, a cheerful pair of pixies competed with conkers, and a group gathered around sparkling marbles, trying to hit the largest one. They motioned him over and pouted when he declined. The air filled with *awws*.

Wheedle frowned. *Where'd they get the toys all of a sudden? And when did they start wanting to play with gargoyles?*

The Great Cavern was noisy with monsters and imps enjoying themselves. They all seemed to have forgotten they were ever in a battle.

All except Wheedle, Maggie, Sam and Bladder.

What makes us different? Wheedle wondered.

The largest ogre, the one that had chased and grabbed Sam, sank to the ground, reaching towards a fluffy, grinning bogie. Maggie threw two handfuls of dust at him, and the ogre looked up sleepily.

When Sam screamed, Wheedle shot down the wall before even checking to see why his boy was so alarmed.

He stopped to orient himself, glancing towards the dais.

Sam's position had not changed. He lay at the feet of the banshee, but the lumpy great ogre, a grin still on his face, had risen and was staggering towards Bladder. The stone lion roared at the ogre and stretched his stone wings as wide as they would spread. He looked huge and fierce. For all Bladder's grumpiness, Wheedle had had no idea his pack mate could be either of those things.

'It's all right, it'll be all right,' Wheedle said to himself, keeping his voice soft and low, but that's what both the ugly and the lovely song were saying, and they lied.

The souls that had escaped when Sam broke the sword had done a thorough job of paring back the old monsters. Most of them were gone. Even the one bearing down on Bladder was a head shorter than Thunderguts, but Wheedle knew he was big enough to pulverise a gargoyle.

Sam's voice echoed across the cavern. 'Bladder. Run!'

The ogre's docile grin faded and the creature frowned. Bladder's bellows reverberated. The deep animal sound shook the walls, making the dirt fall like rain on the mob. But instead of scaring the ogre, it woke it further, and a vile hunting expression filled its face as it reached for Bladder with deadly claws.

All three sirens sang louder. Sam saw Maggie glare in the direction of the barrel. She'd figured out what was creating the melody that bewitched her monsters, and she paced behind Sam, clenching and re-clenching her hands. They both watched Bombottom and Bladder circle each another.

'Hurry up, ogre! And when you're done with him, squish the little siren too,' Maggie called.

Sam raised his wounded body to crawl closer to the dais edge. He had to help Bladder.

Maggie snorted. 'Samuel, darlin'? What do you think you're doin'?' She walked forward, pushed him down with one bare foot so he fell on his wounded finger. He cried out as the pain renewed. His head cleared, but Maggie must have realised the effect. She opened her tin and blew a pinch at him, then the agony drifted away. It floated a long way off. Not just the pain, everything. Even Bladder's sad face seemed distant. Sam knew the fairy dust had befuddled him and he couldn't even get angry about it.

Bladder's roar faded and the happy racket in the Great Cavern softened. Sam peered at the fight as Bladder and the ogre glowered at each other.

'Get on with it,' Maggie said.

The sirens' songs lessened at the sound of Maggie's voice, but they did not stop singing.

Bladder glanced at Sam, his stern stone face saddening. He mouthed, '*Are you* OK?'

Sam didn't know.

Maggie knelt by him. 'Don't worry, my darlin', it'll be over soon. We'll put a stop to that little siren's singing and you can be the king you're meant to be.'

Spigot settled into the couch between Amira and Hazel. They didn't mind hugging up to him, despite the fact that he was made of stone, and though Spigot suspected it was to get closer to his popcorn, he felt pleased watching a movie with them. A nice song played over the dialogue and they smiled at each other. Wilfred sprawled across the other couch and Great-Aunt Colleen remained in the kitchen ('close to the tea,' she said). Uncle Paddy and the babies were sleeping upstairs and the film took their minds off the battle that might or might not be going on under their feet.

And Nugget.

Nugget was going to be fine. Spigot had not failed to look after Nugget. Wheedle would be pleased.

A manic pecking beat at the front door.

Spigot and the shifter children ran to open it.

'What's going on?' Great-Aunt Colleen yelled and hobbled in from the kitchen.

Hazel opened the door and Yonah flapped inside. 'What?' Amira yelled.

Yonah flapped to the floor crying.

Spigot didn't need an explanation. Something awful had occurred in The Hole. He could tell, because Yonah's glow was so faded she'd turned a filthy white.

As the dove settled on the rug and sang out her distress, Spigot realised he could make out the notes of other, competing songs from far away. One a horrible grating noise, and the other a melody of longing and loneliness so beautiful it made his heart ache.

Then Yonah, as if exhausted by her journey from below, collapsed on the carpet.

Spigot looked up at the open front door to see Nugget jump over the threshold and head towards the kerb on the street outside. The lovely song was coming from the drain, and Nugget was following it.

Spigot took off, shrieking as he ran, trying to get Nugget's attention.

The stone bird heard the padding of soft, shoe-covered feet behind him.

'Not you three', Great-Aunt Colleen called out, but the shifter children were keeping pace with him.

'Nugget!' they yelled together.

Yonah was there too, flailing with the last of her energy. She whispered a resigned chirp and fluttered on to Wilfred's shoulder, clinging to his jumper. She jerked about, unable to steady herself against the rise and fall of his racing feet.

'Nugget!' the children screamed again.

The little gargoyle did not look back as she dived into the drain. Spigot jumped in after her, the children falling behind him through ghostly bars.

Great-Aunt Colleen's protests snapped off as the magic closed over them.

The group landed in the dark. All four sniffed the air, picked up the scent of the newly flesh-and-bloody gargoyle and followed her into the darkness. Yonah bobbed on Wilfred's jumper, glowing weakly.

'It's going to be all right', Sam repeated. He said it a third time, realising his words had taken on the tune of the little siren's song. His eyes widened.

That's what they all believed. Humans, monsters, ogres. That's what the songs told them.

I'm dreaming, he thought, and I don't know how to wake myself up.

Maggie caressed his hair. He closed his eyes, shutting out everything else. Michelle often did this to Beatrice and, sometimes, when she thought he was completely asleep, she would sneak into Sam's room and stroke his head as if he were a baby too. Her baby. It felt so good, so why was his face wet?

It's not Michelle.

Sam opened his eyes. Maggie's hair trailed over him.

'Sam, wake up,' Bladder yelled out, just before Bombottom grabbed him by the neck and tried to drag him forward. The stone lion dug his claws into the dais.

Sam moaned.

'Settle, my baby boy,' Maggie said, and she sounded like Michelle. She could be his mother. She was, in a way, wasn't she? Maybe she was enough. He saw a trail of fairy dust float from her fingers and settle on his face.

Now she's bewitching me. The songs won't work, but with enough fairy dust ...

Sam dragged his gaze back to the two monsters facing each other. He hadn't thought of Bladder as a monster for a long, long time. Bladder had gone up against ogres before, Sam remembered. It never lasted long.

And it never turned out well for the lion-faced gargoyle.

From the corner of his eye, he saw a small blur of soft brown. It sprinted through the middle of a pack of goblins rolling dice with leprechauns. When it stopped and looked around, Sam recognised it.

'Nugget!' Sam heard Wheedle yell. Sam peered up to see the stone bull racing down the cavern wall, heading in the same direction as the little gargoyle.

Wheedle's voice distracted Bladder and he must have lessened his grip for a moment. The ogre swung the lion above his head.

'Wheed, Wheed.' Nugget stopped briefly to wave to Wheedle and then she headed on all fours towards the cage.

Spigot dashed in behind her, followed by the three shifter children.

'No!' Wheedle yelled.

Sam laughed and cried. Gargoyles were fragile. Humans doubly so. He didn't know why that was funny, or why Bladder was sobbing.

'Hush, hush.' Maggie stroked his head. She sprinkled more dust on him.

It's a lot of dust. But dust doesn't affect me as strongly as it does other people, he thought. *I can still wake up. If I want.*

The siren baby continued singing. The monsters and human-types turned to face Bladder and Bombottom. Some even cheered as if it were entertainment.

The shifter children chased Spigot through a cluster of trolls, who were counting their taloned toes. Spigot shrieked at the kids to keep going and one of the trolls grabbed Spigot into a hug. The stone eagle writhed and squirmed, but the troll cuddled on.

The shifter children slowed and then ceased running. They had been in the cavern long enough for the song to affect them. They peered open-mouthed towards the cage.

As they stopped, Wheedle reached ground level. He'd descended the wall at such a break-wing speed, he hit the bottom with a crack. Two goblins fought over who would put his leg back on. For some reason this made Sam sadder.

'Close your eyes, darlin'. It's not your concern any more,' Maggie said.

Sam eyes fluttered as he began to drift off.

'Sam!' Wheedle yelled.

He felt so sleepy it took effort, but Sam opened his eyes again. Wheedle was staring at him from behind a pack of pixies playing conkers and pointing at the fight in front of the dais. Bombottom waved Bladder above his head to the sound of applause, his claw clamped on Bladder's neck. The gargoyle gagged.

Maggie stared at Bombottom, Bladder writhing and wriggling to get free of his grasp, but Bombottom had turned to face the little siren, her song overpowering the dusting he'd had.

'End it, you stupid idiot,' Maggie screamed at the ogre. 'Why am I the only one who can keep a clear head here?'

She blew another handful at Bombottom and one at the ogres circling the shifter children.

Bombottom grinned with malice.

'No,' Sam whispered as the ogre lobbed Bladder up and out, throwing the gargoyle at the wall of the cavern. The gargoyle bounced off the solid surface with a thunderous crack. The sirens stopped singing, and for a second Sam saw fear on the faces of all, monster and human alike. Bladder screamed.

Wheedle screamed too.

Bladder fell, rolling legless in the air, and hit the ground. White dust smoked up from where Bombottom had thrown the gargoyle, and there was another distinct crack, followed by many snaps, thumps and a solid thud like a small building collapsing.

Then the songs began again.

And somebody sobbed. Sam wondered if it was him.

The one dissenting gargoyle was dead, and Maggie had forgotten Sam in the moment of her triumph.

It's OK, we've put Bladder back together before, Sam thought. *We'll just do it again.*

'One problem sorted,' Maggie said, and opened her tin.

She blew a handful of dust towards the trolls surrounding Amira, Wilfred and Hazel. It shot over the pack of pixies in front of them, as if knowing its intended destination, right into the trolls' faces. Their befuddled expressions cleared.

'Grab those humans,' Maggie said.

Sam found himself admiring Maggie's control of the dust. *She's sedating me and waking them,* he thought.

The trolls studied the children and Spigot. One troll licked a fang.

'Not good,' Sam said. He wasn't sure why it wasn't good.

'Not important,' Maggie crooned.

Important. The word echoed. Maybe it was an angel voice. Sam looked around. Daniel lay in the muck on the floor of The Hole, his usually glowing face aged and pale. Sam could see Yonah dangling off Wilfred's jumper by one claw. Only her beak opening and closing weakly suggested she was still alive.

Important, the voice said again.

Sam knew he needed to wake himself, but it felt so much easier to sleep and let it all go. He could fix Bladder later. Everything would be OK later.

Nugget ran towards the cage. The Kavanaghs were inside, as enchanted as everyone outside.

Sam lifted his head.

'Stop fighting me, Samuel.' Maggie took out her tin and blew another gust of dust into his face. The air sparkled around him. She sure was using a lot of the stuff.

Wheedle gave Sam a despairing glance and took off after Nugget once more.

Nugget laughed.

Sam heard soft splashing by the cage and followed the sound to see droplets running down the side of the sirens' barrel. The little siren pushed herself out of the water, leaned on her white-feathered arms and scanned the cavern. The small siren's song changed as she saw Nugget heading in her direction. Even Sam understood it; she'd called to Nugget. She'd called for a friend.

Is *Maggie a friend?* the voice asked.

Nugget ran on her back legs, racing across the cavern floor towards the barrel and the little siren. She yipped and giggled. 'Fren,' she said.

'No, not friend!' Wheedle called, and Spigot shrieked out the same warning. The little gargoyle continued running.

'Bombottom, I thought I told you to ...' Maggie pointed at the little siren.

Sam heard a thumping, clanging noise echo out across The Hole. It was Wheedle's heart, giving a single beat. Even Maggie turned at the noise. She looked between Wheedle, Nugget and the little siren, while Bombottom glanced at her, waiting like a good boy for her to finish the command.

Almost killed me by not being careful. He's careful now. It might upset her, Sam thought. *Good.*

Nugget waved at the little siren, and the siren waved back, her song stronger.

It seemed to speak to Sam too. *You need real friends, Sam.*

He lifted his head again. Maggie snarled and she blew more dust in his face.

Sam settled, listening. Every time he moved, Maggie had blown more dust at him. He was starting to sicken from it. He wanted sleep to come.

'Nugget! No! She's the enemy. We're at war!' Wheedle's voice called out above all the other noises.

Friends? Enemies. Who's who? Sam thought.

He lay still. If he moved, Maggie might dust him again.

That's not what a friend would do.

You have to wake up, Sam.

I have to wake up.

Sam bent into a ball. He'd curled up the first time because …

I hurt my finger.

That's right, he'd broken his finger. Badly.

Sam felt the wounded finger. Even a touch hurt. It cleared his head a little. He wanted to wince but, if he did, there would be more dust. He poked it again. It hurt. No, it agonised!

And if he didn't do something, Wheedle and Spigot would be broken alongside Bladder.

I can fix them.

But you can't put Hazel, Wilfred and Amira back together if they get eaten. Or the Kavanaghs. In fact, everyone who isn't a gargoyle.

That did it! He grabbed his finger hard, and bit down on a cry. It cleaned his head. His body still felt groggy, but his head could think. He watched Maggie, whose attention flicked between Nugget, then the ogre, then Sam. And back again.

Then the little siren sang. *Why can't we all be nice to each other? Why can't we just play?*

'Play!' Nugget yelled.

'No!' Wheedle called after her.

Nugget hurtled past pixies sharing boiled sweets, past young ogres, who grinned as the tiny gargoyle clambered up the side of the cage, grabbed the lip of the barrel, and jumped into the water. Sam couldn't see them, but he heard the childish cheers as the babies found each other.

Wheedle rushed through Sam's army. He yelled, 'Come on! It's not going to be all right unless we do something.'

Sam had to wake himself.

The little siren's song grew friendlier and happier as she and Nugget crawled to the edge of the barrel. Sam saw them dangle their small legs over the edge as the water washed over the top of the cage.

Sam had to get his friends out, had to release his family and put Bladder back together. He realised it'd be easier to go back to sleep. He even wished for more fairy dust so he wouldn't feel so bad.

Wheedle hesitated for a second near the dais. Sam saw the gargoyle stare about. He looked at Spigot and the children cradled in the arms of the trolls. The song was winning out over the dust. They had done Maggie's bidding, but they rocked the limp shifters like babies. The children allowed them. Only Spigot struggled against his captor's embrace. Then Wheedle looked at Sam. Sam couldn't do too much, or Maggie might realise his thoughts were clearer than she'd like.

Wheedle turned to the cage where Nugget was in claw's reach of two wet witches.

Sam imagined Wheedle's distress. What if Maggie told the sirens to hurt the baby gargoyle too?

Can Nugget swim? Sam wondered.

He watched the bull-faced gargoyle crash through a nest of pixies hugging and playing with each other's hair.

OK, Sam thought, *as soon as Nugget is safe in Wheedle's hoofs, I will move.*

The little siren's song continued spreading happiness, cheering the monsters around her, infecting them with good spirits. Even Gouttière, Plomberie, Égout and the other gargoyles began smiling.

Maggie knelt again next to Sam, her tin open and ready to dispatch another dose of dust at a monster under the spell of siren song. Sam peered at the tin. It was mostly empty. She'd wasted it keeping him settled.

She was even swaying to the song herself.

She doesn't have enough fairy dust on her to charm everyone. Not even enough for herself. Maybe we can get out of this alive with all the prisoners. We just have to keep the sirens singing.

Maggie stood up again, seeming to forget Sam, who lay as limply as possible. She was as interested in the gargoyles as he was. She studied Spigot wriggling in a giggling ogre's arms. She turned and watched Wheedle pulling at the blanket over the cage. Her chin jerked up and she swore. Sam guessed she'd noticed Nugget too, splashing in the barrel.

When at last she stooped to pat Sam once more, he shut his eyes again.

'Now, can you tell me, darlin' Samuel, why your gargoyles aren't charmed by the little one's song? If she must sing, then it should be everyone who's bewitched, don't you think?' Sam watched her through his blurred vision as her interest returned to Bombottom, who stared slack-jawed at the little siren. Maggie went to take a pinch out of her tin, directed her finger at the ogre and then thought better of it.

Sam lay quietly, pretending sleep. Maggie dropped the dust on Sam instead; the sparkles falling from the air muffled the pain in his hand. Part of him wanted to go with it. His finger was throbbing, but he had a strong need to answer her question. 'I don't know,' he said. 'I was wondering too.'

'I've had to use a lot of dust to charm you, and a lot to break the charm over Bombottom. She's of a different magic to the other sirens, and a creature of your making. Maybe she's more useful than I first thought. I could control all of the monsters with her little voice. I've noticed some trying to slink away. Even now there's those that hide from me. How are we supposed to conquer the upstairs when there's so much disobedience about?'

Maggie touched Sam's head. 'Now sleep, my dearest. You're safe. It'll all be sorted by the time you wake.'

He wanted to do as she said, and sleep crept in. He could close his eyes and not witness what would come next, no matter how bad.

No, you have to wake up.

He grabbed his finger again. He bit his lip at the pain and tasted blood. The pain revived him. He let his eyelids remain almost closed and turned, pretending to get comfortable, giving a gentle moan as he tilted his head so he could continue to watch Wheedle.

Wheedle stood at the foot of the cage. 'Come down, Nugget. Come down, my girl.'

The guards, a pair of barely adolescent ogres, grinned at the gargoyle and pointed upwards. They'd long forgotten what they were there to do. Wheedle looked back at the dais to see Maggie bending over the prone body of Sam, whispering in his ear. He would have to deal with all that later; she wouldn't kill Sam.

Wheedle grabbed at his bull chest. 'What?'

His heart thumped of its own accord again, beating rhythmically.

No time for that. He had to save Nugget first.

He put his head over the lip of the barrel.

Someone don't know much about sirens, Wheedle thought.

Sam had told Wheedle they were like sea birds, which didn't need to be wet, but someone had chained the older sirens in the water.

One of them paused her song long enough to hiss at Wheedle and the sound echoed throughout the cavern, making the humans in Sam's army jump. Wheedle had no time for her; his gaze was caught by the soggy lump of fur and feathers splashing in the water in front of the adult sirens. The tiny siren had wrapped her arms around Nugget, and a furry Nugget was hugging her back.

Fur? Where did the fur come from?

The adult sirens did not seem to have a problem with Nugget. The younger one's eyes smiled when Nugget made the little siren laugh, and the older one waved a finger in the air as if conducting their songs together. Despite one song being beautiful and the other being ugly, Wheedle noticed something similar about the rhythms.

The baby siren was adorable too. *Almost as sweet as Nugget,* Wheedle thought. Had her singing addled his brain? Made him see her as charming? She had a little girl's face, curly-haired, coffee-coloured skin. And she had real arms and legs, unlike the older sirens, whose bird legs and winged appendages reminded Wheedle of neglected budgerigars. Their torsos were also birdish and half-plucked, whereas the child had the downy smooth white chest and stomach of a swan. She looked like a lovely little girl in a feather dress.

It had to be the song making him see her that way.

'Nugget, come now', Wheedle said.

Nugget pouted, but swam towards Wheedle.

Wheedle had no time to be surprised by Nugget's wet fuzziness. The little siren had ceased her singing. The other sirens folded their wing-like arms and glared at Wheedle.

Then they sang again.

'Sleep, my darlin' Samuel', Maggie was saying. 'You don't need to see this. I will wash them all from your memory. Don't worry, my babby boy.'

Sam watched Wheedle talking. His hand ached all the way to his shoulder, as if the broken finger could not contain its pain and needed to spread. He could think though. He watched Wheedle carry Nugget down the side of the cage. The baby siren's song had stopped. That wasn't good.

Nugget couldn't be hurt by sirens, but there were enough monsters on ground level to kill her.

After Nugget, the next most vulnerable were the shifter kids. They weren't marked with anything to make them unappetising, and Spigot had climbed up the goblin holding Wilfred and was pecking at its claws, trying to detach Yonah from the shifter boy's jumper.

Sam yanked on his own finger again. A horrendous pain shot up his arm, making him sick up on to the dais. He bit his tongue to stop from groaning.

When the baby siren's song stopped, everything went very quiet. The larger beasts blinked their eyes as if coming out of a pleasant dream, and the little ones gawped, finding dice or counters in their hands and blushing.

The air was gritty and filled with dirt.

Wheedle raced towards Sam with Nugget in his arms.

Sam didn't like the idea of Nugget anywhere near Maggie.

'He pulverised 'im,' something said. 'He won't have survived. Look at all that dust.'

Sam scanned the cavern to see who was speaking.

And who they were talking *about*?

More than one voice joined in. Sam peered up. Maggie gasped as he rolled away. She reached for her tin.

Despite the pain, Sam bowled himself to the edge of the dais and fell in the dirt. He twisted himself so he landed on his unbroken side, but the resultant jolt still jarred pain through him.

'Sam?' Maggie called. Her voice sounded clear. She didn't need to fight the song any more.

Sam rocked to his feet, cradling his arm, but he was up and away, fleeing from the last of the pixie dust Maggie blew after him. He ran past a leprechaun who got the dust right in the face before falling over backwards.

Sam raced by imps and monsters hiding their toys and backing away from each other. He had to find where the bits of Bladder lay. He'd put the lion back together before, more than once. Only, the puffs of powder that had flown up as Bladder fell made him think that maybe some bits were too small to ... He stopped, his feet refusing to take him further, refusing to let him see anything.

His heart beat loud, then Wheedle was beside him with a frowning Nugget in his forelegs. Sam had a second to consider that she was wet. Like a dog. The stone bull's nostrils flared as he hoofed the ground. 'He'll be in nice-sized pieces. He'll be in pieces. We can put him back together.'

'Look at this,' a pixie said, padding towards them. He held a solid piece of Bladder's wing.

'See. Pieces,' Wheedle reassured Sam.

Dust filled Sam's eyes, They watered so much, he had to cry to clear them.

'Sam?' Maggie called behind him. She scurried towards him from the dais. 'You cannot save him now. You cannot save any of them without my help.'

Sam closed his eyes. *What if she's right?*

The pixie holding the wing scrunched up his little fists and the stone piece crumbled into millions and millions of particles. A brownie held up two chunks of mane, and they dissolved too.

Wheedle cried and stamped a foot on the ground, his heart pounding in his solid chest. Sam crumpled next to him.

Bombottom, no longer dulled by the singing, was already striding steadily towards the sirens' barrel.

'Why don't you eat them?' Sam heard Maggie saying.

Sam turned back to see her talking to the largest remaining ogres. She pointed in turn at the goblins holding Wilfred, Hazel and Amira, and then directed her eyes towards the barrel. 'Bombottom, once you've scooped up that little siren, bring me the prince back. Unharmed.'

CHAPTER 19

Sam was in pain. Not just in his arm. Everywhere. He didn't know where it came from. But Bladder was dead and Maggie's army outnumbered his.

The polar bear had bent into a fur-bagel. The fairies lay in collected heaps and a few goblins were counting them. One-i'-the-Wood remained curled with his children. Kylie drooped against Russell's leg. At first Sam thought she was dead, but then she lolled her head, telling him there was some life left in her. Monsters converged on the humans and human-types and blinked. Daniel's marks were holding, making Sam's friends appear rancid and inedible.

It wouldn't stop the monsters killing them. Not for long.

The earth shook as Bombottom thumped towards the cage and barrel.

The sirens screeched as Bombottom reached in and removed the little one from her family. The baby cried. Sam didn't think the little siren could have sung even if she'd wanted to. Bombottom held the baby siren gently (as least he'd learned that lesson) and he winked at Sam. Sam guessed the stupid thing thought he was doing what Sam wanted.

The great ogre stomped over and put the baby in Maggie's arms, then walked towards Sam smiling.

'I couldn't leave her there,' Wheedle said, looking at Nugget. And then he cried. 'Should I have left her with the sirens? Then the song ... Can't you order them to stop, Sam?' Wheedle asked. 'They think you're the ogre king.'

The older sirens screeched, pulled against their chains, sang songs that hurt everyone's ears, but they had no songs to baffle ogres. They were not concerned with Maggie's bidding any more.

Sam marvelled. The baby siren meant that much to them?

There was no more singing, and without a song, humans began waking. The shifter children too. They gasped to see the ogres looming over them.

The Kavanaghs peeked through the heavy blanket over their cage; Sam could just glimpse their grey features. Fear reached for him. It was mightier and stronger than Bombottom's fist.

One-i'-the-Wood was back under the blanket, helping them out of the cage, Sam hoped. That's what they'd all risked their lives for.

He looked to where he'd seen his shifter friends last. Their eyes and mouths were open in wide silent Os. The monsters took steps towards them, and the young trolls holding them scarpered to let the ogres have their prey. The adult shifters, still dazed, gaped around with furrowed brows and twisted mouths, as if wondering what to do. Spigot, Amira, Wilfred and Hazel backed in to each other.

'Spigot!' Wheedle yelled and ran.

Sam shot after the stone bull as Spigot squawked and positioned himself between the advancing ogres and the dazed shifter children.

Then Wheedle was at Spigot's side. The gargoyle turned on the ogres. 'You'll have to come through me first', he said.

'And us', yelled Gouttière as his pack marched towards the children, stone fangs showing. The other gargoyles filed in with him.

Sam ran to them, though he knew it was hopeless. The ogres would smash the gargoyles, and then pluck up the shifter children.

And Nugget. She had been safer in the sirens' barrel.

Their defence would give Hazel, Wilfred and Amira only a little extra time alive. Yonah hung upside down from Wilfred, her tangled claw still trapping her to his jumper.

'You don't have to', Wheedle said to Plomberie.

'No one has ever called me beautiful before. For a few moments of my whole existence, I feel wanted. I 'ave a purpose.'

Gouttière nodded, peered at Amira's terrified face and gave her a strained smile. 'Be'ind me, Princess', he said.

'Smash them all', Maggie said. 'Except the prince. Don't you dare hurt him.'

'Please, no,' Sam cried out. 'Please.'

The ogres stopped moving. The ones at the front of the troop were old, with twisted grimaces, but the few at the back hid their big soft faces in their hands. One peeked over Bombottom's shoulder, watching Wheedle with a sad expression.

Sam elbowed the stone bull. 'Who's that? He's staring at you.'

'Cob?' Wheedle said.

The ogre shrank at the sound of his name, but Bombottom moved forward, leering over Wheedle.

Wheedle shoved Nugget at Spigot. 'Well, it looks like we are all going down together!' He didn't look one bit frightened to Sam. Sad, but not frightened. Sam marvelled at Wheedle's courage.

Nugget hung limply in Spigot's wings. 'Fren', she sighed, and peered over to where Maggie held her siren playmate.

'Wait,' Wheedle hissed urgently. 'There's only six Old Ones here.'

Sam peered at the gargoyle. 'What do you mean?'

'The new ones, young ones. Most of her army is made of them. You have to look closely – some of them are huge – but it's the faces. Look at their faces. They're terrified.'

'So?' Sam said.

'Where are the others, Cob?' Wheedle called out. 'Why are you doing this?'

The young ogre peered around Bombottom's elbow. 'Have to, Wheedle, or she'll do to us what they did to

Bladder.' His eyes brightened with tears. Sam stared with wonder at the clear gem that travelled down the ogre's face. He must be dreaming. Ogres didn't cry.

'What are you doing?' Maggie shrilled. 'Destroy the gargoyles and eat those children.'

Spigot held Nugget tightly, looking for a break in the crowd to whisk her through. It was his fault she was there. He studied the ogres, looking for a weak spot. Few of the ogres appeared eager to kill. The bloodthirsty ones pushed towards the gargoyles while the younger monsters hung back.

He'd seen Cob's face too, the ogre's huge paws rubbing at his eyes and runny nose.

Why are the younger ones so different? What's changed?

'Hold! Hold! Hold your ground!' Gouttière yelled to the gargoyles.

The rest of Sam's army had awakened from the horrible lullaby, and the sirens' caterwauling echoed across the Great Cavern as they clawed at their chains and hurled yowls at Maggie. The sound of their pain meant no enchantment filled the huge space.

Sam's army had wakened wounded and defenceless. Too many swords had been bent and damaged to make the silver tree, and there were a hundred monsters and imps for every member of Sam's army. Even though it would take twenty pixies to take down one adult, there were enough to do it. If they wanted.

Those that could still fight battled to reach the shifter children and the gargoyles, and Sam heard the shifter parents yelling their children's names, but the goblins held them off.

An old ogre reached out a claw and grabbed Plomberie by the throat. Wilfred yelled and grabbed the gargoyle's stone rump, pulling her backwards. The gargoyle gagged. The younger monsters turned their heads. They didn't want to help the murderers, but the half a dozen vicious, older beasts were enough to destroy all the gargoyles and eat three unprotected children.

Spigot's gaze returned to Cob's face. *What's changed?*

He looked down at Nugget and then up at her new friend, the little siren, squirming in Maggie's arms.

Spigot's grey eyes widened. He knew. He knew what had caused all these weird things.

He knew the humans couldn't understand him, but he hoped someone would. He opened his mouth to screech a word he loved, one that would solve everything. He looked for Wheedle, who was baring his teeth at a growling, older ogre.

Bombottom threw back his head and bellowed. The ground and air shook with the sound of war. A circle of red clay gargoyles barricaded the children, encircling them, the last line of defence, while the gargoyles made of stone and granite charged at the ogres. As they collided, the cavern filled with a sound like rock hitting rock, and there were awful cracks as gargoyle limbs and gargoyle heads broke apart.

As the older ogres charged forward, the younger monsters – ogres, trolls, goblins – huddled back. They weren't joining the fight, but they weren't helping Sam's army either.

Spigot yelled his word with all of his might, but no one heard him over the din.

Then a light flashed, a wall-shuddering roar exploded over them all and a glowing bead knocked Spigot to the ground.

Sam lay on his back, winded. The explosion had blown him closer to the dais and he could hear the wailing of ogres and the crying of trolls and goblins. Pixies and brownies wept.

The roar had been so powerful it had toppled Maggie. The beautiful banshee lay on the dais floor. She could have been sleeping. She looked so lovely, the little siren so recently in her arms huddled next to her.

Sam squinted at the brightness. It wasn't a single light. It was a group of tiny lights, beautiful and sparkling. He had seen something like them before.

They dropped like stars towards the ground.

But instead of hitting dirt, they veered in all directions. Glowing pink, blue, orange, green, yellow and white, they shot into the gargoyles, throwing them back across the dirt with such force that some of the stone creatures flew, despite their wings being made of mud and limestone. Even the gargoyles that lay in pieces did not escape the eager orbs. Each torso glowed.

'What 'as 'appened?' Sam turned his head to see Gouttière sitting up and holding his head. It hadn't fallen off, but nearly. Sam heard the sizzle and then the gargoyle exhaled in relief.

Plomberie groaned, legs scattered around her. They weren't only hers. Grey granite pieces lay everywhere.

The Great Cavern was full of ogres in prone positions, huddling on the floor with paws over their eyes, while Sam's army sat crumpled on the dirt, staring, confused.

Only Bombottom remained upright. The ogre's meaty arms and claws were still waving above his head in an attack stance, although he scanned the scene with a stunned, stupid expression.

Sam's head hurt, his finger pointed at an odd angle to his hand and his body ached, but all his pain melted away as he saw something emerging out of a cloud of dust. It was one of the most beautiful things he'd ever seen: a great living, breathing orange-brown lion bounded towards the shifter children, its wings spread larger than Daniel's.

Sam struggled up and ran forward.

'Oi!' the beautiful lion yelled over to Bombottom. 'You leave them kids alone! They're friends of mine.'

Bombottom roared at the lion and grabbed at Gouttière. The gargoyle's monkey face twisted in pain and panic. With everyone else cowering, Bombottom menaced them all, looking dangerous. The ogre bared its fangs at the children and lifted the gargoyle over its head. 'Will smash!'

Cob's face appeared behind Bombottom's shoulder. He was a head shorter than the old ogre, but he was holding something in his fist. Sam watched as the young ogre brought a lump of stone crashing down on to Bombottom's head. It thwacked hollowly, and the ogre hit the ground. Gouttière fell on to the ogre's back, which softened the fall a little. The gargoyle cracked anyway, but only one leg fell off.

'I'z always liked gumgoyles,' Cob said. 'Doan hurt 'em.'

'Hey, Cob?' the winged lion said.

Cob frowned. 'Who are you?'

'It's me, Bladder,' the great winged lion replied. 'Sammy, you look pale. Why're you all looking at me funny?'

Wheedle rushed forward. 'I think you need to look at yourself, Bladder. Very closely.'

Bladder picked up a paw. 'What in the world ... ?' He patted his face. 'I'm furry.' He swung a golden wing around so he could see it. 'An' feathery. Well, would you look at that.' He flapped the wings just a little and lifted ten feet off the ground. 'Whoa!' he said, and those below cheered.

When he landed, Wheedle ran into his forepaws, putting his dirty tear-stained snout into the magnificent ruff of the flying lion, and a crowd of shifters and gargoyles pushed forward to pat him and welcome him back.

Sam glanced over to see One-i'-the-Wood holding the blanket to one side. Daisy offered Michelle her hand as she climbed through a hole in the side of the cage. Then he saw the top of Nick's head.

It's all going to be OK, Sam thought. He smiled. It was all he had the energy for before his knees gave way.

Spigot lay in the dirt laughing. He couldn't help himself.

'Get up, you duffer,' Bladder said. 'I don't look that funny.'

Spigot wasn't laughing at Bladder.

Pixies and brownies stared at him with boggling eyes.

Spigot laughed harder. He couldn't help it. Nugget squatted next to him; she giggled too.

He found it impossible to breathe, which was silly, as he'd never had to breathe before, but he guessed, maybe from the light-headedness that comes with lack of oxygen, that the changes beginning inside him were the same ones that had started in Bladder all that time ago. And they'd ignored them all.

He slapped himself, hardly surprised to see a chip fly off his beak. It wasn't just the monsters that were changing.

He tried to get up and fell over again. Everyone saw him, the crazy stone eagle who couldn't stop giggling. He lay there, getting back his breath.

He opened his mouth to squawk and surprised himself by speaking like Bladder and Wheedle. 'Sam,' he said.

'Ooh,' Wheedle gushed. 'He said a word everyone understood.'

'Sam,' Spigot said again. He shook his head and waved his wings around, including everything in the Great Cavern in his wave. 'Sam,' he said, pointing at Nugget and the little siren. 'Sam!' he said, pointing at Bladder. 'Sam,' he said, beating his own birdy chest with his wings. 'Sam.' The old beasts began retreating to the darkness, while the younger ogres and trolls came close enough to peer at him. He pointed at them and repeated, 'Sam.'

The monsters, imps, fairies, humans, half-humans and anything else present studied him like he'd gone completely barmy, and maybe he had. Spigot fell on the ground again, chipping off a bit of his wing and not caring. He laughed at the Great Cavern's ceiling and said 'Sam' quietly. If no one else understood, at least he did.

'Hey, where is Sam?' Daniel asked.

Sam lay in a crumpled heap not far from where Spigot was writhing in the dirt and the gargoyles were checking each other for cracks. He was halfway between the dais and the wall Bladder had been smashed against, and he wished he could see more. People, animals and fairies were running around the golden lion. Pixies seemed to be giving directions. He couldn't see any of the big ogres on that side and it didn't look like anyone was trying to kill anyone. He saw Daniel turn away from Bladder.

What is he looking for? he wondered.

Bladder's mane glowed stronger than Daniel's hair. Sam closed his eyes and let them flutter open again. As bad as he felt, he didn't want to miss anything. Bladder made a most magnificent lion. Daniel and the small group of angels managed to hover off the ground again – hope had reignited to fuel the heavenly beings – and Sam saw the cherub fluttering towards the shifter children.

She better thumbprint them quickly, Sam thought.

But it didn't look like anyone wanted to eat them. He could only see one soft-faced ogre, Cob, and the poor thing looked terrified. Sam turned his head in the other direction and felt a little seasick. Maggie was crouched on all fours on the dais. Her red hair lashed her face as she turned to look at her new guards: a group of gargoyles, some older shifters and

Two-i'-the-Wood, who jabbed her with a twiggy finger. A frown scarred her beautiful features. Next to her, two ogres sat on the edge of the stage, six well-armed 'thropes pointing their swords at them. Had this been battle, six wouldn't have been enough, but too many of the younger monsters and imps were scurrying around trying to be useful to the humans. With Maggie defeated, the old ogres had no one to lead them. And the young ones didn't want to follow.

Something reflected near the base of the dais, and Sam saw Maggie's silver tin lying in the dirt. It had been trampled under too many feet. Sam wanted to tell them not to hurt Maggie, but he found the words did not come. She'd been willing to kill them all to get him back, and he thought her lucky that fairies hadn't joined the group keeping her captive; she might have got more than prodded.

A 'thrope woman had picked up the baby siren and was carrying her back to the barrel. Wheedle watched nervously as Nugget followed them, and the two infant monsters waved back and forth at each other.

Kylie came sniffing through the filth, gave an excited yap when she came upon Sam, and licked his face. 'Are you all right?' she asked. 'She can't hurt you now.'

'Hey, Kylie.'

'Can you sit up?' Kylie asked.

Sam strained to get himself into a seated position, and his hand ached. He felt foggy, fuzzy, as if his body were creating its own fairy dust to dull the pain that was going to hit him soon.

'I'm tired, Kylie,' he said.

'Tired is good. It's not dying.'

Sam was relieved to see Daniel push his way towards the three shifter children and give them a quick thumbprint. 'Just in case,' the angel said.

Sam realised they could all see the winged being. Amira's eyes were wide; her mouth was so far open he could see the back of her throat. The darkness of The Hole, probably, making the angelic glow obvious.

Sam watched as a group of pixies, brownies and other imps poked Cob the ogre in the back, away from the unconscious Bombottom, and forced him closer to the dais and the gargoyles.

Gouttière, Plomberie and their stone packs peered at Cob, eyebrows raised. The young ogre had just saved a gargoyle's life.

Cob climbed on to the dais. 'Doan hurt us, will you?' he said to the gargoyles. His eyes darted to Maggie, but she looked as frightened as the others.

Sam wanted to tell Cob it would be OK. 'Sam?' Daniel called out.

'Over here,' Kylie barked.

It felt like every gaze fell on him. He struggled under the weight of their attention.

'Let me see him,' Bladder said.

'Coming through,' Wheedle added.

From near the cage, Richard's voice yelled out. 'Is he all right?'

Daniel's face was abruptly nose to nose with him. 'Sam? What's the matter?'

'I can't smell anything but that awful fairy dust,' Kylie said.

'Hey,' Milkthistle replied. 'You watch what you say about our dust.'

Sam let his good hand fall. He'd yanked his busted hand so much to wake himself from Maggie's spell that it looked like One-i'-the-Wood's twiggy fingers.

Daniel grimaced. 'He's in shock. Don't worry, Sam, it'll be fine in a minute.' Then the angel took his broken hand and held it. The first second was an agony, and he almost passed out to escape it, but then the pain ran out of him, from his shoulder to his elbow, out of his hand and away. 'See,' Daniel said. 'When the body is in pain, it doesn't know what it feels like to *not* hurt, but when a body is healthy, pain, even recent pain, becomes a distant memory. It's very like a heart that way.'

Sam sat up.

A crowd had gathered around him; members from Sam's army as well as many monster faces studied him. Everyone looked as nervous as Cob.

Bladder breathed egg-sandwich breath in Sam's face. 'Someone restrain those harpies before they sing again.'

'I don't think they will,' Wheedle said.

Sam followed the bull's gaze to the barrel. The older sirens hugged their little one, while Nugget splashed around in the water.

'My family?' Sam said. 'Are they all right?'

'Just having a little refreshment,' One-i'-the-Wood's voice responded. 'Three be sortin' them out some tea.'

'Tea? Where'd he get that from?' the voice of a parched shifter asked.

'My children are always prepared to make a cuppa.'

'Sounds lovely.'

'Samuel!' Maggie screamed from the dais. 'It's not too late.'

Several hands helped Sam up. He walked to the platform and gazed up and over the edge. Maggie's had acquired some extra fairy guards, and they were poking her with their needle swords. She didn't seem to notice.

'Too late for what?' Sam asked.

'We belong together, you and me.'

Sam nodded. She was part of his history and his life. Maybe it had occurred to her too.

'We are monsters, you and me, no matter how we appear. We must have power, both of us. Look at you with your army. Can you not see it?'

Sam sighed. She still didn't understand. 'I don't have power over these people. They're my friends.'

'You don't need friends, Sam.'

'Yes, I do. And family too. In a way, you're my family as well.' Sam climbed on to the dais and reached for her. He held her hand. 'I don't want power over you, Maggie. I love you.'

Maggie shrieked. At first, Sam thought it was anger, but then she began to glow. Her hair turned grey as the fairy magic burned off and she looked fragile: not a crone, just an old woman with a sad expression. Where Sam's hands had been on her arms, her skin greyed further, like granite, like dust.

She stared at him and a tear slid from her eye as her face crumbled and she fell to the stage in a pile of dust.

The two old ogres pushed past the half a dozen guards who had been stabbing swords into their buttocks and ran as fast as they could to reach any exit.

The 'thropes' voices lifted in a gleeful cheer, but faded as quickly. Sam put his face in the crumbled pile.

Daniel put his hand on Sam's shoulder, disturbing the dust. A little green stone spilt out. A banshee bead. It was all that was left of Maggie.

'Sam?' Spigot said.

Wheedle stared at Spigot. *What is that bird going on about?* His first word: 'Sam'. He'd kept saying it.

Wheedle looked at all the things Spigot had gestured at. The whole cavern, including the piles of beads; Nugget and the little siren up in the barrel; Bladder; himself; even the young monsters. What did he mean?

Yonah had appeared too and was cooing beside Spigot. Wheedle moved closer and sat quietly at the edge, watching over the shifter children, a few fairies and a lot of bewildered gargoyles. His heart beat quicker and it felt good seeing Sam wander by, although his face looked so long he could have been a goblin.

D.I. Kintamani and Dr Kokoni walked over with Nugget and the little siren. Both were soggy and dribbled water down the shifter parents' clothes. Wheedle glanced up at the barrel; a flight of pixies was working on unlocking the sirens' chains. He wasn't too sure who'd said that was OK, though they hadn't tried to harm Nugget at all.

He took a closer look at Nugget. Her surface was flattened and dark. She was made of real fur, not fur-shaped stone.

'How did *that* happen?' Wheedle asked.

'It just came off, in the bath,' Wilfred said. 'The concrete stuff. It dissolved away.'

'Like it did with Bladder,' Amira added.

'Yeah,' said Bladder. 'It did feel like peeling a layer of skin.'

'Sam,' Spigot repeated.

Wheedle stared at Spigot. 'Sam? That's all he keeps saying.' He frowned at the stone eagle. 'Oh my goodness. Of course.'

'Sam?' Bladder asked.

'Spigot's the smartest out of the lot of us. He always was. *Sam* did this. He changed us. He changed you. You've been getting weirder ever since he put your heart back together.'

'Weirder? Who are you callin' ... ?'

'Don't interrupt. You've been eating funny for a gargoyle. Like you need real food, and not just for taste.' Wheedle reached for Nugget, who put her arms out for him. 'Sam sneezed on the bean that hatched Nugget, and he breathed on the one that hatched the little siren. We've been thinking they were bad first efforts, but what if they are exactly the kind of monsters Sam would produce? He's made them lovely, sweet and living. They're not monsters at all. What if they're the way Sam will always make them?' Wheedle peered at the pixies struggling with the sirens. 'Do you remember when we first met Cob and his company? They were nice. What if, when the old king dies, the new generation become more like their new king? These young ones weren't hatched long before Thunderguts was ashed, and they wouldn't remember him. They're too young. They would be waiting for their new ruler and their new ruler's way of being.'

'Sam's the new king?' One-i'-the-Wood asked.

'The new ogre king? Maggie's been telling us he is: what if she was right?'

'And those lights, Sam caused these too?' Gouttière asked.

Wheedle looked around for Sam. He was sitting by himself, his face all covered in ash. Best to leave him alone for the minute. 'I don't know. Maybe.'

'It's burning in me. What is it?' Plomberie asked.

'A soul,' Daniel replied.

The pack of gargoyles chatted and checked, asking each other what they felt.

'I am different, it is true. I feel more like ...' Gouttière started.

'Myself,' Plomberie finished.

'I just feel gassy right now,' Bladder said. 'Is this what happens when you get a real body?'

'Only if you eat too much egg,' Daniel said.

'I didn't know that,' Bladder said. 'Thanks for the tip.'

The pack turned on Daniel. 'You knew this would happen?' Wheedle said.

'The souls, yes. Always', Daniel replied. 'But the rest of it only became clearer recently.'

'Sam?' Wheedle looked for him again.

Sam wandered over to where the Kavanaghs stood sipping their tea.

His family was free. He wished he felt happier.

He felt selfish. He wanted everything: happy Kavanaghs, happy friends, happy pack, happy monsters, but a happy Maggie too.

All that was left of Maggie was lying at the bottom of a pile of dirt.

Richard grabbed Sam. 'Sam. Our Sam. My Sam.' He sobbed. Sam couldn't tell why – whether it was exhaustion, relief, happiness or all of them. He felt it himself and surrendered to the embrace.

Then he shared the same with Michelle and Nick. 'You came back to us', Michelle said.

'Of course I did. I wasn't going to leave you in the cage forever.'

Nick and Michelle laughed. Richard continued to sob. Michelle stumbled, weak and pale, and a trio of trolls pulled up a few rocks for them to sit on. The trolls looked shyly at Sam and blushed at his thanks.

'Sam', Wheedle called. The crowd around the gargoyles had grown, and a few of them were monsterkind. The hubbub grew as people, fairies and monsters chatted amongst themselves.

'You go, let us catch our breath here', Michelle said.

Sam dragged himself over to where a huddle of angels, gargoyles and others talked with great energy. Kylie barked at him to hurry.

The throng, as large as the one Sam had seen on his hatching day, parted for him, and though there were many human faces in the group, there were ogres and trolls too. A boggart waved its sinuous arms at him. A group of pixies ran alongside him like eager children at a parade.

He turned to see the Kavanaghs sitting, and half-smiled when he saw a cherub put her hand on each head, the colour of life returning.

Finally, Sam stood in the centre of the crowd and stared at Bladder. He couldn't help it; the winged lion gave off more colour than anything else in The Hole, even the fairies. He leaned in and embraced the warm fur.

Wheedle held out his hoof. 'Sam?'

'Whatever it is, Wheedle, can it wait?' he said. 'I just want to go home.'

'I don't think it can, Sam. I need you to breathe on this.' Wheedle held a bright green bean. It was Maggie's bean. Hot tears pricked Sam's eyes.

'Why don't we do it another time?'

'It's important, Sam.'

'I don't have any fairy dust.' Then he peered at the bead. Even if he could bring Maggie back, would she be as fragile as Nugget? And who would she be? What would the dust do to her?

'There might be some in the cave,' Cob said. 'Or a fairy could give you some.'

Milkthistle growled.

Wheedle grinned. 'Just breathe, Sam. I'm guessing the fairy dust doesn't help anyway. If anything, it slows things down.'

Sam shook his head. *What was the point?*

'Sam!' Spigot shrieked and exhaled cool gutter air into his face. When Sam didn't move, the stone bird did it again. Yonah clambered up the gargoyle's neck. She looked a lot whiter and more chipper than she had half an hour before. She rubbed her snowy cheek on Sam's.

'All right,' Sam replied, and he exhaled. The tiny egg did nothing. It sat in Wheedle's hoof looking stoneish, rockish, lifeless.

Just as Sam expected.

The crowd sighed. A unified sound of disappointment.

'I told you, no dust. If the fairies give us some dust, maybe ...'

The nugget tipped. Sam didn't see Wheedle move his hoof, but he must have.

The stone cracked.

The crowd oohed.

A huddle of pixies squealed and ran off. Sam expected they didn't want Maggie back. He touched the egg with a fingertip. It felt warm. He smiled. It couldn't? Could it?

Wheedle grinned.

Sam felt a hand on his shoulder. Michelle. He turned; the Kavanaghs and Daniel stood with him.

A chip of the egg flew off and a little glow like white opal shone through the small hole, then the top of a head poked out. A flash of bright red hair. The shell cracked away and a tiny cheerful face appeared with pretty green eyes and a button nose. Wheedle put down the creature before it became bigger than his hand. The limbs grew out, straight and slim. The focus of the green eyes never left Sam's face. A brownie screamed.

'Maggie,' a young ogre said in a despairing tone.

When she was no bigger than Beatrice, Wilfred wrapped his jumper around her pale infant body.

'Tham?' little Maggie said.

Sam's eyes felt hot. They ached. He put a hand to her cheek. He pulled it away as if stung. 'She's warm.'

Daniel reached down and touched her other cheek. Maggie snuggled against the angel's touch. He slid two fingers to her throat and bowed his head. He let them sit there for a few seconds. The angel blinked. 'She has a pulse.'

'What does that mean?' Sam asked.

'It means she has a heart, Sam.'

Baby Maggie sent sparkles at Sam, as light and colourful as any Beatrice gave off. 'Tham?'

Nugget and the baby siren scampered between Sam's knees and hugged the new baby.

Sam reached out to touch Nugget. She looked furry. She was furry!

Nugget and the little siren clapped. It set off a string of clappings and cheerings until Bladder roared in his rich, living roar and everything quietened.

An ogre reached out and grabbed Sam around the waist and put him on the dais.

'His Majesty, Samuel Kavanagh, the ogre king,' Wheedle called out.

The crowd thundered so loudly again, even Bladder couldn't quieten them, and he didn't even try as the three monster babies clambered up his fur.

CHAPTER 20

Sam's head felt much better after a sleep, and he had no doubt the ministrations of angel hands helped. Nick mixed batter while Richard cooked and Michelle served the guests crushed around the dining table. Great-Aunt Colleen admired the winged lion lying inside the back door, licking his platter and eyeing up the new batch of pancakes. Yonah pecked at the crumbs scattered on the floor around her.

Nugget was sitting on the table while Beatrice smeared maple syrup in her fur.

Every now and then, Nick would look at Wheedle, Spigot, Bladder and the new tiny banshee curled against Wheedle's chest. She wore one of Beatrice's onesies and sucked her thumb.

'How did she end up so adorable? Had I not seen her, I'd've been prepared to dislike her immensely', Great-Aunt Colleen said.

Wheedle shook his head. 'Sam's made her his own way. She's something new.'

'She's a beautiful baby,' Michelle said.

'I'm wondering, does that make you a grandmother, do you think?' Great-Aunt Colleen laughed.

Michelle mock-hit her.

Sam blushed.

Knuckles rapped at the back door and they all looked to see the angel that had arrived.

Michelle gasped. 'I don't think I'm ever going to get used to this,' she said.

'When miracles happen for you, I suspect it's hard not to see angels everywhere,' Nick said. 'I find it easier to see angels than to process my brother coming back to me after all this time.'

'Oh, my,' Michelle started. 'We missed your birthday. It was three weeks ago. You're thirteen.'

'It's all right,' Sam said. 'Daniel sorted a cake, and the gargoyles and my shifter friends threw me a party.'

'Wilfred, Amira and Hazel knew too.' Michelle teared up.

Bladder chortled. 'You know, if you'd told me two weeks ago that Sam would be running the kingdom before Christmas and I'd be a real lion, I'd have said you were crazy. It seems we are required to believe at least two unbelievable things a day from now on.'

Sam walked outside, followed by Bladder and Spigot. Wheedle handed Maggie over to Nick and he and Richard came too, with Michelle hurrying at Sam holding a winter coat.

'Put this on,' she said.

'It's not cold downstairs ...' Sam started. He wanted to say it, then worried that it would sound silly to her. He closed his eyes, took a breath and said it anyway. 'Mum.'

Michelle pulled him into a hug. 'I'm always going to worry about you, you know. It's a mother's job.'

As he walked to the drain with Daniel and the gargoyles, he heard the Kavanaghs talking.

'I'll give the babies a bath.' Nick said 'babies' like it was a question.

'They eat a lot, these gargoyles. Especially that Bladder, and if they're staying with you, you might want a bigger house,' Great-Aunt Colleen said.

'We will figure it out,' Richard said. *Not Richard*, Sam thought. *Dad.*

'I think it's brilliant!' Nick said. 'But it's going to take some time before Uncle Paddy's used to it.'

Sam liked the new look of The Hole. White light globes in the street lamps, fairy lights everywhere, coloured doors on the burrows. Just ahead, at the mouth of the tunnel they were ambling down, he caught a glimpse of the dais. The new throne upon it was made of wood and painted gold.

Daniel handed Sam a clipboard. 'So, messages have been sent to the various kingdoms affected by the change in monarchy and, of course, Titania already knows, so she's sending an envoy. D.I. Kintamani and T.C. Angelina will be present. As requested, the different monster and imp groups have been asked to elect a representative so conversation and debate don't get out of hand.'

'That was your idea, not mine,' Sam said. 'It was a very good idea.'

'But as king you must affirm it, and then it becomes a request.'

'None of these things occurred to me. If you hadn't told me ...' Sam sighed. 'I'm going to make a lousy king.'

'You're an improvement on the last guy,' Bladder said.

Sam stepped into the Great Cavern. They had come to the king's entrance, which followed a red-carpeted path to the dais and the throne. Sam stopped and surveyed his kingdom.

He felt awed by its size. He always had, but somehow realising he was the ruler of the place made him feel smaller.

He watched the inhabitants. A few younger monsters sat in rings chatting and giggling. Pixies chased each other along the outer edges, and brownies and leprechauns played marbles and threw balls at each other. The imp groups mixed. Boggarts danced as goblins sang and trolls looked at a variety of musical instruments, figuring out how to hold them.

As soon as they saw Sam's small group, the trolls flung the instruments away and the boggarts and goblins stopped their happy-making and hurled themselves to the ground, scraping at his feet. The brownies and leprechauns stood, forming little walls between Sam and the game areas to stop him seeing what they'd been doing, and the pixies ceased chasing each other. Many shied at the glow Daniel cast, and most stared at Sam and trembled. They shuffled back into the shadows of the mounds of beans as Sam's group passed.

'Come on, King Sam', Bladder said. 'Let's get you to your throne. Walk ahead.'

Sam looked at his pack.

'You need to go first', Wheedle said.

Sam led the way. He did not feel even a little bit like a ruler, but sad faces looked to him, and he knew, no matter how much he didn't want to do this, someone had to.

When he stepped up on the dais, the small audience in front rose. The elf, Edgar, Titania's representative, was dressed in a formal three-piece suit with an ermine robe over the top for good measure. Milkthistle was with him. Another little person sat next to them. Sam didn't recognise her, but she looked a lot like Edgar and wore a green outfit with a peaked cap. D.I. Kintamani and T.C. Angelina were in uniform and they gave him friendly waves, and, as ordered, one each of the monster and imp clans stood together in a nervous cluster and stared at him with wide eyes and pursed mouths. Even the two old sirens waited in their barrel at the back.

Only Gouttière the gargoyle stood by himself, looking relaxed. Sam peered around and saw Marée, child of Eulimene, the mermaid, standing on two legs and gawped at her. Her dress was a shimmering blue-green. She smiled and mouthed, '*Legs aren't bad.*'

'Hi', Sam said. 'I'm Samuel Kavanagh, er, King Samuel, of The Hole. It's great to see you all here. You are all very welcome.'

'Well said, Yer Majesty,' One-i'-the-Wood replied.

Sam jumped at being called 'Your Majesty' and he was sure his greeting was anything but well said.

D.I. Kintamani winked at him, and Sam relaxed, reminded that even the representative for the Shifter Authorities was just Wilfred's dad. He looked around at Daniel. He had no idea what to do now.

Bladder purred and stepped up beside him. 'Don't worry, Highness, we've got you covered. Just say what Daniel told you, and we'll do the rest.'

'I have asked you all here today to discuss the future of The Hole and of monsterkind itself, where we go from here and how we continue to interact with the various supernatural establishments of Earth. Under my ... um ... leadership ... things are going to change.'

'You were supposed to say "majestic authority",' Daniel said.

Sam had enough trouble saying 'leadership'. He wasn't even six months old yet. He bet that Thunderguts was a couple of centuries old before he took over from the Jabberwock. How was he supposed to do this without any knowledge of what it was to be a king?

'How, Your Majesty?' A young ogre shuffled forward and a mob of mixed imps and monsters shuffled with him, as if terrified of being separated.

'It's Cob,' Sam heard Bladder say to Wheedle.

'What do you want to know, Cob?' Sam said. 'I really don't want monsters thinking of kidnapping and eating people any more.'

'Or fairies', Milkthistle shouted.

Sam looked at the fairy. Milkthistle bowed apologetically.

'No, I agree. Don't take fairies either, or steal their dust. In fact, let's not steal anything.'

'Is you gonna have us killed, Your Majesty?' a troll asked.

'What's your name?' Sam asked.

'I'm Underbridge', the troll replied.

'Don't forget to call 'im "Your Majesty" every time', a small voice said. 'Or Highness, or Big Guy.'

'Your Majesty', Underbridge added.

'Well, Underbridge. My plan isn't to kill any monsters either. Maybe if they try to eat someone, we can lock them up in the dungeons, but I'd hate even doing that.'

'The Old Ones say you'll kill us off the way you kilt so many of them, all explosions and the like', a troll said. 'An' you dusted Maggie down.' A pixie tugged his arm. 'Your Majesty', he added, then went on. 'We seen them souls t'other day en we dint know if they might get us deaded, but they was scary, and the old trolls say they kilt off nearly all the old guard when you let them loose last time.'

Sam gazed at the gathering. There were small groups of ogres, trolls, goblins, boggarts and bogies, but none of them were old and the space wasn't crowded.

'Where are the old monsters?'

'They went down lower, into the caves, Your Majesty', Underbridge said.

'Is this all the younger ones? I'm sure there were more of you during the battle.'

The tiny group of monsters and imps maintained its huddle. They all shook their heads.

'They stayed in the sub-caverns, Your Majesty', Cob answered.

'Then why did *you* come?' Bladder asked.

'His Majesty ordered us, an th'uthers fought you might come down to the caverns with an army of souls if we din't send someone, Your Majesty.' Cob bowed at Sam.

'No, I won't be doing that', Sam said.

Imps in the shadows stepped closer to the dais. 'Really?' a pixie voice asked. It squeaked and Sam watched its little shape dash back towards a hill of nuggets, toppling a few more to the ground as it raced.

'An' I came just for meself ... Your Highness', Cob started. He winced. 'When King Funderguts died we dint know what to do, we just wanted to play, an' Her Maggisty came and tol' us we were meant to run around upstairs an' make the humans miserable, and we thunk "well, she'd know", but we still wanted to play, an' the big ogres said we no' sposed ta play, we is silly for wanting to play, so I sneaks off and plays with trolls and goblins and we hide when we do it.'

'Pixies gets to play all the time', the elected little troll said.

'Except when they is tol' to do errands for the ogres and trolls', a pixie replied.

'Which is lots', said another, 'and then they might feed us to the witches anyway.'

'They doan like that', Cob said.

As Cob talked, bigger creatures began edging forward.

'So, why did *you* come?' Bladder asked.

'Cos you're His Majesty's *friend*,' Cob said, the last word whispered.

'Because I'm his friend?' Bladder asked. The gargoyles looked at each other. 'I don't understand.'

'We met. At the talk, remember?' Cob asked.

'Yes, I remember,' Bladder said.

'An', I know it was a short time you was there, but we was friends for that time, wern we?'

'Yeah, I think we were,' Bladder replied. 'We can still be, if you like.'

'Oh, that would be ever so nice,' Cob said in a rush. 'Anyway, I fought, if you can be friends with us, and with the new king, maybe you can tell 'im not to kill us?'

Sam smiled. 'I wouldn't kill you anyway, but being friends with Bladder does ... What's the word, Daniel?'

'*Entitle*, Your Majesty.'

It sounded weird when Daniel called him that.

'Entitle the friend to privileges.'

'Above his station,' Daniel added.

'I'm not saying that,' Sam replied.

'Majesty?' Cob edged towards the dais.

'You are entitled to friendship privileges, Cob.'

'What's that mean?' asked the elected pixie.

'Games, parties, sharing food, family films,' Bladder said. 'Stuff like that.'

'Oooooh,' the elected monsters said.

The creatures at the sides of the cavern moved closer, and from the burrows and tunnels nervous faces appeared.

'An' you're definitely sure no one has to get kilt, Your Honour?' Underbridge asked.

'Majesty,' a pixie corrected.

'Definitely sure,' Sam replied.

It was only a small crowd, but it was a great cheer.

The group of elected monsters moved forward, less huddled, until they were at the edge of the dais. A troll picked up a pixie and put it on the platform so it could see Sam and Sam could see it.

'What does you want us to do then, Your Majesty?' the pixie asked. 'Does we do chores, cleaning and the like?'

'You can do that, if you like,' Sam replied.

'If we … like?' the pixie asked, and turned to the group. 'Do we like that?'

'Sometimes,' said the elected brownie.

'I like hopscotch, Your Honesty,' said a young puck, and clamped its hand over its mouth and stared wide-eyed at Sam.

'Well, play hopscotch then,' Sam said.

'Can I, can I, can I … ?' The troll shook its head. 'No, it's all right. I won't offend Your Majesty's ears.'

'Does it involve hurting or eating anyone?' Sam asked.

'No, not at all. I wants to play in the snow.'

The little cluster shrieked together. This time, the puck clamped its hand over the troll's mouth.

'Well, then play in the snow,' Sam replied.

The puck dropped its hand.

'Really?' asked the troll.

Sam laughed. 'It sounds like a wonderful thing to do. Go and do it. I hear there's lots of places where it's snowing right now.'

'Can we bake?' asked a voice.

'And ride bicycles?' asked another.

'And play marbles?'

'Arts and crafts?' yelled the elected brownie.

The groups of pixies and brownies and young monsters that had been hanging back in the shadows came rushing forward and threw all sorts of other suggestions at Sam.

'An' what about dancing and parties?' Cob asked. 'Is we allowed them too?'

'Yes, of course.'

Daniel coughed.

'Ooh, but you must clean up after yourself and try not to disturb people who are sleeping,' Sam added.

'We will clean up ever so well, and we won't be too noisy. Not ever ever ever,' Cob agreed.

Sam wondered about that, but smiled anyway. He looked over to where Daniel pointed at the non-monsters in the cavern. 'Now, why don't you sit down quiet for a while as I attend to my guests.'

'Yes, Your Majesty,' Cob said, and motioned the monsters down.

A peace filled the Great Cavern. Not silence – the monsters shuffled like eager toddlers and more than a few pulled out knuckle bones and marbles and played in the dirt whispering rules to each other and giggling behind hands – but it was quieter and calmer than Sam had ever seen it.

One-i'-the-Wood watched the happy faces about him. He lifted his leaf cap and smiled with blueberry lips. 'Well done, Yer Majesty. See what happens when you give a little bit of "yes"? I bet it feels nice too.'

'It really does.'

'Don't think you can't say "no" occasionally. I'm learning that with my own brood,' One said, but he beamed and winked at Sam.

Daniel coughed very loudly.

Sam remembered his assembly representatives, and turned back to them. 'Many apologies to my guests. I probably should have talked to you first.'

Edgar rose with a grumpy expression, but D.I. Kintamani spoke before the elf could say anything. 'I expect it's hard to know where to start, and your own people often need reassurances first, so no need to apologise.'

Edgar grimaced, opened his mouth, but shut it again.

'How can I help you, Edgar?' Sam asked.

Edgar bowed low and flourished a hand so his ermine robe swung over his shoulder. 'Her Imperial Majesty Titania, Empress of Fae, Sovereign of the Sunfilled Seas, Monarch of the Magic Skies and Queen of Faeryland greets you with all honours and dignities accorded to your crown. She recognises your royal status as king of monsters and ruler of The Hole and hopes there will be peace between our peoples.'

'Of course there will, Edgar, you know ...'

Edgar glared.

'Let him finish, Sam,' Daniel said. 'And pay attention – you might learn a thing or two.'

'If there is to be an alliance between the fae and monsters, the whole of monsterkind, impkind and all of their ilk must cease and desist from hunting and hurting fairykind.'

'Yes, of course,' Sam said.

'An ambassador of your people is requested and will be offered protection within our realms and accommodation for themselves and a full staff will be provided, to make this possible.'

'Well, yes ... I don't know if anyone will want to go. Let me ask.'

Edgar bowed low. 'May I approach Your Royal Personage?'

'OK.'

Edgar trotted closer, followed by Milkthistle. He motioned Sam over. Sam got on his hands and knees so he could talk to the Fairy Envoy.

'OK, King Samuel, first off, try to sound a bit more formal,' Edgar whispered. 'Let's not "OK" and "all right" our way through a royal audience. Remember, you're in charge. You need to be in charge, or it'll be chaos. You tell whoever you want to go where you want them to go, and they've got to go. Then you'll sound kinglier. Although we'd much prefer a happy ambassador, that's true too. So, you didn't hear it from me, but we've had many a puck and pixie defect from The Hole and come to live with us. I'm sure more would have tried. Again, you didn't hear it from me.'

'Got it!'

'Got it, Lord Edgar,' Edgar said. 'I'm Lord Edgar in formal company.'

'Got it, Lord Edgar,' Sam repeated.

'Your Majesty, although you have not requested a fairy ambassador, can I suggest you tell us you need one so we can send someone to help you get all your etiquette right?'

Sam looked up at Daniel. The angel shook his head.

'Not yet, Lord Edgar, but I will keep it in mind. Thank you.'

For the first time, Edgar smiled at Sam. It did make his face look merry.

Edgar shooed Sam back to his throne and went back to his spot.

'So, one more time, Your Majesty,' Edgar continued at a louder volume that carried throughout the cavern, 'an ambassador from your people is requested. What say you?'

'Yes, I think that sounds good, Lord Edgar. I will consider who to send, and who will attend them. You will have my decision by the end of the day.'

'Nice reply,' Daniel said.

The pixies all seemed very attentive now. Sam looked to the elected pixie official and nodded. The pixies understood straight away and squealed in excitement.

Wheedle watched too. He still had a stony exterior, but he could feel his heartbeat, and he had made sure he didn't eat as much curry the night before because Bladder had described indigestion, yet he'd been hungry for it, a real empty gutter gurgle feeling. He was excited for wings. Bladder had shown him how well his worked and Wheedle couldn't wait to soar up in the sky. And he was starting to feel weather changes. Just a little – not the way he realised Nugget felt them, not yet. He understood now that's what made her cry so much. The poor thing had been cold and hungry. She'd be playing on the floor with Beatrice now, Michelle giving her the occasional cuddle and pieces of fruit. She might have only looked part monkey in the face, but she was all monkey in personality.

Spigot itched. His feathers, the real feathers growing under his marble skin, pushed up. A few barbs poked out, but he shuffled around to cover them. The worst were the ones in his ruff. They drove him crazy. He looked up, trying to concentrate on what Sam was saying, but it was so hard. He looked over at Yonah perched on Daniel's shoulder. Ah, Yonah. Would she still like him if he had feathers? Maybe she'd like him more. Were they friends only, or would she ... ? No, she flew so much higher than he could; she probably only liked him because he was part of Sam's pack and Daniel's ward. Spigot sighed.

Yonah peered back at Spigot, who stopped fidgeting. *Keep still, keep still*, he told himself. *Look cool*. Yonah cooed at him, and his new heart melted like a sucked toffee. She turned back to the audience of monsters.

'Yonah', he whispered.

Wheedle turned, grinned and winked at him.

He felt his beak get hot.

Sam listened to the requests of all the visitors. It ended with the little person in green who'd been sitting next to Edgar approaching the throne and unrolling a scroll.

"'I, Nicholas – High Regent of the North Pole, overseer of the Magic Manufacture Corporation, servant of Christ's mass, in the line of Balthasar, Melchior and Gaspar, also known as Weihnachtsmann, Kanakaloka, Grandfather Frost, the priest who bears gifts, Joulupukki, Old Man Christmas, the Christmas Gnome, the Christmas Brownie, St Nicholas and Santa Claus, and a hundred other titles, recognised by millions of children the world over – present to you my emissary, Holly. Greetings to you, King Samuel of The Hole.'"

Sam exhaled. This Nicholas sounded very important.

Holly the elf continued reading. "'Many apologies for not attending your coronation in person. Unfortunately, you have caught me during my busiest season and though I will be able to visit you on December the twenty-fourth, please be aware I won't have time to stay. Your rise to succession as king of monsters comes as a surprise, for it is an unprecedented event when the monster king is also amongst those on my 'Nice' list. Ogre kings and most of their subjects have only ever been on my 'Naughty' list till now. Congratulations.

"'To make up for the offence of missing this most auspicious of occasions, I send an invitation for you and a small party of friends and attendants to have dinner in the North Pole towards the end of January.'"

Wheedle gasped. Bladder woo-hooed and Spigot squawked.

'Tell him you are grateful for the invitation and will happily attend,' Daniel said. He added, 'You will have a wonderful time.'

'Ooh, he'll be happy to hear that, Holy Attendant,' Holly said to the angel.

'It is important Sam says it too,' Daniel said. 'Most individuals here can't hear me.'

'Completely understand.'

Sam repeated what Daniel had told him to say.

Holly darted forward. 'Your Majesty, do you mind if I ask a question?'

Sam scurried from his throne again and leaned over to talk to Holly.

'Father Christmas says you might want to bring a brownie or two. We know they like to make things and he's always on the lookout for extra staff. There's never enough.' Holly dropped her voice. 'He pays in toys and sweeties. You might like to get the elected troll to come along too. We have a lot of snow.'

Bladder rested contentedly on his forepaws. Who knew everything would turn out so well? White Wings had a self-satisfied look on his face, but it didn't upset him the way it used to. They all deserved to feel good about this.

Then the angel leaned in to Sam's ear. He spoke so softly even Bladder could have missed the words if he hadn't been straining. 'Now, Sam, repeat after me ...' and Sam did.

The strange thing was that, soon, Bladder stopped hearing Daniel at all and the words seemed to be Sam's own. But he guessed that's what happens when an angel whispers in your ear.

'I, King Samuel of The Hole, welcome all my people and the friends of monsterkind to this kingdom. Together we will make changes. Together we will change. There will be no more killing. It will be replaced with playing. No more stealing; we will make our own things. We will replace despair with hope, and regret with relief.' Sam smiled at them all, and they smiled back. Bladder noticed the crowd had grown and still more imps and monsters sidled out of the shadows. 'Yet, I am young, very young, and it is fit for me to grow and learn some more before I can always be with you, so I am appointing regents to rule in my stead. Members of my pack, Bladder, Wheedle and Spigot, will watch over you until I am old enough to take on this role completely, although I will always be your king.'

Sam looked up at Daniel. 'Really? I don't have to do it now?'

Daniel nodded.

Bladder laughed. Sam was doing a great job. He could tell by the boy's face that he wasn't feeling confident, but the glowing gazes of the monsters and imps rested on him, and Bladder knew they adored their new king. Not as much as Bladder himself did, but well enough.

Bladder thought the heart inside him would break apart again, it felt so huge and full.

CHAPTER 21

There is a house a little way outside of Brighton in England. It's a large house, and if you happen to be on the right back road at the right time of day, you might look up and see a winged lion, a winged cow or an eagle sitting on the roof. In cold weather, they could be wearing anoraks. If you're the type of person who glows, you'll see an angel and a dove too, and if you need somewhere to stay there is a whole floor devoted to free bed and breakfast managed by a cuddly corgi named Kylie and her human assistant. Do leave sugary treats for the cleaning staff.

Bladder looked over the roof of the new house. He could hear Sam talking to Nick and Wilfred on the stairs inside.

'Hazel wants to crush me?' Sam asked. 'What did I do?'

'No, she has a crush *on* you,' Wilfred replied.

'That doesn't sound any better.'

Nick's laugh carried to the furry gargoyle's ears. 'It means she *like* likes you?'

'Well, I like her too.'

'Enough to kiss her?'

'Oh,' Sam replied. 'Oooooooh?'

Then Wilfred and Nick laughed so hard, Bladder laughed too.

Daniel landed next to Bladder. 'It looks nice. It came together quickly.'

Bladder did feel quite pleased with Sam's new 'castle'. 'When I told the leprechauns Sam needed a bigger house – out of the way to accommodate state visits, areas to raise the younger monsters and just make it easy for them to visit their new king before he takes on full leadership – they handed over a pile of gold without flinching. Two days and a thousand brownies later and the whole family is moved in. The top floor is out of bounds to anyone except the Kavanaghs and their guests. Monsters and fairies, as nice as they are, do get a bit much sometimes.'

'And Titania organised a portal to Faeryland?'

'Sam tends to use it to visit the twiggy family, but it's so the pixie ambassadors don't have to be away from their packs all the time.'

The pair fell silent and peered down at the snow-covered lawn. Nugget played with Melody, the siren baby, as well as Baby Maggie, five tiny new pixies and a dozen identical newly hatched beige-coloured boggarts with pink ears. They were all bundled in puffer jackets to ward off the gentle snow falling on them. They kept the garden statues busy retrieving a ball, but the stone shapes looked delighted to do it. Bladder had to admit Sam's hatchlings were incredibly cute. Even Maggie. And they got cuter each time.

'You've made sure you have some private space in the house?' Daniel asked. 'Being regent is a tough job.'

'Big-screen TV, huge bed, private fridge constantly stocked with sandwiches. The works. The job's gotta have some perks.'

Daniel smiled. Below, Michelle and Richard came outdoors with Beatrice between them. Nugget ran to them and hugged Richard's leg, and a statue of a faun took baby Beatrice and carried her around to say hello to the hatchlings.

'So, I've been wantin' to ask.' Bladder peered at Daniel. 'How come it changed so much? The monsters, I mean. How do you turn that kind of nasty around?'

Daniel patted the lion's back. 'What are you all made of?' he asked.

'Sighs.'

'Which are ... ?'

'Sadness, regret, misery, despair, awful things.'

'And if you pour resentment and anger on a child, it will build to fear and hate. As soon as Sam became king, it changed. Thunderguts was no longer there being hateful and angry, so when Melody sang, and when they realised Sam wanted them to play, they became more themselves. That's what children want, even unhappy ones. A way to make themselves feel better.'

'But they're more than playful, they're lovely. Some of them even made Father's Christmas's list.'

'Love does that. It wants everyone to be the best version of themselves. I bet you like being on Santa's list.'

'Yeah.' Bladder sat up straight so his woolly red scarf could be shown to its best.

'And it will be the first of many regular presents, because of what Sam does. If you pour love and hope on regret and sadness, even despair, what do they become?'

'Dust.' The winged lion watched the little banshee.

'Bladder.'

Bladder thought for a while. 'I think I would say "compassion". Does that sound right?'

'It does indeed. When did you become so wise?'

Bladder purred. 'Daniel, I think I will always love Christmas best.'

'Because of the presents?'

Sam's pale face and cold red nose appeared over the edge of the roof. 'Hey!' he said, waving at them. 'I've been looking for you.'

Bladder shook his mane. 'No. It's because it celebrates a time when a child came into the world and changed everything.'

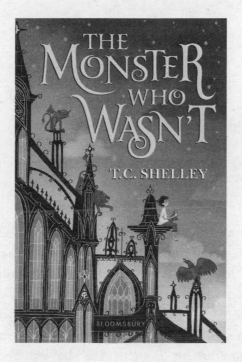

CHAPTER 1

Old Samuel Kavanagh studied his granddaughter's face. His son and grandson had brought her for the evening. It took him a lot of work to keep smiling so his boys wouldn't know his thoughts. They worried about him enough. He peered at the sepia photo of his wife on the dusty sideboard. Despite his smile, she'd have seen through him and right into his thoughts. She'd have shared them.

He missed her.

The ten-week-old baby girl lay on his lap. She smiled at him, exposing bare gums. She'd been born with a full head of ebony hair, as they all had. His grandson reclined at his side, perching on the chair's arm. Only two years into his teens, he watched his grandfather with Kavanagh black eyes, the young man he'd become hiding politely beneath the surface.

Then Samuel turned to look at his son – greying at the temples, hovering over his daughter with lines of concern carved into his forehead. What wouldn't the old man give to lift that load from him?

He sucked his tongue, feeling the air move from that bottomless place in his stomach. He held it back, but the sigh won, hissing out into the room. Regret and misery, pain and weariness blended and solidified.

The baby laughed, and her music burbled into the polluted air. She watched her laughter turn into a bead of light and circle the old man's head, dancing and casting sparks over his thin hair. The baby reached for it and the sparkle ducked between her fingers, teasing her. It shot upwards joyously and got caught in the toxic fog of the sigh. It hit against the sigh's insides and gleamed through the dark surface.

The blend coughed and spluttered and struggled, but the laugh and sigh stuck together. The mixture sagged, its serpentine tail curling in as the baby giggled again.

Samuel's grandson grinned. 'I've never heard Beatrice laugh before.'

'Ah, Nicholas, it's a wonderful sound, isn't it?' The old man ran a finger over the baby's face.

Unnoticed by the older humans, the muddle turned in the air, tightening into a tiny black lump. The laugh held it in the room for a moment, sparking as it soaked in the loving atmosphere. When it grew tired of fighting itself, it flitted towards the old man's bathroom and slithered down the rusted plughole in the basin.

The visitors didn't stay long. The baby's giggles settled to whimpers, and she began to fuss.

The old man stood to see them off.

'Sorry to leave you, Dad', his son said. 'Your show's on next. We'll let you watch it in peace.'

His grandson kissed him on the forehead.

Familiar music wisped from the television as Samuel waved them out. He saw the glow of their car's backlights heading south.

He leaned over and picked up his wife's portrait, setting it on his lap and stroking the picture frame.

'I don't know why, but I think they'll be fine, Annie, my darling', he said. 'And I'm not worried any more; maybe my prayers have been answered.'

He settled to watch his show, but he would never move again. He drifted away remembering his grand-daughter's giggle.

At the window, a pair of pretty green eyes looked in on Samuel Kavanagh. They had witnessed everything. They'd seen with some surprise the sigh rise smoke-like and congeal into a small and scaly cloud, and they had creased into a smile as the old man breathed his last. Then their owner turned away and slipped into the darkness.

The tiny black gem fought with itself as it travelled the pipes, turning a normally quick journey into a struggle lasting days. The laugh itself wanted to burst free, find fresh air, see the sky and head for a bright star singing a singular, irresistible note. But the sigh was heavy; it needed to sink and merge with dark water running through rusted pipes into murky sewers.

It looked odd too. It was not pure regret – not merely loss and wasted opportunity. The laugh had brightened it, and though the nugget was black, like all last sighs, it gleamed. It had held back long enough in its absorbent state to nab the humour, the kindness and the love of a family. It had soaked up a lot of humanity.

It took five days for it to arrive in The Hole.

It zipped over the heads of the monsters gathering in the centre of The Hole's Great Cavern, the huge hub of the monsters' lair, deep under the Earth's surface. One end stretched three football fields from the other. The cavern walls rose high and dingy, so high not even a monster's nocturnal eye could see the roof.

Near the middle, a thunder of ogres played football with a gargoyle's head. The little sigh flew over them and joined the hundreds of other sighs flitting around, gnat-like, into the faces of red-coated leprechauns and pixies wearing newspaper hats and hessian skivvies. The trolls batted at them. Boggarts climbed head first down impossible walls to watch sighs fall into a heap inside a circle of rocks. They were overshadowed by a rough-wrought throne on a raised stone platform.

It was Hatching Day. A day of celebration, a day to listen to cracking and crunching of hard dark shells as the latest crop of sighs spat out grubs and pups of the various monster breeds. The monsters had gathered from every corner of The Hole to see if there were any new members to their packs. Some even came down from the world above, abandoning attics, cellars, bridges, tunnels and other human-built residences to have a look at the new additions. The stronger the beast, the closer to the throne and the circle of dark eggs they shoved themselves, which annoyed the weaker imps, as they couldn't see much at all.

At the front of the crowd, trolls shoved leprechauns, which in turn bit their toes. One ogre with a head like a damaged pumpkin grinned down at a clutch of shivering pixies and sucked his fleshy lips. Towards the back, a batch of brave brownies waited for their moment. After the goblins and ogres pushed forward and settled, they squeezed between comfortable bums to fill gaps. Being breakable, the gargoyles hung at the rear of the mob, away from ogres' feet, and listened to the few snatches of news that were passed back to them. They readied themselves to rush forward and grab any new gargoyles before ogres crushed in the hatchling heads.

Ogres on guard circled the mob, making sure no one ate anyone else before the new-mades hatched. It was exciting. A festival of sorts. Even the footballers stopped their game and pressed close, elbowing banshees and goblins out of the way.

When the ogre king entered, an avenue formed as the crowd parted so he could ascend his throne upon the flat stone. The king was the largest of all the monsters. He had two fangs like elephant tusks poking from his top lip, and though his left hand was of the same compact muscle and meat as any ogre's, his right curled into a solid stone fist. It weighed on the end of his wrist.

The creatures bowed low, muttering 'Your Majesty' and 'King Thunderguts' under their collective smelly breaths as he passed. A pixie squeaked as a boggart trod on it, desperate to get out of his way.

King Thunderguts blinked at his scraping underlings and took one large step to ascend the platform. As he did, the sighs hiccupped and bumped each other in front of him, rolling, some already cracking in a hurry to become little monsters.

The ogre king's attention was caught by the sight of a sparkle. He studied all the beads and spotted one shining. Even among hundreds of dark jewels it stood out, with its unnatural and (Thunderguts's mouth felt sour as he thought it) *pretty* glow. He shifted from one hip to the other; he knew he should waddle down there and pick it out. It was lovely, and nothing so lovely could produce a half-decent monster. It would be best for all if the thing was destroyed. No point telling one of the underlings to do it. They'd be holding up every bead and button until teatime before they got the right one.

He stepped forward, ready to descend into the pit of sighs to collect the shiny little reject, but before he could, a panting, puffing crone in bedraggled, venom-green rags shoved through the crowd.

'Majesty, Majesty.' The frail creature pushed past a bear-eared ogre. It flinched and stepped aside for her. 'Majesty?' She stood wheezing beside the platform.

The king nodded and a troll with a nose like a cowpat lifted her on to the dais.

Thunderguts leered at the crone, studying her twisted face, and stepped to his throne. He wiggled his huge behind between its long-suffering arms and sat down. His red eyes widened but even the strongest of the cavern's yellow lights could not make them glow.

'What's got you so excited, Crone?' He spoke low, although the crowd's attention had turned back to the black beads in the pit, watching them pop and jump like fleas in a pot.

'It's happened. And the bead, it's a little different. I think this one will take.'

'Well, which one will it be, then?'

The hag looked out over the myriad black stones. She shook her head; there were so many. Then she smiled and pointed at the glowing gem among the dull black nuts.

The ogre king chuckled. 'You're sure it will work?'

The crone sighed and opened a small metal box. It was full of sparkling powder. She took a pinch and snorted it, clicking the tin closed again. 'It has to, I won't last much longer.'

'Well, get down there and grab it before some oaf forgets himself and steps on it.' The king lifted his stone fist on to the arm of the throne and issued an exhausted grunt. 'It's time to hatch these beads!' From the comfort of his seat, he tupped his tongue to the top of his mouth and bellowed his heavy breath all over the new nuggets. Then he watched with the rest.

A goblin helped the crone off the edge of the dais and she hobbled through the mob. The monsters shuffled aside for her, jostling and pushing and peering back at their ogre king. Thunderguts felt their curious glances on him. His people knew he didn't normally wait to watch the new ones emerge once he had set the hatching in motion.

Crowds of monstrosities and imps huddled closer and raised eyebrows as the first of the black gems snapped and erupted. A dark boulder began hatching before all the rest, expanding as the ogres cheered. Its surface cracked and a claw burst through the top. Two ogres helped the young ogre climb out and they leaned forward to hear its first word.

'Meat?' the confused creature said. Its new pack shouted encouragement and the little ogre tried to grab a yellow-jacketed pixie.

Next a batch of brownies burst out of their kernels like popping corn. *Pop! Crack! Knisper!* Adult brownies gathered them in arms before the trolls could shove them into their mouths. At a safe distance they stopped, pushed together and laughed as the hatchlings struggled to speak.

'Slackle', one said. The brownies giggled. It tried again. 'Spackle.' The tiny creature looked around to eager faces. 'Sparkle.' The brownies hoorahed and the whelp repeated the new and exciting word.

Leprechaun arrivals received approval for their cries of 'gold', 'profit', 'coin' and 'commerce'. One excited cub yelled 'business' over and over until it vomited. The leprechauns shook its tiny hand.

'Shall we call it Kean?' an old leprechaun laughed.

9

The fledgling yelled out its name – 'Kean, Kean, Kean' – until it vomited again.

Thunderguts's gaze narrowed. He ignored all the hubbub and excitement, focusing on the sparkling nut. It was one of the last to hatch and the crone almost had it, but as she bent down, a newly hatched pixie grabbed it away. The bead cracked in the little imp's hand. The pixie yelped in pain and dropped it, staring at its fingers.

The crone held back.

At first, the hatchling grew like many of the other larvae, its shape bubbling and popping. Legs snaked out, arms appeared like worms. It spread the usual pale leaves, although Thunderguts flinched to see the odd budding of straight, slim limbs.

Nearby ogres and trolls squinted at each other. Goblins shifted. Nobody knew what to expect: a puck, perhaps?

Thunderguts raised an eyebrow and smirked as the shiny nugget grew. A head formed: one ear on each side, two eyes facing forward, the nose too short (even for a puck) and a mouth filled with small, even teeth with no sign of a fang. Hair sprouted like dirty wheat from the top of its head, but not its chin. Hands burst from the stumps of arms, small and dainty.

A troll grunted its distaste.

The soft, pale thing opened its eyes, and the monsters nearest him inched back, muttering. Even the new-mades shuffled away.

'Good grief. It looks human,' something hissed.

'Let's not start imagining we can hatch our own humans, shall we?' a green-vested leprechaun said, waving calming hands in the air.

'Nummy', said a small ogre.

Thunderguts grinned, drool collecting on his bottom teeth as the new creature sat up and sneezed.

The crone pushed the other new-mades aside. When she reached the creature she leaned down and kissed it on the mouth, making several brownies yuck and gag as she did so. Kissing was not normal monster behaviour.

They all heard the hiss as a long sliver of fresh air filled the new-made's lungs. Then the crone stared at it, as if she was waiting for something.

Thunderguts's voice carried across the space. 'Is it ... is it ... all right?' he asked.

The crone grinned, her eyes disappearing into the crimping folds of her face. 'It's perfect', she cried back.

The ogre king laughed. As enormous as the cavern was, his bilious chortle filled it. The noise startled the remaining new-mades and many cried.

'Got nothing to do wivvus. S'not one of ours. S'get outa here', a goblin said. It bombed past the crone, pushing her out of the way as it snatched up a tiny goblin.

'Let her work!' Thunderguts bellowed, and jumped from his throne. Monsters nearest him backed away, desperate to escape the king's flailing fist. A sprite hustled forward, seized three fresh pixies and fled with them. Other waiting packs, wanting to collect terrified hatch-lings, forced themselves in, grabbing at grubs.

In the midst of all the mayhem, a brownie scuttled between the crone's legs. It tripped her as it snatched a pair of soft-haired mewlers. Sprites and boggarts scooped up more pups.

'Oi! Oi!' yelled Thunderguts in growing frustration, and jumped down into the pit. 'Get out of her way. Stop!' He threw his stone fist around and hit an oversized leprechaun in the face. The imp flew backwards into the throne, clanging on to the chair, sending shudders through the ground.

The crone dragged herself up and reached for the strange new-made imp once more. Everyone else was trying not to touch the deformed creature, but the growing pandemonium threw it up and over piddles of pixies and a glut of shivering tommyknockers. The crone crawled towards the new-made imp, but it bumped further away. A gaggle of boggarts tripped in front of her, dragging at hairy cubs. The crone sat back on her bony bum and screamed frustration into the cavern roof.

Thunderguts's bellows reached the crone across the chaos. 'Hurry up and get that ...' Thunderguts could not find a word for the new imp. 'Bring it to me. It's mine.'

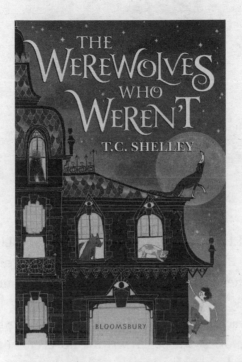

T.C. SHELLEY studied Creative Writing and Literature at university. She has been teaching English for over twenty years and her first school was classified as the most remote in Australia. She loves an audience and long before she took up teaching was writing and performing her poetry and short stories. She began writing novels to entertain her daughter, who wisely suggested that she try to get them published. Shelley lives with her husband, her daughter and two dogs in Perth, Western Australia.